Night at the Vampire Castle

A CHOOSE-YOUR-OWN ROMANCE

WRITTEN BY HARI CONNER

WITH ILLUSTRATIONS BY
Hari Conner, Alex Assan, Anine Bösenberg, Vincent Cecil, Otava Heikkilä, Shazleen Khan, Rowan MacColl, Ashley McCommon, Mal Marwood, Harriet Moulton, Lio Pressland, Bayleigh Underwood, and Val/Bishop Wise

Andrews McMeel
PUBLISHING®

HOW TO PLAY

- This book is for **adults of any gender**.
- The book will tell you what to do and how to play. No experience required.
- When you see **GAIN THE MARKER,** you'll need to make a note (using the Notes page at the back of the book, a journal, or notes on your phone—anywhere you can check later). This keeps track of what you've done, which might affect your story.
- If you reach YOUR NIGHT ENDS, it's game over. You may have been killed or devoured. Start again or backtrack.

YOU CHOOSE WHO YOU ARE

At the start, you'll find out a few general things about the character you're playing—for example, you're living in London, you hate your boss, and you're able to walk and travel. But you choose whatever appearance you want: **It's up to you to imagine your gender, how you dress, and what your body's like.** These aren't specified in the book.

YOU CHOOSE WHAT YOU WANT

This is a romance book, but it's not restrictive about what that can mean. There are sensual scenes on all the main routes and with some extra non-vampire characters. You're in control of your character's choices and choose whether you want intimate scenes. **For the three main characters, you can choose options with or without sex,** and it won't affect you advancing their romance story.

TAILOR YOUR EXPERIENCE

TAKE IT EASY: If you want **more control** over what happens or to avoid starting over, try making notes of the page numbers you go to and where you pick up markers so you can "rewind" and take another route you prefer.

MAKE THINGS INTERESTING: Once you've reached THE END, **achievements** can be found on page 266, to show you more of the possibilities you can explore.

WARNINGS FOR WHAT YOU'RE GETTING INTO

IN THIS BOOK, YOUR CHARACTER MAY DIRECTLY EXPERIENCE: blood; vampires; peril; death; being alone in the woods at night; sexual scenarios, if you choose them; being bitten against your will, fed on, or eaten; and late capitalism.

OTHER CHARACTERS MIGHT MENTION: violence; murder; eating animals (raw); experiences of surviving abuse, war, disease, police, and oppressive regimes; and general life experiences of homophobia, transphobia, and racism.

TURN THE PAGE TO BEGIN.

PROLOGUE
THE FORBIDDEN ROAD

It's only after an hour of trundling through the darkening forest—in a truly terrible borrowed car—that you realize you're on the forbidden road.

Your tough-as-nails old gran had gone deadly serious when she'd pointed it out on her old map of Romania, getting you to memorize the location. "For-bidden," she'd said clearly in her thick, familiar accent. When you asked why, she'd just looked at you knowingly. "You take this road only if you don't want to come back."

But when you think about what's waiting for you at home, you're not in a hurry to get back at all.

QUICK START: Turn to page 6. For the full story, keep reading.

LIVING THE DREAM

You've finally got a solid job and your own (rented) place in the city, just like you always wanted. You're living the dream. Aren't you?

You live in a dingy, wildly overpriced flat that you tell people is a "studio apartment" like the listing did, even though everyone's tacitly aware that means "one small room." It came "fully furnished," which means the room's dominated by a sagging particleboard wardrobe and a rickety bed frame with sharp corners you're always smashing your shins into. It's "complete with kitchen" (cabinets and a two-ring electric hob), "bathroom" (cupboard sized, peeling plastic tiles, wet black mold), and a "view" (onto a stained concrete wall).

The front door locks only if you wedge it shut at a certain angle, the taps drip, and the hot water follows its own mysterious system, so each shower is an exciting surprise. Rats and sirens fight to keep you up at night, but seldom win out against the people next door who love to argue loud and have sex louder, sometimes at the same time. Your landlord tells you he's a "good guy" while jacking up the rent, continuing to never fix anything, and trying to make *you* feel bad for *him* about it. The rent costs most of your income, and you mostly can't afford heating. It is not the worst rental you've lived in, in London.

After all, you live a mere half-hour power walk then an hour-long commute on the Tube from the city proper, even if there are no available seats or masks in sight as strangers cough down your neck. A childhood friend—who bought a house in the north with his parents' money and his equally smug wife—once told you with relish that every journey on the Tube was as bad for your health as a cigarette. You'd never bothered to look it up, in case it was true. Instead, you just vibrated toward the city each morning with your face crammed up against the glass in the stuffy, shuddering carriage, wondering why you bothered to quit smoking.

Your job manages to be both mind-numbingly bullshit and enormously stressful. You have twice as much work since they "had to" let go of everyone who'd been talking about unionizing in a "restructuring" (purge). You were told it was for the good of the company and it made profits look better for shareholders—and to avoid getting fired, you tried to look like you might give a fuck.

The clock ticks down agonizingly slowly to the end of each day, when you're expected to swap to unpaid overtime. On Friday evenings you watch older coworkers knock back eight pints and lurch dismally home to families you're not sure they like and wonder whether that will be you one day.

A poster in an excruciatingly overpriced shop near where you work reads, *When a man is tired of London, he is tired of life*—and boy, are you tired of life.

The joyous, vibrant cacophony you loved about the city is being fenced off, pushed out, and shrunk down until profiteers deem it manageable. Old venues, shops, and pubs fall to property developers and the oncoming, horrifying creep of gentrification—extortionists conquering new territory and former havens. In some places, only the last hints of color haunt old neighborhoods like ghosts. Now you walk past gray buildings and smiling ads on identical chain stores, the same as anywhere else in the world, and can't afford the coffee.

Your favorite Chinese restaurant closed down, replaced by a new ghost kitchen boasting algorithmically generated images that look nothing like the graying lumps that arrive with exhausted, underpaid bike deliverers. You trudge past boarded-up high streets and unaffordable affordable supermarkets whose shrinking packet sizes and empty vegetable shelves remind you about the collapsing climate and this wet island hacking itself delusionally out of Europe.

The background noise of loss—and the awful empty flat you'll have to go home to eventually—have turned London's glittering trends and enticements hollow. Most are out of your price range anyway. You usually just go to terrible parties you wish you hadn't, and can't remember when you last had the energy for anything else.

You are *living the dream*. You just need a break.

A SERIOUS, PROBABLY NON-HAUNTED BREAK

In the email you sent to your boss, you made it sound like you had a sudden meltdown—a serious personal upheaval that meant you had to "step away" and please, please not come back to work for a while. But the truth was it had been a slow breaking, the exhaustion seeping into you until it tipped over into something else: Your mum called it "a bit of a tizzy," your boss called it "irresponsible," your remaining friends called it "fuck it" energy.

Your plan was to go stay with your gran in Romania to rest up and think things over. Your friends thought that was crazy and your gran's house sounded "definitely haunted," both of which you denied. You may not have seen your gran in a while, but her enigmatic laughter hadn't sounded *that* strange and distant down the crackling phone line.

Besides, once squeezed into the cheapest economy seat on the cheapest red-eye flight, your breath eased with every mile you put between yourself and London.

Your heart felt lighter as you left the bustle of Bucharest behind. Your train spanned the fields, closing the distance toward the Carpathians' rocky slopes, still shrouded, for now, in pockets of the last unfelled old forests in Europe. Arriving in Sighișoara, you went wandering to kill time before your next slow train and found the ancient, cobbled streets of the rural town mostly deserted in the offseason. The clawing fingers of the future seem not to have reached the pastel-painted medieval squares of the old town yet. You ate in an empty tourist restaurant you could actually afford, feeling as if you'd been borne back not just to childhood visits, but centuries before.

NOTHING TO SEE HERE

The platform was empty, so you just had to assume the train was the right connection—even if it hadn't come up on the boards and, unlike the other trains, this one was made up of only two rust-pitted and seemingly deserted carriages that rattled as they moved.

The narrow, overgrown tracks of the unusually disused railway line definitely looked charmingly rustic, bare branches scraping at the windows as you slowly pulled past another boarded-up station. That must be normal for the countryside—and the closed cabin at the front *must have had a driver.*

It was a relief when two other passengers joined you farther along, climbing the outer steps to pry open the creaking doors. One was tall and sinewy, face pale behind an old-fashioned mourning veil, the other's crumpled suit and hat leaving little visible but the thick hair on the back of their hands. You flicked to the back of the dog-eared '90s travel guide you'd found in a charity shop, frowning and figuring out how to ask when your stop was.

But you'd seen the sign and made it safely enough to the bare little platform where your tiny, smiling grandmother had held out her arms toward you. You hadn't seen her in years and barely remembered coming all the way out here to the old farm as a child. But the way she beamed as she told you that you looked "very tired and old" made you laugh, and everything settled into a comfortable rhythm for your stay.

You couldn't afford to actually travel around all the ancient, picturesque towns in the far-off hills or the fairy-tale Transylvanian castles promised by the faded front of the guidebook. But it felt good just to wander the ordinary farmland, to feel surrounded by fields and trees, to have such bad Wi-Fi that you were forced to do nothing or help your grandmother around the house. It'd been a soothing few weeks, and you were reluctant to leave.

But now, as heavy rain begins to fall on the forbidden road, you start to recall every small, strange thing you'd seen on your trip in one disquieting whole: the unexplained howls from the forest at night, the eerie, dilapidated buildings at the edge of the village. You remember the corpse of a deer you'd found rotting in the woods, crawling with maggots and strangely emaciated. It was torn open as if by something big: just bears, your grandmother had told you one dark evening, grinning as she sipped at a little glass of plum brandy.

THE TERRIBLE CAR

Your gran had turned out to be busy on the one night you needed to be driven back to the tiny rural station to go home, and she was taking the car with her.

"It's a party! Old friend," she'd said, patting you robustly on the shoulder, totally unconcerned. "But Andrei, two cars. You borrow car with Andrei, everything okay."

Andrei was her nearest neighbor. He'd lived in the village all his life, taken over his father's farm at twenty, and spoke much better English than you spoke Romanian. He was tall and shy, with dark eyelashes, big, rough hands, and a nervous smile he flashed apologetically as he agreed to lend you the spare car.

When you saw it, you realized why.

The car was squat and square and weirdly dented at the back, like it had backed into a pole a long time ago. The passenger door was rusted shut, and the other had a window patched unevenly with duct tape. The seats were worn thin, so you could feel the springs, and the engine rumbled alarmingly—but it was the only option you had.

As you shuddered the engine into an uneasy start, Andrei nodded approvingly, telling you to leave the car unlocked at the station with the keys inside. Before you left, he pointed up at the darkening sky, then gruffly and slightly shyly passed you a neatly folded note with his phone number and name in looping handwriting. "In case you are in trouble," he'd said. "*Any* trouble."

It was late afternoon by the time you were on the road out of the village, dark clouds rumbling over the horizon. The ramp onto the highway had been blocked off with flashing barricades—some kind of collision, metal scattered over the tarmac, dark splashes of red. You followed the diversion signs winding up steep uphill tracks into the mountain forests. There was nowhere to turn or pass, but you met no other cars along the way.

It was only as night was falling that you realized you were a long, irreversible way down the forbidden road.

TURN TO PAGE 9.

LET'S BEGIN:
IT IS A DARK AND STORMY NIGHT

So this is where you find yourself: Night is falling, dark and stormy, and you're on the forbidden road.

You're driving along intermittently surfaced tarmac shadowed by forest. Bare, spidery branches are giving way to thick firs and spruce as the road climbs, and dark gray clouds seep down over the mountain, wisping through the trees like ghosts.

As thunder rumbles overhead, the car's one working headlight sputters alarmingly. Heavy raindrops are now pelting down in a drumbeat on the roof, the road darkening as the sun dips below the horizon. There's only a tiny pool of light from your crappy headlight, illuminating the falling rain.

You start as you feel something on your neck—the roof is leaking, cold water dripping steadily onto your head. When you focus back on the road, your windshield wipers have shuddered to a stop halfway across the glass—not that they were doing much anyway.

Just in time, you notice a sharp hairpin bend, the road dropping steeply off into blackness immediately in front—

The tires skid as you manage to swerve the car around in the encroaching black, veering into a boulder on the other side to save yourself. There's an awful screech of metal as it scrapes along the side and a horrible clunk, but the car just about slides by, shuddering forward. There's an alarming noise clattering under the hood, and water is leaking through the roof in earnest now.

> You're sure everything's fine. Just keep driving. **TURN TO PAGE 10.**

> Bring the car to a stop. **TURN TO PAGE 13.**

KEEP DRIVING

You force the car onward. It clatters and staggers, then gradually picks up speed again.

In the blur of relentless rain, you make out the next sharp turn and the trees ahead of you only as you're heading straight for them.

With a heave, you force the wheel around.

You avoid the tree, but there's a thump as your front tire bumps along the edge where the tarmac crumbles away into the forest, and as you shudder along, trying to get back on the road, the remaining headlight winks out.

You're plunged entirely into darkness for a few terrifying seconds. There's no hint of the steep mountain road or trees visible in the pitch black. You brake, and the car takes a while to stop on the slippery surface.

You hear yourself breathing hard.

You restart the car twice before the headlight just about flickers back on. You've managed to stay on the tarmac, but it was a close thing. A moment longer and the car would have been sent hurtling off the road and into the forest, down the steep, rocky slope.

The headlight sputters again in the freezing rain. Its halo of light seems to already be fading. It's casting an increasingly weak glow a foot or two out into the storm—just about still working, but you suspect not for long.

> You're sure it's *definitely* still fine. Really just try to keep driving. **TURN TO PAGE 12.**

> Stop the car. **TURN TO PAGE 13.**

EMBRACE THE NIGHT

You slam the car door shut behind you, hoping your eyes will slowly adjust to the gloom. You're not used to the darkness, only the halo of sickly streetlight orange in London where you can't see the stars. The sensation of the world now being the same with eyes open or shut is jarring. This will be a great story to tell your friends, you try to think cheerily, in the face of the bleak, wet nothing that surrounds you.

Eventually, you can make out a dark tree line against the sky, a smear of dark purple left by the setting sun. And among the trees, farther up a slope, you see an unmistakable glimmer of light.

You shuffle gingerly toward it and feel your feet meet the edge of the hard surface of the road. You tread down into the earth of the forest. You feel your heart beating in your chest. There's nowhere to go but forward.

It takes a long time to make progress, each of your steps tentative in the rain and absolute darkness. You feel out along the ground and hold your arms ahead of you, trying to avoid the trees, and eventually get into a rhythm. The light ahead is a ways off but must be above the treetops, as it stays visible—you're getting closer.

You suddenly flinch as your outstretched hand scrapes along thorns that tear at your palm. You manage to stop yourself from walking right into the thicket, but your hand prickles with sharp pain—the thorns must have drawn blood.

Through the hammering of rain falling on branches, you hear a sound far off in the forest.

There it is again. You're not sure whether it's your imagination, but it sounds closer this time. It's the crack of a tree branch, maybe a big one—loud enough to hear over the patter of rain. There's another noise, definitely the same thing, definitely closer—something moving toward you in the darkness. Something moving fast.

> Try to turn your phone light on. **TURN TO PAGE 16.**

> Run toward the glimmer of light in the trees. **TURN TO PAGE 17.**

REALLY JUST KEEP DRIVING

You confidently struggle with the unpredictable gearbox until it clunks, and the terrible car jerks forward again. In the last light, you see the road turn steeply downhill—just as the headlight dies.

The car hurtles forward into the dark, wheels failing to find purchase on the wet road.

You're slammed forward with a crunch of metal and the loud bang of an airbag that doesn't fire right.

You come to consciousness sideways, lying on wet tarmac and the broken car window. You figure out which way's up from the water pouring down on you, the whole structure of the car seemingly crumpled in. Slowly, wetly, you're able to extricate yourself and drag your body out onto the dirt of the forest floor, scraping your leg along the twisted metal to escape. Along your calf you feel the welling of hot blood, which seeps out with each pound of your heartbeat. Your head rings, your breath is loud in your ears—are you crying?

There's a noise in the forest, but all you can do for now is lie still next to the crumpled wreck of a car, panting on the ground. The noise comes again, closer, and you woozily prop yourself up to search for your phone.

You pull it out and turn on the light, and your heart jumps in your throat.

For a second, the small, blinding light illuminates a ring around you, the mangled wreck of the car, and a humanoid figure standing in the darkness beside it. The thing stands over you, eyes like a cat's reflecting the light, and before you can make sense of it, your shaking hands let the wet phone slip down into the dirt, extinguishing the light.

Just for a moment, you feel a screaming, searing sensation in your chest as you're torn apart. And then you feel nothing.

YOUR NIGHT ENDS, AND SO DO YOU.

You've met your end. To go back to the start of the section, **GO TO PAGE 9.**

HAUNTED FOREST

Very slowly, you inch the car to a level patch of ground just off the road and come to a stop. You sit for a minute, listening to the rain hammer on the roof.

The glow of the old radio on the dashboard fades into the darkness. The remaining car headlight illuminates the falling rain and a half circle of pitted tarmac in front of you that cuts off at the sharp drop. Beyond that, there's nothing but the night.

As you lean back with a sigh, the headrest squelches with freezing water that's now soaking your back. The body of the car is twisted where you scraped along the rock before, and the roof's now doing very little.

You try to turn and half crawl around in your seat, checking the car for any kind of emergency kit, flare, anything. There's nothing but dust and old chocolate wrappers. You've only got a cheap carry-on bag, and when you search through it, it's just clothes, socks, toothpaste: nothing of use.

Your phone has no signal—as usual out here—and the battery symbol is blinking red in the corner: less than 10 percent. You could have sworn you'd charged it before you left.

It's a cold autumn night, and the temperature's dropping. You can already see your breath steaming. The engine makes another alarming noise, and you're suddenly aware that you're trapped in a metal cage. You need to look for help or shelter.

The headlight flickers—running down the battery of the crap, unpredictable car, you realize. You crawl through the working door and switch the light off. The road plunges into darkness.

› Use the last of your phone battery as a light to navigate. **TURN TO PAGE 14.**

› Save your phone battery for emergencies and move in the dark. **TURN TO PAGE 11.**

LIGHT AND SHADOW

Your phone light casts deep shadows in the looming trees.

You follow the road for a while, searching for any road sign or hint of a turnoff that might lead to a house, like the ones farther down the mountain. The phone battery symbol blinks down to 8 percent . . . 7 percent . . . then you stop looking. It's old and, like most phones, not built to last—it could switch off at any time. You try to move as fast as possible, checking the roadside in the small halo of light the phone casts through the driving rain. Just as you're starting to wonder whether anyone would live this deep in the forest along a supposedly dangerous road, you see a slight opening in the trees and move closer.

Off to the right, leading up the slope into the forest, is the start of a dirt track. It's very overgrown, as if cars don't come this way often, but a few steps off the road, metal bars glint among the branches—once-grand entrance gates left open so long that the forest has grown around them.

And down the track, you think you see a distant glimmer of light.

Using your phone light, you navigate along the path as best you can, avoiding overhanging branches and occasional patches of encroaching brambles. Your heart lurches as your phone finally switches off, the harsh light abruptly swallowed by the night as the battery dies.

◆ Gain the marker **DEAD PHONE.**

But you can now see the light ahead clearly, a beacon above the treetops, even through the rain—a high window? As you draw nearer, treading carefully in the darkness, more points of light become visible below. You emerge from the trees out into a clearing and squint through the hammering rain, trying to decide which to head for—is it one big building, like an apartment block?—when a bolt of lightning crackling through the clouds gives you an answer.

In the brief flash, you see you're standing in front of a castle—not quite the red-roofed fairy-tale spectacle on the front of your guidebook but a less photogenic cousin hunched among the trees. You see a glimpse of forbidding walls in dark, discolored stone—high gothic rooftops, turrets of towers crawling upward from the sides of a main building. A narrow walkway leads over a plunging unseen drop toward a main door, and as darkness falls again, you hurry toward it before the afterimage fades in your mind.

Your feet reach the stone of the walkway, and you cross as fast as you can, hands following a rain-slick wall until they reach the entrance archway. You feel around in the dark, fingers brushing cold bolts, and find an uneven metal knocker on the weathered wood of the huge door. You lift it with numb fingers and knock it heavily against the door.

In the hammering rain, you stand grim and shivering. You think you hear a noise far off in the forest and are about to knock again when the heavy door swings inward without warning. A few steps above you, a large, broad-shouldered figure stands looming over you, unnaturally still, silhouetted against a dim light from inside.

A quiet, commanding voice asks you a question in a language you don't understand. You say, "*Scuze*"—you're pretty sure that means "sorry"—before replying in English that your car went off the road and you had nowhere else to go.

"So I see," the low voice replies in perfect English and an accent you can't quite place—maybe French and something else, old-fashioned and smooth.

Through the rain, you hear another strange noise from the forest, closer this time, and the figure steps quickly back from the doorway, voice sharp. "You'd better come inside."

You hurry up the steps, and in a movement so swift you barely see it, the figure slams the heavy door behind you as if it weighs nothing, then remains still with a hand against it for a moment, as if listening. Straining your ears, you hear the noise again, but more distant now—and then there's nothing but the rain.

TURN TO PAGE 18.

IF A BODY FALLS IN A FOREST

You hurry to find your phone in your pockets, forgetting where you put it in your panic. There's another crack of movement close by, much closer than you would have thought possible.

You're shivering, hands slick with rain as you manage to pull your phone out, fumbling for the light setting. In the faint glow of the screen, you realize some of the wetness is blood streaking from the palm of your hand, smeared in the dark over your clothes and across the phone screen as you finally hit the right button.

Just as the light flares to life, the noise comes again right ahead of you and the phone slips from your shaking hands in a confusion of bright white light.

In the instant of it falling, turning in the air, the beam of light flashes upward. You see a last moment of images thrown into sharp relief: wet, bloody leaves at your feet, black brambles ahead, and two shining eyes of a humanoid figure standing perfectly still among the dark trees.

Then the phone lands face down in the mud and the light winks out.

For a second, you just hear the rain and your own ragged breathing, then a brief moment of screaming sensation. There's something sharp and hot at your throat—blood, your own blood—and then nothing.

YOUR NIGHT ENDS, AND SO DO YOU.

You've met your end. To go back to the start of the section, **GO TO PAGE 11.**

RUN

Without stopping to think, you take off toward the faint light above the trees at a run, no longer carefully feeling out your footsteps. You stumble into trees and over logs and branches, hearing yourself make a spectacular amount of noise.

Far behind you, you think you hear hoarse exhalations, like some kind of inhuman parody of laughter, as something follows, moving toward you at a pace. You don't turn back or stop to check, only stagger blindly forward. Above you, the light grows larger, and now you can see other points in the trees—but you're not fast enough. Whatever is following will reach you before you make it to the light.

Out of nowhere, you feel a strong arm at your waist, pulling you tight to an unseen body, lifting you off your feet, and drawing you forward in the dark. You can't quite make sense of it, but suddenly you're clasped against someone, moving swiftly through the night and silently avoiding each tree and wayward branch.

Close to your ear, a low, urgent voice says something in a language you don't understand. You whisper back "What?" in your panic, your Romanian all forgotten.

The low command comes again in a smooth, old-fashioned accent you can't quite place—maybe French and something else—"*Stay quiet.* I could hear you a mile away."

You try to steady your breathing and realize you can still hear the hoarse panting through the rain behind, closer than ever—but the lights are right ahead of you now, and as lightning crackles through the clouds overhead, you see where they were coming from.

In a brief, stark flash you see you are rapidly approaching a building: the dark, forbidding stone walls and gothic rooftops and turrets of a castle, its great wooden door open to the storm. The dark-cloaked figure with arms tight around you seems to cross the last stretch in an impossible bound and all but hurls you both through the door, turning to slam it shut behind you and then hold very still, listening.

You lean forward, catching your breath. You notice the place where the thorns scraped your hand. Barely a scratch and the bleeding's already stopped, washed off in the rain. Straining your ears, you think you hear the strange hoarse noise again, but now distant—and then nothing but the storm.

TURN TO PAGE 18.

INTO THE CASTLE

In the dim light of the entranceway lamp, you now see the figure more clearly: the rough stubble along his jawline, the long hair braided back out of his face with wisps of loose curls falling carelessly around his eyes. He's shrouded in a large black coat, collar high against the castle's chill. You're not sure if it's a trick of the low light, but instead of a rich brown, his skin looks almost ashen, dark eyes haunted.

Finally, he seems satisfied that whatever was outside has retreated and fallen quiet for now, and then he turns from the door. His features are firm and serious, regarding you with a frown. "This is a bad place to be after dark," he says solemnly. "There are dangerous things in this forest."

He steps away from the door and walks into the house, speaking darkly, half to himself. "You may owe your life to the rain, covering your noise and scent, but . . . you must not venture out again tonight. You shall remain here."

You stand, numb and dripping in the entranceway. All you can do is agree—that definitely sounds better than the forest outside.

As if recalling the correct procedure, the figure turns back to you, his low voice smoothing over into something less severe. "I beg your pardon. You may call me Casimir. This is my home."

You introduce yourself back, and he nods, but he seems either uninterested in taking the conversation further or unsure how to.

Instead, he walks forward and gestures for you to follow.

You emerge into a large unlit chamber, its shadowy contours just visible by the reflected light from the entranceway behind you. It's all stone and all empty—barring a table or two along distant walls and a huge woven carpet so threadbare, it's basically just scraps of decaying gray. It may be dry, but the room is just as cold as outside.

Two sweeping stone staircases curve upward to another floor, and along the balcony, archways lead away into darkness.

Casimir seems to realize the state of the room. "The chambers we use are farther into the house," he says in apology, his face briefly softening into amusement. "I'm afraid we're not much used to guests." He smiles ruefully, and you see a roguish flash of very white teeth and very sharp canines.

Oh, you think. *This guy is definitely a vampire.*

Casimir leads you away toward a side door, turning to light an old-fashioned lamp on a nearby table with an actual candle inside. He faces away as he strikes a match, so you can't see his eyes. "You will be careful," he tells you smoothly, "not to stray from my side. Parts of the castle are also dangerous. The stonework is not all secure."

He turns to look at you, eyes hard. "Do not go into the dark." His tone invites no argument.

Through the door, he leads you through a twisting nest of corridors, dark coat sweeping out behind him. It's not long before you reach a path with actual carpet underfoot and what look like gas lamps fixed to the walls, glowing orange in the silence.

You pass by more turnings into empty dusty corridors, half-open doorways where you glimpse dank, disused chambers within. As you hurry to follow Casimir's quick stride, you find yourself very aware of how easily you could get lost here.

You turn a corner, where Casimir passes by a particularly large and uneven archway, leading off into a shadowy passage. Its rough edges remind you of teeth, a mouth disappearing into pitch black. You think you can hear the rain beyond and realize you've paused, straining to see what's inside.

Then something moves in the darkness.

You think you see the gleam of a cat's eyes, reflective pinpricks in the far distance—but no, they can't be. They're too big, too far from the ground.

› Remain where you are and stay on the path. **TURN TO PAGE 20.**

› Go into the darkness. **TURN TO PAGE 31.**

STAY ON THE PATH

The glimmer of eyes seems to disappear, but every hair on your body is standing on end. You realize you're holding your breath.

Suddenly there's movement close by, and your nerves seize—Casimir appears right behind you, one strong hand holding tight to your arm, forbidding you from moving forward. "I see you've met August," Casimir says in a smooth voice that doesn't match his unflinching grip. "They won't hurt you," he says, though it sounds more like an instruction aimed at the ominous corridor.

No creature pounces from the shadows, only a pale figure who slips out into the light ahead of you.

August wears a tailored suit over a silky blouse and a smile with no hint of friendliness—and no effort to hide the pointed canines. "Charmed, I'm sure," says August in a bored period-drama lilt.

"They grew up in England," Casimir tells you gravely, as if explaining that August has some sort of unfortunate disease.

You might have expected "they" to sit strangely in his old-fashioned voice, but he says the pronoun with a decided precision, daring you to contradict him. You introduce yourself back, trying to project "I get it" and a more general air of "Don't eat me."

But August seems to take little notice of you, addressing their reply to Casimir. "We're having a guest for dinner, are we?" they say delightedly, smiling like a cat with a mouse. "I'll tell Raisa. You shall have to give me time to dress." It's unclear what could possibly be more "dressed" than their current outfit, but you stay quiet.

Casimir seems to consider for a moment, then nods solemnly. "Very well. But you'll behave, August," he says in a tone of warning.

Before you can ask who Raisa is—or who August is, for that matter—Casimir turns to stride off down the gaslit corridor again.

You make to follow, but August interposes, their languid movement easily outpacing you somehow and blocking your path.

"How *intriguing*. We don't often have company," they say, slinking around you as if to examine a mildly interesting trinket from the best angle. "What a *treat*." The sharp smile never drops from their face.

Then with a breathy exhalation of laughter, they're gone, slipping back into the darkness.

TURN TO PAGE 23.

POLITELY DECLINE

You try to say no as politely as possible.

August gives you a withering look. "Dreadful behavior for a dinner guest taken in wholly out of kindness. Don't you know how much this stuff *costs*?"

"August." Casimir's sharp tone seems to have some immediate power over the tall figure beside you.

At his voice, August leaves you alone without protest, slipping back around the table in a flash of red. They move with perfect poise but sit down dramatically to signal their displeasure, pouring themself a large glass of their own.

TURN TO PAGE 33.

THEY'RE HAVING YOU FOR DINNER

Casimir leads you into a gloomy hall with a long, dark table down the middle. He puts the lantern down with a click that echoes around the stone, then goes over to a large fireplace stacked with logs, crouching to light it with a practiced ease.

The room is stark but clean, more recently lived in. Above you, the high vaulted ceiling stretches away, cobwebs among the beams. It's warmer than outside but not by much, and the sparse lamps on the wall do little to brighten the mood.

As the fire springs to life in the grate, Casimir stands smoothly. "I must see to the preparations—I will return soon." He sweeps out of a far doorway and up a stone staircase before you can say anything else. You go to stand near the fire and spend a while trying to dry out and find some warmth in the huge dark castle.

It's August who arrives first, walking in as if to a large dinner party and not a dark and empty stone room.

They pause in the doorway, leaning against the arch with an effortless elegance. August is now confidently wearing a nonchalantly draped blazer over a dress and neat brogues, but they're observing you sharply, like a cat waiting to pounce. You realize they're waiting for you to say something—maybe even to ridicule them.

But nothing about August looks ridiculous—they look born to wear outfits that snatch the attention and breath out of a room. They also look like they might have been born to ruthlessly behead anyone small-minded enough to tell them dresses belonged on a different sort of body.

> You find that attractive. **TURN TO PAGE 24.**

> You respect that and would prefer to do so from a distance. **TURN TO PAGE 26.**

WHO DOESN'T FIND "MURDEROUS" AT LEAST A LITTLE ATTRACTIVE

August seems to gather your look is decidedly appreciative, and their shoulders relax into a more authentically debonair set as they come farther into the room, a small smile playing at their lips.

Then—in a strangely fluid, inhuman motion—they're right beside you.

August moves behind you to trail a finger along your shoulder blades, as if appraising. The touch is so soft, it barely makes contact, sending a shiver through your body. "All alone, are you?" they murmur. "Raisa is foraging for whatever food there is to be had; she'll be here soon." It's hard to focus on who Raisa might be or anything else as August's lips move close to your ear.

"Are you hungry?" they ask with a low, breathy laugh. "I am."

"*August.*" Casimir's low, commanding tone cuts through the room from the far door, and you feel August immediately straighten beside you. They glide around to the other side of the table and sink into an exquisite pose in a dark wood chair to watch you primly from a distance, smile sharp and dangerous.

Casimir sweeps down the stairway into the room, eyebrows low and serious—perhaps their natural state. Now that he's without his heavy outdoor coat, you see he's solidly built. His striking suit is a soft, expensive black over smooth cream ruffles, open shirt baring a jagged triangle of dark skin and an unhidden swell to his chest. It might be a '70s style or something much older—either way, he wears it well.

Casimir reaches the table, and his eyes sweep over August to you. His eyebrows stay low, but he gives you a nod deep enough that it might be a formal bow and gestures slightly stiffly for you to sit. Only once you're seated does he move to pull out his own chair at the head of the table—a large, heavy seat that looks about halfway to a throne. He sits down, shooting August a hard look of warning.

"*Sorry,*" August says in a musical tone, "I ought not to play with my food."

TURN TO PAGE 25.

RAISA DAN

From the other end of the hall, you hear a clanging, then someone bursts into the room carrying a haphazard arrangement of plates and cutlery.

Casimir clears his throat, controlled but slightly exasperated. "This is Raisa. She—"

Crockery and glasses clatter down on the table as Raisa lets them go, catching one of the plates as it makes a bid to escape to the floor. She skims it down the table like a Frisbee, where it skids to a halt in front of an amused August.

"Shit, hold on!" Raisa calls brightly in an accent that sounds just like the ones in your gran's village, and disappears out of the room. She emerges again with a couple of covered trays and a loaf of bread under her arm. As she brings the scattered dinner things over in too many trips, she steps into the light of the fire, and you get a better look at her.

Raisa is wearing mostly black—frayed jeans tight to her curves, combat boots, a weathered motorcycle jacket splashed with patches. Her skin's not quite the milk-white of August's but a very pale tan that doesn't look like it sees much sun.

She throws herself into a chair near August, unceremoniously uncovering one of the platters and stabbing a piece of what looks like very rare meat with a fork to help herself. "Nice to meet you!" she says warmly, through a mouthful of what you hope is venison.

"Please, help yourself," Casimir mutters to Raisa, deadpan, serving and arranging strips of meat and vegetables from the other platter carefully on your plate. He sits back and gestures that you're welcome to eat.

TURN TO PAGE 28.

YOU RESPECT AUGUST . . . FROM A DISTANCE

August seems to notice your lack of concern at their choice of clothes, and their shoulders relax minutely into a more authentically debonair set.

"*Awful* manners for Casimir to leave you all alone like this," they say, slinking over to one of the dark wooden chairs a little way from the fire and gesturing vaguely for you to sit down.

For a moment, August is still, poise on hold for a moment as they look wistfully into the dancing flames in the fireplace. "He's . . . withdrawn into himself over the years, since he took over. Gets lost in his thoughts. I think he's been alone here for too long." Their eyes slide away from the fire and back to you, glittering and sharp again. "Apart from us, I mean."

You realize they're waiting for you to ask who "us" is, so you do.

"Raisa, I believe, will be fetching us dinner, so you'll see her soon—though who *knows* what we have in the pantry."

There's a noise from the far door, and you see Casimir descending the stairs.

Without his heavy outdoor coat, you see he's solidly built. His striking suit is a soft, expensive black over smooth cream ruffles, open shirt baring a jagged triangle of dark skin and an unhidden swell to his chest. It might be a '70s style or something much older—either way, he wears it well.

Eyebrows low and serious, he gives you a nod deep enough that it might be a formal bow before sitting down in the large, heavy seat at the head of the table. He looks halfway to a king on a throne, troubled brow and all.

TURN TO PAGE 25.

TELL THEM PART OF THE TRUTH

You give an extremely selective account of your life back home, thinking it might not be a great idea to tell a bunch of vampires the intimate details of your life.

You have your own place, you say—you do *not* tell them what it's like. You're taking a break from your busy job where you could be about to get promoted—because, well, you could be. You wax lyrical about the delights of London, you don't mention you can't afford them, and you stay nice and quiet about everything else.

August responds with mockingly sympathetic "ooh"s and sad "oh"s that sound extremely insincere.

You describe your poor, dear grandmother, alone in the village, how you're kindly pausing your amazing life to come and look after her, weak and ailing as she is. Casimir, who seems to be listening quietly, frowns at this, leaning back in his chair. "I don't know anyone by that description in the villages nearby," he says simply. "I have lived here a long while and know the locals very well."

You falter and stop making stuff up about how sweet and ailing your gran is. His tone is not one to be questioned.

Raisa makes a noise that sounds like she's trying to stifle a laugh.

August's perfect, manslaughter smile is cold. In the silence that follows, they maintain eye contact as they finish skewering the cork of the wine with their very sharp knife, pulling it neatly from the bottle with a pop. Their nails click as they place it down on the table.

The quiet goes on for exactly long enough to make you acutely uncomfortable, until Casimir takes mercy by moving smoothly to another topic, as if nothing happened. "The river by the north road will burst its banks in this rain," he's saying when you almost jump out of your skin.

August has appeared soundlessly beside you, holding the dark bottle of wine with a smile about as sharp as the knife they opened it with, offering to pour you a glass. It smells strange and extremely strong.

- Drink the wine. **TURN TO PAGE 29.**
- Politely decline. **TURN TO PAGE 22.**

DINNER CONVERSATION

You sit with the three vampires at the long table in the hall. It might be the weirdest company you've ever had for dinner.

Casimir, as if as an afterthought, has put a couple of strips of meat on his own plate, but he only pushes them around with his cutlery and doesn't take a single bite. August seems not to bother with the food at all, instead reaching for a bottle of wine left sideways on the table by Raisa.

August keeps their eyes on you as they take a very sharp steak knife to the neck of the bottle, expertly splitting the red wax open in one clean slice. Their voice is casual as they turn the blade in their fingers. "Tell us about yourself. You're an outsider; aren't you a tourist? Why come into the mountains on a night like this?"

> Talk honestly about the minor crisis you had back home. **TURN TO PAGE 30.**

> Tell part of the truth, but make it seem like you have an amazing life back home and are kindly visiting your poor, frail grandmother. **TURN TO PAGE 27.**

> Answer as little as possible. **TURN TO PAGE 32.**

DRINK THE WINE

August pours, and you sip at the almost-purple liquid. The wine is like none you've ever tasted before—strangely thick on your tongue, with an unusual heady scent you can't place. Even a mouthful has your head swimming a little.

You place the glass carefully back on the table and find that August is still standing there, smiling like a car crash. They pour again and keep on pouring. They stop only when forced to, as the dark liquid approaches the brim—the glass is big enough that they probably got about half of the bottle out.

"Oh, I beg your pardon," drawls August in the least sorry voice you've ever heard in your life. They seem to be perfectly at ease, unaware of how close they're standing to you, waiting for you to drink. Nothing else to do, then—or nothing else to do safely. The room is tense and silent.

You take a gulp, and they break back into their murder-weapon smile, which does not put you at ease. You put the glass down, and they top it up once more before slipping back around to their seat.

You take a few more careful sips, trying not to spill any, as Casimir seems to murmur something to August in a warning tone. But you soon find yourself unconcerned that you can't make their conversation out.

This wine is *great*, actually.

You find yourself sipping at it absent-mindedly. Maybe this whole situation isn't so bad either. The candlelight and the fire in the grate seem to twinkle invitingly in the dramatic room. Your limbs relax, and your tongue feels loose in your mouth. You drink a little more, and must keep on drinking a little more, because after a while you realize the very large glass seems to be empty.

◆ Gain the marker **FULL OF WINE.**

TURN TO PAGE 33.

TELL THEM FRANKLY

You answer honestly about how things have been pretty grim, starting with the job you had to get away from: how your boss asked a coworker whether she'd "thought about the team" when she asked for time off to go to a funeral, how everyone's complaints about dire work hours got greeted with "stress awareness" seminars and pizza instead of better work hours.

The vampires seem attentive, so you keep talking, and it all spills out: the rent hikes, the energy bills, the price of food; everyone sick all the time but nobody wearing masks or getting allowed time off work; your cousin working sixteen-hour overtime shifts at the hospital who can't afford new school shoes for his daughter.

Raisa listens with rapt horror and at one point bangs her hand down so hard, a fork flies off into the shadows. She looks grimly understanding about unpaid overtime and ready to flip the table by the time you're done. August's initial lack of sympathy gives way to sincere noises of distaste and a few cold interjections—you wonder whether anyone else has ever called your landlord an "unfeeling swine." Casimir stays quiet but seems to listen intently, his expression growing increasingly stormy.

◆ Gain the marker **A CRISIS SHARED.**

None of them seems to have recent similar experiences to share—do vampires even have jobs?—but the quiet that falls is more comfortable than before.

Casimir, as if trying to return the favor of holding a conversation, manages to say a few sentences about how he expects the storm will affect the rivers. August tells you how picturesque the mountains will look in the snow soon. Raisa thoughtfully chews a piece of bread, looking like she's thinking about how she could get to London to hurt your boss.

Seeming to remember the bottle of wine they were opening, August pops the cork out with a practiced skill and slips round the table, offering you some. Casimir looks disapproving, giving August a look of warning, but stays quiet. The open bottle smells strange and extremely strong.

› Accept the offered strange wine. **TURN TO PAGE 29.**

› Politely decline the wine. **TURN TO PAGE 33.**

GO INTO THE DARKNESS

You step out beyond the gas lamps' glow into the all-consuming void ahead of you.

A few steps in, you feel a cold breeze and hear the rustle of trees off to your side in the gloom, and you think it must be a large open window—until you stumble.

Like missing a stair on the way down, your feet plunge into some kind of crack in the floor. You tumble down into the pitch black, just managing to catch yourself with shaking arms as they scrape down the rough walls on either side.

But your legs hang down in the cold night air. You feel a hot trickle of blood where your hands scraped against the jagged stone, can almost smell it. And in the forest to your side where the rain blows in, you think you can hear something moving.

For a moment, you hang in the pitch-black stillness, with only the sound of your heavy breathing and the rain through the broken wall.

And then everything quickly ends. The speed is merciful, and you at least don't have to see what comes for you. There's only an instant of searing pain as you register you've been dragged down by the legs out into the forest. You thump to the wet earth and lose consciousness before the life is drained out of you.

YOUR NIGHT ENDS, AND SO DO YOU.

You've met your end. To go back to the start of the section, **GO TO PAGE 18.**

ANSWER AS LITTLE AS POSSIBLE

Thrust into a bizarre dinner in a haunted-looking castle in a dangerous forest, you think it might be a good idea to be more cautious and not tell a bunch of vampires about your life.

You answer very briefly, saying only that you came from London and have family in the village, then let the room lapse into silence.

August looks as you expectantly, waiting for some further entertainment. When they realize none is forthcoming, they lean back in the chair with exasperation and pick up the bottle of wine again.

Casimir frowns at you but nods solemnly and returns his attention to his plate. He slices piece after piece of meat and doesn't eat any of it.

You're very aware of the clink of cutlery on china.

The only person who seems to be enjoying themself is Raisa, happily chewing on a piece of bread—but after a while, Casimir gives her a strange look. "Don't make yourself sick," he says, quiet enough that it's almost inaudible.

Raisa waves this away, but you realize she hasn't eaten much overall. "I know what I can handle," she says. You wonder whether she has a wheat intolerance.

Suddenly August is noiselessly beside you—though you could swear you didn't see them move—holding the dark bottle of wine. You notice the cork, intact but neatly skewered by the steak knife, sitting back by August's place at the table. The knife gleams in the firelight.

With a smile that looks about as sharp, August offers to pour you a glass.

- Drink the wine. **TURN TO PAGE 29.**
- Politely decline. **TURN TO PAGE 22.**

AFTER DINNER

After dinner, Raisa checks her old digital watch and swings her boots off the table. "This was great," she says with no trace of sarcasm, "but I've gotta head out."

Casimir scowls as if he disapproves, but Raisa ignores him to talk to August. "It's the big party of the year. Everyone interesting in the whole country will come. Mara in the village plans decorating, drinks, everything!"

"You know I can't. Anyway, it's *raining*," August replies lazily.

You hear a scrape as Casimir stands, frowning down at the table. His hands still grip his cutlery in a tight, unconscious flex, despite not having taken a single bite of his food. He glances at you as if weighing his words carefully, then turns to Raisa, low voice almost a growl. "You *know* dangerous things are abroad in the forest tonight." He seems to loom over you all in the low light. August sits perfectly still, watching him from the corner of their eye.

But Raisa just stretches, completely unmoved. "I'll be on my bike, and nobody can touch me once I'm there. Anyway, nobody's out to get *me*, old man." She turns toward you, eyes bright. "Even the human could come!" she says, leaning closer with a warm grin that seems like it's just for you. "It will be *fun*."

"All this risk to spend the evening in a house full of *werewolves*?" Casimir mutters.

Right, of *course* there are werewolves, too.

But Raisa just exudes untouchable confidence. "Yeah!" she replies with a bold grin.

Casimir exhales and flexes his jaw, then carefully puts the cutlery down. "I can't control you, Raisa. I can only urge caution," he says darkly before turning back toward the stairway, cloak swirling behind him.

August stands with languid grace, eyes flicking toward you. "I can take care of our guest," they say with a sharp smile that seems to draw you in. "Keep you comfortable."

- Go with Raisa to the party. **TURN TO PAGE 196.**
- Go with August. **TURN TO PAGE 82.**

◆ If you have the marker **A CRISIS SHARED . . .**

Casimir also hesitates on the stairs for a moment, then looks back at you. "Unless you'd prefer to join me in the study? It's . . . usually warmer."

With this marker, you can also choose to go with Casimir. **TURN TO PAGE 68.**

THE GARDENS

You walk along the arcade around the gardens, and as you turn a corner, you see the woman again.

She's sitting on a bench with a thin flower in her hand and wearing an old-fashioned dress that flutters as if in an unseen breeze.

She looks up in surprise as you approach, her hair swirling around after her like she's underwater.

"You came to see me," she says in a strangely hoarse voice that echoes around the cold stone. But she sounds excited, as if longing to speak to someone. "How I've waited—nobody has come to this part of the castle for many years. Few walk the halls now, or not in any place I can reach."

She drifts closer to you, head tilted sadly to one side. The soft blue pallor of her skin looks strangely insubstantial, as if she's not quite solid.

"But how did you come here? I hope it is not as a guest of Casimir?"

Your heart sinks. You explain it was too dangerous to drive in the storm and briefly describe the man who invited you inside.

She shakes her head slowly, frowning. "That isn't him," she says, and doesn't seem to be able to answer when you ask what she means.

› Ask how she came to the castle. **TURN TO PAGE 38.**

› Ask whether there's another way back indoors. **TURN TO PAGE 89.**

REALLY, REALLY STAY IN BED

Okay, you really do just stay in bed. You hear strange ominous noises all night and resolutely refuse to confront them or discover any mysteries or secrets. You hear cackling and chains rattling, a distant scream, alluring moans. You stay perfectly still.

You're in a vampire castle, but you're determined not to encounter any more vampires or get to know them.

The door is actually still open, wide onto the blackness. At one point you think you see the strange blue glow just out of sight—you do not go and look at it. It's not going to get you that easily.

The candle burns low, then burns out. You lie there in the darkness, listening to weird, unidentifiable, probably haunted sounds deep within the rooms beyond.

Slowly, the gray light of dawn creeps into the room.

In the thin daylight, you realize the noises have stopped, and the room looks strangely ordinary: a slightly dusty stone chamber.

You get up and put your clothes back on. You leave the nightclothes—chosen just for you by your unseen hosts—folded on the bed. You make your way downstairs.

In the light of morning, the castle is cold and ordinary and, as far as you can tell, entirely empty of people. You can't find your way back to the dining room or anywhere you really recognize. In fact, nowhere you go leads to any sign of habitation, any sign of the people you met last night. You almost wonder whether the whole thing was a dream—if not, there's certainly no note, no sign that anybody here wants to see you.

Eventually, you open another door at random and daylight floods in. You realize you've opened a side door and can see a path leading back down to the road.

TURN TO PAGE 264.

BUMP IN THE NIGHT

You take the pewter candleholder August left and put your slightly damp shoes on.

As you step out into the hall, there's no wind, nobody in sight—and no warning when the door swings heavily shut behind you.

You test the handle to make sure you can get back in and find it . . . stuck. The door won't budge, no matter how much you rattle it or pull with all your strength.

You stand in the stillness. You're alone with your flickering candle in a very dark stone corridor.

Time to explore, you suppose.

Away to your left, you see a glimpse of the same indistinct blue glow far down the hall, in the direction you heard someone crying. You think you see it move slowly around a corner and out of sight.

To your right, beside the stairway you came up, more steps lead upward to the noises above.

› Follow the blue light. **TURN TO PAGE 46.**

› Go up to the attic. **TURN TO PAGE 53.**

REMEMBRANCE

You sit down with the spirit on a bench in the walkway. The rain patters down in the garden beyond.

You're not sure how many stories you have to tell, but you try. You tell her about your first real friend and times you went to visit family as a kid. You tell her about your favorite meal and what happened when you first tried to make it yourself. As you speak, her form seems to become more solid, the soft blue glow growing, starting to light a circle around her.

You start with small, simple things, but slowly, seeing her light up makes you think about how life is the small things. It's made up of little moments listening to the rain, trying not to burn your tongue on a hot drink, getting to know a person.

And in turn, she tells you the small things from her own life. She tells you about her grandparents and the songs her mother used to sing her to sleep with. She tells you the sounds and smells and intricacies of Paris long ago. She tells you how she always wore a raincoat when the clouds looked dark but somehow never had it on when it rained. You laugh together. As she goes on, you think about how many times these stories have been shared in different times and places, traded between people with everything and nothing in common.

You talk for a long time until the glow is very bright, her body almost indistinct. But you know she's smiling as she places the flower she's been playing with in one of your palms. The light leads you by the hand out into the rain, and you trust her enough to follow. Down beyond the graves is a dirty, hidden-away corner where an old well sits forgotten, still covered by a half-rotted roof, and you place the flower by the base of the well. It's a token of remembrance.

As the petals touch the ground, there's a rush of air in the graveyard. Wind swirls in a circle, and far away, you hear the door back into the castle banging open. The light beside you soars up in a long arc to crash against the roof of the well, which crumbles down into the dark, burying her remains for good. The indistinct figure of light rises up, up into the air until it's high above you. Then it's lost in the wind and the storm—free out into the world at last.

You turn back toward the courtyard door and see August standing framed in the dark archway, wearing an old jumper and an expression that looks both thoughtful and very surprised.

TURN TO PAGE 84.

THE VAMPIRE'S BRIDE

"It was very long ago," she tells you in her hoarse, breathy voice. "I met Casimir in Paris. He would take me to the opera, to the finest parties, dress me in silks and jewels. He seemed enchanted with me and promised he'd bring me back to his grand family home and make me his wife.

"But he turned cold. After arriving at the castle, I fell ill, overcome by sudden weakness—but he was seldom there to help or comfort me. He was mysterious. He would disappear for long stretches. He was so pale, and rarely went out in the daylight—even then he had a parasol, gloves he would never take off."

The mention of Casimir's "pale" skin throws you—not the man who hosted you earlier this evening, then.

"And he had dark moods. I grew to hate him—even before I came to understand the weakness was from his feeding on me in the night. By the time I realized what he was, there was no way for me to reach home. I had no money, no friends. The locals refused to come near the castle."

Her fingers fumble at her neck, and you realize she's unbuttoning her high collar.

She peels it back to reveal a bloody mess.

Her throat is torn as if by claws that ripped into her vocal cords. Around the wound are the dark bruises of fingers, punctures from two sharp teeth digging in, over and over again.

"When he killed me, he made it slow. There was nobody to mourn me.

"I was not buried among his ancestors. He tipped my body down a disused well and forgot it. There is no stone to mark my resting place. I dream of many things: freedom, of course. I do not know what strange forces hold me here. I dream of feeling the sunlight again, of stories and laughter. I dream of the loving touch I longed for from a husband and never experienced while I lived. All I want is for some living soul to remember me."

Her hand reaches up to slide over yours. The sensation is strange, like trying to touch sand or water, but you *can* feel her. She looks at you imploringly, standing close. "*Please.*"

> Show her the loving touch she longs for. **TURN TO PAGE 40.**

> Tell her stories about your life, and listen to hers, so she'll be remembered. **TURN TO PAGE 37.**

FORGOTTEN BONES

Drenched and shivering in the rain, you test the rope, then slowly lower yourself into the pitch-black circle of the well.

The sounds of the rain and the storm grow more distant as you descend into the dark. You hear them far above, but around you there is total stillness—only broken by slow dripping and the sounds of your wet clothes moving as you continue downward.

The knots make the descent easier, and you reach the bottom sooner than you expect. Your foot makes contact with solid ground, and you wince at the sound of a crunch. Trying to force down your growing terror, you feel around in the dark and find a large burlap sack, half rotting but still intact. Lifting it, you feel the weight of the bones inside. There's nothing else down here in the dried-up well—perhaps the vampires have some other way of disposing of bodies—and you decide there's no need to check inside the sack to assure yourself of the contents.

The body has long rotted away, and the sack is light and easy to carry. You tie it over a shoulder using the dressing-gown belt and move as fast as possible back up the rope, almost slipping in your eagerness to get out of the very dark hole. You come up over the side of the well gasping and lie on the ground in the rain for a moment, very grateful to be back in the open air.

You don't see the dead woman anywhere but have the sense of her watching you. In the graveyard proper, you find an empty patch, and the wet soil comes easily when you dig with your hands. Once it's deep enough, you lay the sack at the bottom and cover the hole back over. It's not six feet and a coffin, but it's a burial nonetheless.

Finally, you find two sticks and a flower among the thorns, the same kind the woman was holding when you had emerged into the courtyard. You place the sticks over the new grave in a cross shape with the flower alongside.

There's a rush of air in the graveyard. Wind swirls in a circle, and far away, you hear the door back into the castle banging open. Stepping back, you see a faint blue light rising from the grave. It moves up into the air, high above you, and is lost in the wind and the storm—free out into the world at last.

You straighten up shakily and head back the way you came—where you see August standing in the doorway, wearing an old jumper and an expression of wide-eyed surprise.

TURN TO PAGE 84.

A LOVING TOUCH

You lean down to where she sits on the bench, holding her face gently to kiss her.

She kisses back with a soft sound of delight, seeming to grow more solid and corporeal with the connection. Your hands move downward with tender care, and underneath them, the body she once had seems to take shape—soaked through from the rain but warm. You feel her soft mouth, her chest moving as her breathing hitches in anticipation, the faint flutter of a beating heart—or the memory of one.

She doesn't speak, but she draws you down to her eagerly. She presses toward your touch, her body seeking the physical comfort and pleasure denied her in life. Your hands slide under the flowing dress that moves dreamily around her. Her back arches as she tugs at your clothes just enough to touch you, just enough to pull you toward her. You yield to her unspoken request.

She buries her face into your neck as she moves against you, her hands clutching at your back like a prayer.

You pour all the care you can into your motions, and the soft glow builds under her skin until she lets out a long, trembling sigh of pleasure. Her eyes close contentedly as she curls into you, but her body seems to be losing shape again, curves indistinct, until in your arms there's only a glowing light in the shape of a person.

You pull your clothes back to rights, and the light leads you by the hand out into the rain. You move dreamlike in her wake.

Down past the graves is a dirty, hidden-away corner where an old well sits forgotten by a gnarled black tree, still covered by a half-rotted roof. The flower the ghost first held appears again in her shining fingers. You take it and place it by the base of the well, a token of remembrance.

As the petals touch the ground, there's a rush of air in the graveyard. Wind swirls in a circle, and far away, you hear the door back into the castle banging open. The light beside you soars up in a long arc to crash against the roof of the well, which crumbles down into the dark, burying her remains for good. The indistinct figure of light rises up, up into the air until it's high above you. Then it's lost in the wind and the storm—free out into the world at last.

The dreamlike feeling fades along with the last of the glow on your fingertips, and you turn back toward the courtyard door.

Framed in the dark archway is August, standing there wearing an old jumper and an expression of wide-eyed surprise, one eyebrow raised.

TURN TO PAGE 84.

FINAL GIRL (GENDER-NEUTRAL)

You have to get out of here. With every ounce of strength you can summon, you force yourself to turn and run back up the steps of the crypt. But as you drag your eyes away, you see a last glance of the woman, eyes widening in fury, mouth gaping wide to show her prominent canines, fingers clawing into talons that stretch out toward you—

You sprint up the steps and out into the rain, slamming the door closed—but there's no key to lock her in, and you hear an unearthly rattle of laughter ringing through from the other side. You run, hearing a slow scrape of stone as the thing in the mausoleum slowly starts to drag the door open behind you.

The way back inside the castle is still shut fast, and the windows are too small to climb through even if you broke them—but away at the side of the courtyard, a crumbling wall leads out to the forest below. Away from the woman in the crypt's presence, the eerie calm has drained out of you and is being rapidly replaced by raw, primal panic. Your every nerve is on fire, your brain screaming at you, every part of you hellbent on escape. Casimir may have told you not to leave the castle until morning, but you know with a cold certainty that the thing behind you will kill you if you stay in the courtyard, and you see only one choice.

You haul yourself up over the wet, crumbling wall with more strength than you thought you had, then drop down with a skid over the other side. In the faint moonlight you can see trees ahead—what must be the forest on the far side of the castle—and you dart into them as you hear the mausoleum door open with an enormous scrape in the courtyard behind you. A death-rattle-hoarse voice rings through the wall—or is it your head?—seeming to echo louder than it should: "I will find you."

Something ancient-wired deep in your brain seizes your limbs with the adrenaline of a prey animal, and before you can think about it, you are running.

The air is cold as you pelt down the hill through the trees, tripping and falling and picking yourself up to continue doggedly onward. You hear sounds of something behind you, hunting you. You're wide awake, your whole mind propelled determinedly forward. Can she smell you? Or could it be whatever else is in the forest?

In the rain and moonlight you can make out the shapes of trees just enough to avoid them as you go. After what might be a terrified minute or twenty—no way to tell—you emerge out of the forest and into what seems like fields, the sky open above you. This isn't the way you came, you realize—you're out on the other side of the hill.

TURN TO PAGE 52.

AUGUST'S EXPERIMENT HAS HAD A SLIGHT ADJUSTMENT TO THE CONDITIONS

Emerging from the stairway is a very surprised August, mouth forming a perfect, dramatic O. They now have an oversized knit V-neck pulled over their red dress—no longer on show for company but still very fully *dressed*. You feel very aware of looking . . . tousled.

August's eyes flick from the sleeping man back to you, your bare legs under the robe, then they beckon you imperiously over.

"That was an *experiment*; you've spoilt tonight's results by changing the conditions," August whispers as you arrive, but they sound positively gleeful. "If he's improved, how are we to know whether the new tea recipe is any better or whether it's all down to your . . . *ministrations*?"

You vaguely apologize, though you're not really sure that's what August wants. "Oh, it's no use now. There's hardly any point trying to make observations now," they say, still sounding delighted. "How *delicious*. Well, don't let me interrupt."

They wave offhandedly toward the chained man. "I've opened that stuck door of yours. I can bring up blankets if you and Luka want to have more . . . time together." August's teasing voice is soft over the man's name, like he's a friend.

August leans in close to you, glittering eyes trying to read you. "*Or* perhaps you're well satisfied and off to try your luck ravishing everyone else in the house, too? If so, you're *very* welcome to join me downstairs," they whisper, a coy tilt to their shoulders. It's a playful flirtation, but it sounds like a genuine offer. Finding you here has apparently dramatically increased their interest in you. "We're all friends here; he doesn't mind sharing," they purr. "And don't worry—I shan't ask for all the sordid details. I'll just have them from Luka another time."

› Stay with Luka. **TURN TO PAGE 60.**

› Go with August. **TURN TO PAGE 64.**

BOTTOM OF THE LAKE

For a moment, you think she's fallen in by mistake. Your eyes open in the dark water, and you're relieved to see her there unhurt, drifting among the reed stems. Her pale eyes are wide, hands gripping tight to the sides of your head. Her long hair floats around her in a huge, ghostly cloud, seaweed-like in the moonlit water.

You try to move upward for air, and her hands do not let go.

Panic rises within you. You're still close to the rock, still not too far from the edge of the lake, and your feet kick off from the bottom to try to propel yourself upward. She smiles back at you, hands vice-like upon your head, and you're unable to break free, unable to get your head above the water to shout for help.

The thing draws you slowly downward and out toward the deepest part of the lake. You struggle and cry, thrashing as she drags you out through the reeds, placid and beautiful. You hear the very faint sound of voices fade away as she pulls you deeper, and eventually the murky water filters out all the moonlight as you're dragged down into the dark. You feel clinging waterweeds across your body and then muddy sediment and unseen wriggling things underfoot as you reach the bottom of the lake.

You try to cry out for help in an involuntary panic, and water rushes into your lungs. The beautiful creature kisses you as you struggle, and the last of your life gives out. The final thing that crosses your mind is wondering whether she was a guest at the party.

YOUR NIGHT ENDS, AND SO DO YOU.

You have met your end. To return to the start of the section, **GO TO PAGE 213**. To restart from dinner, **GO TO PAGE 28**.

BUDDY SYSTEM

Panic rises as you open your eyes in the dark water and see her pulling you through the reed stems, gripping the sides of your head, pale eyes and smile still wide. Her long hair floats around her in a huge, ghostly cloud, seaweed-like in the moonlit water.

When you try to move upward, she does not let go, her hands vice-like, and you can't break free, your muffled shouts only bubbles under the water. You remember Raisa nearby and splash your arms above the surface, thrashing and struggling as loudly as possible. The creature is still pulling you downward and out toward the deepest part of the lake—

Something moves quicker than you can see, and the woman relinquishes her grasp.

You're yanked up and out of the lake, where you splutter and gasp the air back into your lungs. Raisa is holding on to your waist, baring her pointed teeth at the woman whose pale eyes shine just above the surface like a crocodile's. Raisa gives a hiss, and the ethereal woman slips back into the water and wriggles away like a pale eel into the depths of the lake.

You find yourself unceremoniously lifted like a sack of potatoes and carried through the reeds, where Raisa dumps you in the shallow water near the jetty.

"You're pretty crazy, you know!" Raisa says, sounding matter of fact and slightly impressed, slapping you on the back as you cough. "You never heard *rusalka* stories? It's good you have me, huh?" She crouches beside you in the shallows, grinning. "You had fun, though?"

You nod back, stupidly—you *did* have fun, though away from the woman's enchanting gaze, you're able to remember details your mind had brushed aside before: her webbed hands, the strange thin pupils in her bulbous eyes.

"She won't chase you; she's scared. You are safe with me!" says Raisa, drifting out into the lake until she's almost up to her shoulders. She throws her arms out, gesturing at the mountains in the dark. "It's beautiful, huh?" she grins, eyes bright. It is beautiful and wild and dangerous all at once—like Raisa herself. As the wind blows through the trees, rain patters on the surface of the lake, rough and ghostly in the moonlight. Raisa tosses wet hair out of her face, unconcerned. Her cheeks round in a smile as she sticks out a hand, inviting you closer.

- Join Raisa in the water and kiss her. **TURN TO PAGE 218.**
- Go and join the werewolves together. **TURN TO PAGE 220.**
- Suggest you both go back inside. **TURN TO PAGE 224.**

THE LOST SOUL

You move down the corridor, feet echoing on the stone floors, and see the faint glow disappearing out of sight around a corner. You hurry to follow, heading down a winding passageway, then a set of creaking wooden stairs, never quite close enough to see what it is.

You emerge onto what must be the ground floor. The relentless rain hammers above you and against the windows you pass by in the darkness, but otherwise the castle is still and quiet. You strain your eyes to make out the space.

Suddenly there's a crack, and a bolt of lightning illuminates the shape of an arched window. Beyond the glass, a woman with pale skin and a flowing dress is standing in a courtyard, blue against the night—almost the same faint blue of the glow. Her mournful eyes lock with yours through the glass, and she points urgently to one side before the courtyard plunges back into darkness.

Toward the place she gestured, you can make out a door. Finding the latch by touch, you creak it open.

It's dry as you step out onto what must be a covered walkway, sheltered from the rain. You leave your flickering candle on a thick stone windowsill out of the wind, and as a dark cloud shifts overhead, you see the courtyard in the thin moonlight.

You're standing in a walkway that rings a garden, columns and arches separating the dry pathway from the overgrowth beyond. Once-grand fountains, stone now spotted and discolored, loom unmoving among evergreen shrubs hunched close to the ground. Bare branches reach upward from trees that have lost their leaves, stretching like fingers into the night.

The gardens seem to extend far into the distance. Farther away you can make out a cracked statue with a head missing and rows of shapes you can't identify rising from tangles of bracken. Lightning flickers in the clouds high above—and in the flash, you realize it's a graveyard. A large mausoleum looms at the center, its door slightly ajar.

Before you can wonder whether it would be best to just curl up in an empty room somewhere and hope for the best, the courtyard door swings shut behind you in the wind. You half wonder whether August is following you around, doing it on purpose.

- Walk around the covered archway. **TURN TO PAGE 34.**
- Look around inside the mausoleum. **TURN TO PAGE 85.**

THE GUEST ROOM

August slips back out the door, the fabric of their blazer whispering by your arms as they pass.

"I expect Casimir would tell you not to wander around. But I won't." They stand in the pitch-black corridor, only just visible—only a glint of candlelight on sharp, white teeth.

"Although," you hear from the shadows, August clearly relishing being as ominous as possible, "I'd avoid the attic if I were you . . ."

The door swings closed, and you find yourself alone in the room.

Moving around with the candle, you find an ancient wardrobe in dark wood. It's empty inside apart from a thick pair of socks, some very old-fashioned-looking flannel pajamas, and a thick dressing gown, which all seem to be in your size. You wonder whether August bothered picking them out for you earlier.

With your clothes still damp from the rain, you decide to change and find the nightclothes warmer and more comfortable than you'd expected. The candle burns slowly, fighting off the gloom, and you leave it alight as you slide into the cold sheets.

The night is not quiet. Rain and wind howl outside.

Then, far above you, you're sure you hear a heavy thump and some kind of rattling, then a thump again.

In the stillness that follows, you can hear a strange muffled sound close to the head of the ancient bed. You shuffle upward to put your ear to the wall and distinctly hear an intake of breath next door and what sounds like a woman crying.

Who else is in the castle?

- Take a candle and leave the room to investigate the noises. **TURN TO PAGE 36.**
- Stay in bed. **TURN TO PAGE 195.**

QUESTION THE CHAINED MAN

"Oh, oh—I'm locked up for my own good," he says. "I'm an experiment. I mean, I'm new. I'm being experimented on? Maybe that's not the way to say it in English . . ."

You must not look very reassured, because he scrambles on, trying to explain. "But I forgot to—I did it in the wrong order. There is medicine I need on the table, please, quickly. Just bring it over—that is all. There is tea—the medicine is in the tea."

Approaching slowly, you notice that, sure enough, sitting on the table beside the candles is a now-cold teacup with a strainer containing a wet sludge of dried flowers and spices sitting next to it.

You ask whether he needs help getting free, but he shakes his head fervently. "The tea, please, quickly."

- › Slide the tea toward him, and let him chug it. **TURN TO PAGE 56.**
- › Don't give him the tea. **TURN TO PAGE 88.**

GO BACK TO BED

Okay, you go back to bed. You ignore any further strange ominous noises, distant screams, and rattling chains. You stay perfectly still. The candles burn low, then burn out, and you lie in the darkness, not listening to anything that may or may not be going on somewhere out in the castle. You have no more adventures and hang out with no vampires.

Slowly, the gray light of dawn creeps into the room, and the noises stop. The room looks strangely ordinary—a slightly dusty stone chamber.

You dress, you go downstairs, and you see nobody around.

In the light of morning, the castle is cold and ordinary and, as far as you can tell, entirely empty of people. You can't find your way back to the dining room or anywhere you really recognize. In fact, nowhere you go leads to any sign of habitation, any sign of the people you met last night. You almost wonder whether the whole thing was a dream—if not, there's certainly no note, no sign that anybody here wants to see you.

Eventually, you open another door at random, and daylight floods in. You realize you've opened a side door and can see a path leading back down to the road.

TURN TO PAGE 265.

THE RESCUE

With shaking hands, you pull Andrei's handwritten note out of your pocket—slightly smeared in the damp but still readable. You try to wipe your phone screen dry, fingers slipping once or twice as you tap in his number.

You almost cry when you hear his sleepy voice on the other end of the line. You quickly read out the name and number of the bus stop you can see by the light of your phone and tell him the car broke down and something is chasing you. His voice goes from sleep-rough to alert in ten seconds, like he was expecting danger.

"Bad place to be in the dark," he says seriously. "I will come now."

You sit damp and shivering at the bus stop, looking out at the falling rain. You try to make out any sign of movement in the dark trees farther up the slope that disappears up into the night but convince yourself you see nothing. You fiddle with your phone, nervously pressing the button to light up the screen—but the battery is finally dead.

You're alone in the dark, just you and the sound of the rain as it hammers on the shelter roof over your head.

The minutes go by agonizingly slowly—until far away up the hill in the forest, you hear a noise. You haven't figured out whether to run or hide when you jump—something is standing a long way off in the field ahead.

It looks like the shape of a person, but there's something wrong with the way it stands. You think you can see eyes reflecting back the moonlight, like a cat's in the darkness.

You stare back, meeting its impassive gaze. You both know what's going to happen next.

But before the thing can move, you hear the screech of tires on the wet road and see a flare of light as a car bursts out of the trees. It swerves in front of you, and the passenger door swings open before it even comes to a full stop. As something moves at the edge of your vision, you throw yourself inside and slam the door behind you.

In the driver's seat, Andrei is not looking at you as he puts the pedal to the floor—his eyes are wide and serious as they flick from the mirror to the road ahead. As the car lurches forward, something big bangs against the rear window, the jolt shuddering through the metal, but it seems to glance off as the car picks up speed. There's a last horrible scratch against a back door, and Andrei swerves in the road and you're slammed to the side—but it works. There's a thump behind you as whatever was chasing the car lets go.

"Sorry," Andrei says earnestly as the car pelts down the road and you shakily put on your seat belt. For the next ten minutes he's completely focused on driving, keeping the wet tires under control. You turn and speed back along the winding forbidden road, heading far away from the forest and the castle.

You watch the dark trees whirl past as you fly along the slippery tarmac—but Andrei seems to know the way well. You hear no more noises, no signs of pursuit. After a while, the trees thin and give way into fields on either side, and Andrei seems to let out a breath. You see his big hands' white-knuckle grip relax on the wheel.

He seems slightly unsure of what to say.

Then in a frustrated rush: "The borrowed car. I am sorry it broke. I did not know you came this way—why did you go along the death road?"

The forbidden road was common knowledge, then. You explain there was an accident, a diversion—and that you're pretty sure you ended up in a vampire castle but ran away. You wonder whether it sounds ridiculous, but Andrei nods seriously.

When you ask whether he knew about the vampires, he pauses but then makes a small noise of agreement and disapproval. "Everyone in town knows these creatures. In old bad times, they bring us food, if we, uh, give blood in bags from doctor. A good trade. So we do not try to hurt them, but it is better to leave them alone. Not all safe. Some . . . *very* dangerous."

When you turn onto a road with streetlights again, Andrei lets out another long breath, easing slightly. You start to see other cars' taillights leaving red trails in the dark.

He leans back, runs one hand through his hair, and clears his throat. "I have one extra room," he says haltingly. "You will be safe. We must wait for morning to go back, get your bag from the bad car."

When you agree, he nods seriously again. You sit in relieved silence beside him, winding through the rain toward normality. He glances at you as he drives and gives you a small, shy smile. "It's good you called," he says with a relief that mirrors your own.

TURN TO PAGE 235.

THE BUS STOP

You're tiring now, dizzy with the exertion, but hear another faint noise far behind and continue desperately on. As you race across the steep fields, you can feel your limbs growing clumsy while your mind stays sharp with panic.

Then you trip, and you're too shocked to do anything as you go down. You tumble forward in the blackness, smacking into wet, prickly grass and rolling down over and over, faster and faster until you feel like you're about to lose consciousness. And then the steep slope evens out onto wet, smooth tarmac.

You're lying on a road.

You pull yourself slowly to your feet—battered and horribly bruised, with one ankle twisted. But you find you can still *just* put weight on it. No limbs seem broken.

Rain falls in the dark night around you. You must have gained ground in the fall, put a solid distance between yourself and whatever creatures may now be following.

This road is much wider than the one you drove down. And a little way off, you can see a faint square shape, gleaming wet in the moonlight—a bus shelter.

Panting, you limp toward it and collapse down on the seat. Could you wait out the night here? You pull your phone out of your pocket to find the screen cracked but the rest intact.

- ◆ If you have the marker **DEAD PHONE** . . . the screen is black and inert, and nothing happens when you try to turn it on. **TURN STRAIGHT TO PAGE 57.**

- ◆ Otherwise . . . **KEEP READING.**

The phone screen still lights up in your hand, 3 percent battery still holding out—and over on this side of the hill, there's a single bar of signal. You scroll quickly to your gran's number and hear it go to voicemail—not a surprise, as she rarely has any signal. You try the landline but remember she's out at a party as you listen to the phone ring out.

The icon now reads 2 percent. Almost gone. And then you remember the note in your pocket.

- › Call Andrei. **TURN TO PAGE 50.**
- › Give up on trying to get in touch. Wait out the night. **TURN TO PAGE 57.**

THE ATTIC

You head to your right and up the stone stairway, which turns and spirals up several flights toward the shuffling noise above.

Eventually, you emerge into a large stone room high in the castle. Huge wooden ceiling beams slope downward to a dusty floor, and by the dim light of candles on a distant table, you can make out someone else on the far side of the attic.

Chained to the wall—with huge, forbidding manacles around his hands, feet, and throat—sits a short man without any shoes on.

His jeans are loose, shirt sleeves rolled up haphazardly, and eyes half hidden by loose brown curls that tumble around his face. He's paused halfway through cleaning his glasses on the front of his shirt, and where it's untucked you can see a glimpse of his belly, a fuzz of soft, dark curls trailing downward against tanned white skin.

As he sees you, he struggles forward with a jolt, only for the huge chains to stop him after about a foot. The manacles are strangely loose around his limbs, as if made for someone much bigger.

"*Ajutor!*" he calls at you from across the room in a panicked, accented voice—European but not local—and then when you don't respond, "Help, please! There's no time."

› Move toward him to help.
TURN TO PAGE 54.

› Ask why he's chained up.
TURN TO PAGE 48.

HELP THE CHAINED MAN

You hurry forward, telling him in English you'll help, and he replies, "Thank you, thank you—on the table, there is a cup, you must bring it—"

Sure enough, there's a teacup sitting on the table next to the candles, a few feet out of his reach. It's full of a now-cold liquid with flecks of black at the bottom, and a strainer with a wet sludge of dried flowers and spices sits beside it.

You're not sure what you expected the help to entail, but it wasn't fetching him tea.

He asks for the cup again, urgent voice telling you to hurry. You carry it over, and he chugs the whole thing with a shiver.

"Thank you," he says, with real relief. "I messed up. I have to take my, uh, special medicine, every time. I must remember."

You eye the strainer full of dead plants on the table. What are the vampires doing to this guy? You try to find a sensitive way to ask whether he's being drugged.

"Yes, yes, drugged," he says gratefully, as if he couldn't remember the word for it. "Usually one of them comes up to check on me, but tonight nobody came yet."

Will he be punished if he doesn't do as they say? How soon until they come back? you wonder.

He still looks agitated, hands tight where they're still holding the teacup. "But you must leave, quickly, before—before anything bad happens. You are in danger. Please, go."

- Stay to find out more. **TURN TO PAGE 56.**
- Do as he says—go back downstairs toward your guest room and follow the corridor the other way. **TURN TO PAGE 46.**

AUGUST'S EXPERIMENT IS SAVED

On the stairs on the way down, you run into a very surprised August. They now have an oversized knit V-neck pulled over their red dress—no longer dressed up for company.

"Is everything all right?" they ask very warily, body tense. "Have you . . . met Luka?"

When you say that you gave the man upstairs the cup of tea, their whole body sags with exaggerated relief.

"Fuck," they say, sounding more earnest than you've heard them so far. "*Thank* you." And then, half to themself: "All he has to remember is to drink the tea *before* closing the handcuffs. *Must* I do everything myself around here?"

Returning their attention to you, they gesture lazily as they explain. "There are particular plant leaves one can extract a chemical from, which helps make their transformations more manageable. I grew the plants in the gardens for a friend with the condition, and then their friends heard about it, and next thing you know, there's a sizeable population of werewolves on the outskirts of town who all want tea at their time of the month. Raisa made friends with the wolves; Caz says he doesn't like them, but he'd go on a murder spree if anything happened to them. I provide the tea, of course, but I'm always hoping to experiment with improvements."

You nod, trying to process this new information about the number of supernatural beings living in your gran's small rural village. August looks back at you appraisingly, as if revising their estimation of you upward.

"I hope he didn't give you a fright. To be perfectly frank, I didn't really expect you to leave the room. The castle can be rather forbidding nowadays."

Promising to return, they disappear upstairs for a moment to speak to Luka and take notes. Then they glide back down the stairs ahead of you and manage to shove your door back open with their unnatural, fluid strength. "I ought to fix that," they say musingly. Their eyes flick down over you. "Would you like to join me downstairs? If you don't mind getting dressed again, I've a fire lit; it's rather cozy." They give you a sharp smile that looks almost genuine. "I didn't mean to leave you so bored that you felt the need to *wander off*."

- Accept August's invitation and join them downstairs. **TURN TO PAGE 64.**
- Decline. You're done with the supernatural and want to go home. **TURN TO PAGE 49.**

THE TRANSFORMATION

Before you can ask anything further, his eyes widen and hands spasm, empty teacup falling to the floor, where it cracks and rolls away. Through one of the windows set into the attic roof, a thin light is now spilling into the room: The rain clouds have parted, revealing the full moon.

You hear him whimper, but it seems to curdle in his throat into something else—a snarl? He folds in on himself, chains tight as he jerks, shaking his head as if to ward something off. His glasses clatter to the floor. His biceps bulge as if he's flexing them, limbs and torso thickening, growing visibly in front of your eyes. As you step away, his head rolls back with a moan, and his chest swells, popping off most of the top buttons to reveal the hair on the curve of his pecs beneath. Suddenly the shirt is tight to his big shoulders and soft belly—he fits the manacles, and his formerly loose jeans are tight and straining against the hard muscle of his thighs. There's a growl in his throat, thick hair on his forearms . . . but he's not actually a wolf.

He looks paused, partway to animal but definitely still a man—a very well-built, powerful man. His eyes are still sharp with human intelligence, but he looks stormy and wild. His muscles ripple as he flexes against his chains.

"Thank you," he grates out, his voice rough as if restraining himself against some hidden urge. "I was changed not long ago, so I find it . . . hard to control. The medicine makes the change less extreme. But it is not perfect. August is trying to improve it." His jaw flexes, his teeth snap, and he shakes his head, as if trying to stay still. He looks up at you warningly, teeth sharp in his mouth. "I am still dangerous."

You're still standing out of his reach, but you notice his eyes moving hungrily over your body—even though you're pretty thoroughly covered up. He lets out a soft, involuntary grunt that might be . . . arousal?

When he speaks again, his growling voice sounds tight with need. "If you stay here much longer . . . I have to tell you: I can't always resist my animal impulses." He's breathless, eyes wild. The chains hold him back—but you could get close enough to touch, if you wanted.

- Wish him luck with the experiment and head back down the stairs to explore the castle. **TURN TO PAGE 55.**
- Get him to touch you. Let him indulge his animal impulses. **TURN TO PAGE 58.**

NOTHING CAN SAVE YOU NOW

You lean your head back against the bus stop behind you, trying not to be aware of a faint sound far up the hill that sounds like the crack of branches underfoot. You're still wheezing, out of breath—you won't make it far on your twisted ankle and can't summon the energy to run.

You squeeze your eyes shut tight and think about your gran telling you not to go along the forbidden road. What will she say if she hears you're gone? You feel your throat contract and swallow the tears, trying not to think about it.

When you look back up, there is someone in the field.

It looks like the shape of a person, but there's something wrong with the way it stands. You think you can see eyes reflecting back the moonlight, like a cat's in the darkness.

You stare back, meeting its eyes. You both know what's going to happen next. The shape moves faster than you can see in the dark, and then everything ends.

It happens quickly—mercifully quickly—without you having to see more of the thing that comes for you. There's only an instant of searing pain in your neck as you register you've been slammed back against the bus stop. You thump to the wet tarmac and lose consciousness before the life is drained out of you.

YOUR NIGHT ENDS, AND SO DO YOU.

You've met your end. To restart from dinner, **GO TO PAGE 28.**

To go back to the start of the section, **GO TO PAGE 46.**

ANIMAL IMPULSES

When you tell him you like the sound of those animal impulses, he lets out a helpless groan. His chains rattle, pulling taut as he tries to move toward you.

You approach slowly, dropping the robe as you walk, so you're standing with only the thin fabric of the borrowed nightclothes between you. You stay just out of reach of his hands, his mouth. He's straining against the chains now, panting.

"*Closer*," he pleads in a low, rough bark of a voice, unable to stop himself. Instead of moving, you pull the shirt off over your head and watch him writhe, arms bulging against his restraints. His body is humanoid but magnified: big and thick with hair, the taut jeans leaving little to the imagination.

He looks ready to tear through the rest of your clothes, so you pull them off slowly before getting closer, watching his anticipation build. His tongue moves over his teeth as he watches the last fabric fall to the floor. Another low snarl sounds in his throat.

His teeth snap as he strains toward you, his hips shift like he's barely conscious of it, desperate for touch.

You watch his building frenzy for a few more moments until it seems like he might actually rip the chains from the wall, then step forward into his space to press against him.

His body reacts, animal and uninhibited. His hands are rough and impatient on your body, pulling you toward him so he can slacken the chains and move his limbs freely. His strong arms take hold possessively. As you join together, you feel his hot breath and teeth sharp at your ear, animal noises ripped from his throat that build to a panting rhythm as he draws out your pleasure with no gentleness.

◆ Gain the marker **ANIMAL IMPULSES.**

He lets the feeling shudder through you both, basking in the full enjoyment of the sensation.

His weight is heavy on you as his body relaxes. You extricate yourself and pull the discarded robe back around you, finding a folded towel to clean up with by the table, then throwing it to the bulky man so he can do the same. Drowsy with contentment, he slides down the wall to where his chains have enough give to let him curl up on the floor.

You hear his heavy breath fall into the pattern of sleep almost immediately. You're still looking vaguely for your discarded clothes when you hear a creak on the stairs.

TURN TO PAGE 43.

PUPPY LOVE

August doesn't seem crestfallen at all when you turn them down. They return with an armful of blankets and pillows, then turn on their heel with a theatrical whisper of "I'll leave you two alone."

Luka is dozing in the chains but twitches when you draw closer. "The key's in my back pocket, so I can't reach," he mumbles. "I'm all right now. It's safe. Could you—?"

Your hands slide around his muscled thighs appreciatively as you find the key, and then you carefully click open the holds. His big limbs fall, loose and satisfied, and he curls up on the blanket you've laid on the floor.

You manage to slide a pillow under his head, and he nuzzles instinctively into it, already falling deeply asleep. He wraps a thick arm around you in a half doze as you lie down beside him. His body warms the makeshift bed, holding you close, and you sleep better than you have in a long time.

You wake in the early morning in the warm arms of a smaller and more human man, chest still thick with hair but less unnaturally so. He presses sleepily against you, and when you press back, he lets out a small noise of satisfaction, hand trailing over your side. You feel his mouth smiling against you as he kisses down your neck, shifting to press soft bites down your chest and over your belly, then spends the next hour learning exactly what you enjoy. You both fall back asleep, bed-warm and tangled together, and when you both wake properly, there's a steaming teapot and mugs sitting next to a bag of pastries near the stairs, with a note for Luka that turns his ears pink when he reads it. "August is a good friend but very embarrassing" is all he'll say to you, grinning bashfully with a blanket pulled up over his knees.

As if trying to make up for your less-than-conventional meeting the night before, he strikes up a conversation, asking your name with an abashed grin, then how you came here and about your gran. He listens carefully but eats and pulls on his clothes quickly at the same time, finding his glasses to jam them on. He runs a hand through his tousled curls.

"Excuse me, I feel"—he says, and then as if looking for the word in English—"gross? I will wash and see you in a moment." By the time you've finished your pastry and descended the cold stone stairway, now lit gray in the light of morning, you can hear bustling in the room to the left of yours.

As you put your now-dry clothes back on, you're wondering how to find the terrible car and reluctantly thinking about flights. But when you come out of your room, you see Luka sticking his head out of his doorway to meet you. "Come and look," he says with an earnestness you can't say no to.

He leads you over to the arched window of his room that he's thrown open to the cold, gray day. Out of his window the slope descends dramatically into a thick mist that lurks ominously over the trees in the valleys (and, presumably somewhere down there, your abandoned car). Luka is staring out into the morning like it's the best thing he's ever seen, his warm breath clouding in the air in front of him and steaming up his glasses. "It's beautiful, no?" he says.

You peer out at the gray. Farther away, the low clouds brush the distant hills.

The forest extends out in all directions, occasional birds rising over the treetops. It is beautiful, now that you look at it. Close to the castle, the conifers thin to reveal a stream rushing by, and you point it out. Luka gives you a huge grin back. "Yes! It comes from near the top of the mountain. Have you been?" He turns to look at you, eyes bright, dark curls ruffling gently in the cold air. "You have a plane to catch, maybe, but it is a shame. You are so close! The view is beautiful on the other side. The trail is very short, very easy."

From where you're standing together in the window, you can feel his warmth, see his dark eyelashes and pink-cold cheeks close-up. "I know there is some kind of trouble at night," he says seriously, "but the forest is safe during the daylight. I was planning to go out soon—morning is the best time."

- London can wait. Go for a hike with Luka. **TURN TO PAGE 62.**
- Reject Luka's offer—walk back to the car and return to London. **TURN TO PAGE 265.**

HIKE WITH LUKA

Luka beams and starts pulling things out of drawers when you say you'll come with him.

His guest room is more lived-in than yours—clean and full of small personal items, like maybe he stays every month. On the bedside table there's a beat-up old crime paperback in another language next to his glasses case, ChapStick, tissues, and a handful of coins that he sweeps up to put in his pockets.

He puts on a fleece and a serious-looking waterproof jacket over his button-up, then pulls on proper hiking boots. Despite the cold, he's wearing actual shorts that show off the muscled curves of his tanned, hairy legs—but his body is warm as he moves apologetically past you to pack his bag.

You adjust your mental picture of him as he bounces around the room, bundling water bottles and a Swiss Army knife into a backpack with a profusion of straps, which he tosses easily over his shoulder as if it weighs nothing. He's wearing an actual compass on a string around his neck. "The weather is good, so you will be okay!" he says, gesturing at your non-hiking clothes reassuringly. And you are reassured. This guy is extremely prepared.

Outside, you don't tell him that he looks like a dog that's excited to be on a walk. But he's obviously happy in the wide-open space, eager to move, bounding forward up a wet track you would have found difficult to pinpoint on your own. All that remains of the storm are fallen branches and a very thin, misty drizzle that fades away as you continue up the path.

He stops to point out interesting mushrooms and edible berries as he walks and occasionally goes still in a way that reminds you of an animal's ears pricking up. He puts his finger gently to his lips, then raises the hand like he wants you to wait for something. When you listen, you hear birdsong.

At the top of the incline, the land falls away in a breathtaking vista, the haze of mist now clear enough to see the mountains far beyond where they fade into the blue distance. Luka unrolls a thin, dry cushion and spreads it on a flat rock for you to both sit down on, then pulls out cereal bars, pieces of fruit, and handmade sandwiches he's wrapped carefully in foil. You sit companionably together, looking over the hills ahead of you as you eat.

After a while, Luka starts talking in a soft voice, as if to avoid disturbing the wildlife, telling you how the mountains here are different from the ones back home.

"Home" turns out to be a town on the Croatian coast near a national park.

"I grew up by the sea but mostly lived in the mountains after I was bitten—an accident, but a big change, you know. So I trained, and now I work in national parks.

"At full moon, I would go hike far away from people. I love being out in the mountains! So it was okay at first. But it was lonely, and my family want me close to home—I want that, too. One day I met someone else the same as me. She's from a family where they're all wolves. They tell me about a place to get this special tea—her sister uses it to be safe with her children. So I came here and met August, who's making tea that works for me. Soon I can live in the same town as my family again."

On his phone, he shows you absurdly beautiful photos that look like postcards—dramatic mountains rising out of green forests, swiping past occasional pictures of friends around campfires between the fairy-tale waterfalls. You show him pictures in return—they don't look quite as much like a nature photography calendar, but he takes an earnest interest, asking questions and properly laughing at your mildly funny comments.

He talks about his family warmly, and when you ask, he's excited to show you his hometown, grinning kids he tells you fondly are nieces and nephews, the beach in the summer.

You lean closer to see better, and the edge of your hand makes contact with the warm skin of his. You both look up together, meeting each other's eyes. The mountain wind blows through his messy curls as he grins. "You should visit in the summer," he says straightforwardly.

You think about how hot Julys are now in siesta-less London, every year an existentially terrifying record-breaker that turns the Tube (of course you're not on a line with air-conditioning) into a sort of sauna endurance test. On his phone, you look at the shade of the low trees on the hills, the absurdly azure water lapping at the rocky shore.

Luka laughs easily. "Maybe you think it's crazy, but I have a house from my grandmother when she died, with many rooms. It's beautiful, peaceful. I can cook; you can meet my friends. If you want, put your number—we can talk about it." He offers his phone with a warm hand.

› Put your number in Luka's phone. **TURN TO PAGE 65.**

› Decline politely and go back to London. **TURN TO PAGE 265.**

AUGUST'S INVITATION

In the guest room, you pull your mostly dry clothes back on and emerge to August's slow smile. They still look slightly menacing, despite actually seeming pleased to see you this time—you think it's the teeth.

They lead you down through pitch-dark corridors, cobwebs, and dust and into a large, once-luxurious room lit by a fire. A faded settee and a couple of mismatched chairs have been drawn into a disorderly circle in front of the fireplace, and August moves toward them to add another log to the fire. The area around the fire is mostly bare and clear of clutter—just small tables and cabinets with a couple of notebooks and old-fashioned ink bottles on top—which stands in stark contrast to the rest of the room.

In the dancing flames, you see the long shadows flickering over wardrobes and cabinets, boxes and chests, all crowded with things you can't quite make out in the darkness—vases of dried flowers, insects and fern fronds laid out in glass picture frames, a stuffed crow. You move unconsciously toward the unlit parts of the room, trying to get a better look, and see a cabinet with a row of something on top, just-visible round shapes laid out in a long row. Tentatively, you reach out toward one and feel something cool and smooth, then the points of sharp teeth.

August slides up behind you, a lamp in one hand that illuminates the scene. You find your outstretched fingers are resting on the jaw of a canine skull, poised on a metal stick with the mouth open. Below you is a long row of skulls that begins with small rodents down to your left and ends with what looks like bears to your right, all posed dramatically in their place. Some face each other, as if in conversation; others have dried flower stems threaded into the eye sockets, exploding with bouquets.

TURN TO PAGE 155.

THE TOWN BY THE SEA

Luka walks you back down to the beat-up terrible car, which together you manage to start up. Before you close the door, he leans in to press a kiss just beside your mouth. His stubble brushes rough on your cheek. "It was good to meet you," he says in a low voice, and then he steps away, giving you a big, unselfconscious wave as you drive off.

You turn that night and morning after over in your head many times on the rattling Tube into work, where your boss has piled on plenty more projects to make up for your time off. Sometimes you dream you feel Luka against you in the night, but you wake up alone, hot and aching. You don't hear from him for weeks, and you really, really try not to think about it, but when you finally get a message, you feel like your heart's in your throat.

Hello! It's Luka :) It's getting cold here! the message reads, with a dazzlingly lovely photo of snow frozen onto the trees around a very blue lake beside a mountain.

You send him back a photo of a pigeon eating leftover chips on the grimy pavement you took near a bus stop this morning, and he sends back a mock-serious message about the incredible wildlife. You imagine him laughing as he presses Send.

You end up messaging a lot, talking about anything and everything. Luka is happy to ask questions about what you're eating for dinner and the weather, but he also seems to have an endless amount to say about certain topics he gets excited about. Sometimes you ask him to call so you can listen to his now-familiar accent like a podcast. He tells you about the conservation effort to save a species of snow vole in a specific stretch of the Dinaric Alps, then a cult '70s TV series he insists was "the best in former Yugoslavia"—even if you're fairly sure he was too young to have seen it when it actually aired.

By the time you visit in the summer, it feels natural and easy when he picks you up at the airport and pulls you into a tight hug, when he kisses you breathlessly in the front seat of his old car and you both get so absorbed, you almost cause a traffic incident in the parking lot.

He chats happily with the radio playing as he pulls off the dramatic highway that winds along the coast. His inherited house sits just out of town on a wooded slope at the end of a long track. It's all stone and red roof tiles, and as you step out of the cool interior, you emerge onto a sunny patio that overlooks the sea. Luka wraps his arms around you from behind, pointing out the small gate and steep path that lead down to the rocky beach below. He's still half telling you about the paths to walking trails through the woods as he kisses your neck and slides his hands lower with a growl, until you both end up pausing the guided tour for the rest of the afternoon.

In his lovely house, Luka spends half his time with you—at the beach splashing in the sea or lying in the shade, happily doing nothing. The other half he spends typing reports for national parks at the kitchen table, coming over periodically to kiss you so thoroughly that you lose track of what you were doing and he pulls you to bed. In the mornings, he pads around barefoot making coffee; in the evenings, he cooks, and you discover his very specific opinions about the best places to buy fresh seafood and the "real" way to cook squid ink risotto.

There's a full moon while you're there, and its effects apparently last several nights.

Luka spends them drinking new special-recipe tea, handcuffed to the bed frame. You're glad the house is up a long drive away from any others so you can both make as much noise as you want. You surface deliciously satisfied, and he spends the next week kissing the bruises on your thighs and the scratches on your back and bringing you cold drinks in the shade of the trees like you're a member of the royal family.

Occasionally you meet his easygoing friends or visit his lovely family, and his siblings' kids all get excited to try out their English on you. People learn your name in the town, and at the end of July, you're surprised to find yourself offered a job at a little shop on the old high street where the beaming owner insists she wants someone who speaks English for the tourists, three days a week. You tell Luka late at night in bed. He tells you casually that you can stay as long as you want, but can't stop smiling. He tells you he'll have to go to the mountains in the autumn and invites you along without thinking about it.

When you explain what happened to your friends on a call, nobody tells you that staying is a crazy idea. You look really happy, your best friend tells you, before she scrolls hungrily through the pictures you sent and asks when she can visit. Luka says anyone can visit any time, and he really means it.

Your friends arrive on a warm September evening. You sit with a cold drink on a balcony looking over the trees, surrounded by happy people and good food, thinking about the most satisfying way to tell your boss you finally quit. You watch Luka having an expressive and passionate conversation with one of your friends about conservation, hands drawing shapes in the air. Your best friend looks at you across the table, mouthing, *He's sooo sweet!*

You think about the chains and the handcuffs in the box under the bed: "We should keep using them, just in case," Luka had said with a wolfish smile before throwing you down on the mattress and making you feel so good, you briefly forgot where or who you were.

You drag your attention back to the present, where Luka is now excitedly demonstrating how to debone a fish, tea towel over his shoulder. Across the table, your best friend gives you a winey smile. "He's like a Labrador," she whispers.

You just nod and take a sip of your drink to stop yourself laughing too hard.

THE END

Want another adventure? See what else there is to do: **GO TO PAGE 266.**

CASIMIR'S STUDY

You thank Casimir and follow him to the stairs as Raisa disappears noisily off into the castle and August slips away through a far door.

The lamp in Casimir's hand casts foreboding shadows over his features and the far walls. He nods without a word and turns to lead you up into the gloom.

You emerge into a long gallery with grand portraits in ornate frames, but none are of the three vampires you've met. Instead they're almost all of the same man: thin and white, with papery pale skin and hair. The painted man's clothes differ wildly in fashion from one painting to another, but all look deliberately ostentatious—raiments of power, worn eagerly as symbols of superiority.

There's no trace of quiet confidence or humility captured here. In fact, everything about the man in the paintings strikes you as the complete opposite of the one striding before you. You wonder how they could be connected.

The portraits' gazes seem to follow you as you pass by. The pale man is smiling, but every painter has captured something cold in the eyes. In one, he stands with a younger woman with long hair who looks up at him adoringly, holding some symbolic flower. Farther along, you can make out several older paintings with a different wife—she stands regally beside him, dressed in black furs, and you think the two look better matched. Before the lamp moves on, it glints on a plaque at the bottom of a full-length portrait where the pale man stands with hunting dogs at his heels—the plaque reads: COUNT CASIMIR NECULCEA.

The man who called himself Casimir strides onward ahead of you with the lamp, and you hurry to keep up as the paintings return to the shadows.

You reach a spiral staircase of worn, uneven stone. Casimir moves with a steady, effortless stride upward until you reach a heavy door that creaks as it swings open. You're in one of the castle turrets, you realize, as he steps into a warmly lit room ahead of you.

The far wall is mostly taken up by a grand bed carved out of dark, ancient wood, its heavy red drapes carelessly half tossed aside. To one side there's a huge wardrobe with a door open onto dark, expensive fabrics within; on the other, there's a desk it takes you a moment to realize is covered in candles. The white cylinders rise from a sea of frozen wax and half-drowned candlesticks, as if left to drip carelessly down over the sides for many, many years into an intricate, sculptural landscape.

But the main thing you notice—in tall glass-fronted cases and in piles all over the floor—are the books. There seems to be a huge mixture: leatherbound sets with titles in Arabic and golden filigree whirling out around the edges; beat-up paperbacks with pulpy covers; large and small; old and new; French philosophers alongside slim volumes of poetry.

Two plush, comfortable armchairs face the hearth on a beautifully elaborate Persian rug that spans most of the room and looks like it cost more than your whole flat. Tall windows of warped glass look out onto the stormy night, rain hammering outside, but they're swathed and half covered by heavy drapes. There's a warm glow to the firelight, and you feel a welcome wave of heat as you step inside, starting to dry your damp clothes more thoroughly.

Closing the door with the same air of quiet confidence and absolute nonchalance at the fact he lives in a fucking castle, Casimir sets down the lamp on the mantelpiece and unhurriedly begins to shift some of the books piled in the way of the chairs to other parts of the room.

> Sit confidently in one of the armchairs, as if this is a totally normal experience for you. **TURN TO PAGE 75.**

> Wait for him to invite you to sit down. **TURN TO PAGE 71.**

MISBEHAVIOR

You apologize as seriously as you can, standing to move toward him. You're not that unsteady, but you exaggerate it just a bit so you can stumble into his lap. Your hand presses against the curve of his chest, just to make sure your position is secure.

Casimir slowly raises an eyebrow. His expression resettles—less disgusted, more disgruntled. He might still be angry, but he's definitely not pushing you off. "You weren't listening to a word I was saying," he says, low voice even and threatening.

Your faculties are still mostly intact, but your tongue is loose with wine. You tell him you wanted to listen; he was just *really* distracting.

He shifts a knee underneath you suddenly, and you catch yourself reflexively on the arm of the chair. You see him regarding you—he's testing to see how drunk you really are, you realize. He seems reasonably satisfied. "Hmm." The low noise vibrates through his chest to where you're sitting on his thighs. "And how exactly," he purrs, "were you intending to make it up to me?"

You swallow, and he watches your throat move. Not breaking eye contact, he slowly moves his legs to unbalance you, seeming to enjoy watching you flounder. He stops before you tip to the floor completely, but it leaves you undignified, spread over him. The firelight turns the edge of his face golden-brown, his dark eyes glimmering. "If I asked you to kneel, would you do it?" he asks in a tone of voice that feels like it's melting an important part of your brain into soup.

You slide off him and sink the rest of the way down to your knees in front of him almost without thinking, and he makes a disapproving noise low in his throat. "I only asked a question. I wanted an answer, not an action."

He leans forward until his elbows are on his spread knees, gaze still on yours. His face is close and intent. Your breath catches in your throat. "I invited you up to my private rooms, and you've repaid me with rudeness," he says in a low rumble. "You've misbehaved. If you want to be good, you'll act only when I give you permission."

- Sit back and tell him you'll be so good and so obedient. **TURN TO PAGE 102.**
- Tell him you're sorry you've been so bad, and you'd be willing to accept punishment. **TURN TO PAGE 99.**

AWAIT AN INVITATION

You remain standing, hovering by the chair. You hear a soft thump on the other side of the room as Casimir drops some of the books he's moved off the floor onto a table. He moves slowly back into view, placing a slim volume down on the mantelpiece.

He turns to look at you with a raised eyebrow, eyes slowly sweeping over your body before settling on your face. "Are you waiting for my instructions?" he says.

You pause for a moment, unsure how to respond. You can feel the thump of your heart in your chest. But there's a hint of a smile on his face. "You may sit," he says in a low, amused voice. You hurry to obey as he settles himself in the chair opposite you.

You're suddenly very aware that it's just the two of you alone up here in the low light. He looks up at you, running a finger slowly up the spine of a thick leather book he plays with in his hands, and doesn't break his gaze as he leans back to sprawl in the armchair.

You find yourself unable to look away. Although much of the castle seems in disrepair, his pose reminds you of a king at the height of his power—or a creature you've followed into its lair. This is his domain. The wind howls outside the window, and you have the wild thought that if you were to scream, nobody would hear.

He turns the book in his hands as he surveys you, as if waiting to see what you'll do next.

"You're very . . . obedient." He speaks slowly into the silence, drawing out the statement and letting the words roll deliciously around his mouth, as if savoring them—just a little teasing. "Maybe you like following orders."

> Talk to him and find out more about him. (If that was an offer, it seems it will stay open.) **TURN TO PAGE 72.**

> Forget talking—that definitely sounded like a proposition. Tell him you love following orders and you'll do whatever he says. **TURN TO PAGE 100.**

A NORMAL CONVERSATION

His answers come back short, at first.

You talk about your job and family, then ask about his—he tells you he has no need of working any longer and no family living. "You've met the others who live here. They are my family now," he says in a low voice. He frowns when you ask whether he grew up in the castle, as if that was a strange question, and breaks eye contact to look down at the book in his hands instead of replying. But he seems frustrated with himself whenever the room falls quiet.

"I apologize," he says, placing the book on a table at his side. "You have been very honest with me. I have not returned the gesture." He shifts in his chair, leaning back and trying to relax his features—he's at least managing to frown *less*.

"I find myself out of practice. We . . . used to entertain more," he says by way of apology. You ask about when that was, and he seems grateful for a conversational thread to cling on to.

"We used to have a gathering at this time of year—a masquerade ball, close to Hallowe'en.

"At first it was just old connections, people like ourselves—but August and Raisa began to bring the wolves that live nearby and even some of the braver humans. That's where Raisa is tonight—she is determined to continue the tradition, no matter the circumstance."

The furrow returns to his brow, and he rubs a hand over his mouth. "The place felt . . . full of life on those nights. I think I knew how to speak to people then."

You ask why he stopped hosting the party, and he hesitates before replying. "Ten years ago, one of the guests tried to kill me," he says simply. "Someone we had trusted brought a friend, and I bid him welcome, not knowing I had invited a dangerous vampire in." He spreads his hands stiffly, as if relearning an old gesture. "When the screams began, we removed him from the castle fast enough to avoid casualties, but not before guests' blood was spilled—we ourselves only just survived the encounter.

"People of all kinds were hurt that night. I'd told them they'd all be safe, and I broke my word." His voice is bitter, plainly angry at himself, and unforgiving.

"That's the reason the forest around us is dangerous at night now. A vampire with a score to settle waits there for me to forget my caution. He reappears just often enough that we can never be safe.

"He roams the forest, feasting on any human foolish enough to get close—and on deer and bear carcasses he discards on the trails, even in the roads, to terrorize us, remind us of his presence. He means to hunt and destroy me."

You think of the deer carcass you found in the woods and the diversion on the blood-splattered road, and you shiver.

"I would let him, if I thought that would be the end of it," Casimir says philosophically. "But he has grown wild and has no regard for the lives of humans—and I am sure he will not stop until he has killed August, too. So for now we remain here: both prisoners and bait, to prevent him feasting in the town below."

His solemn voice echoes as the tower room falls into silence. You think about the creature, hungry and waiting, out in the dark.

Casimir seems to shake himself out of the gloom.

"This was a poor topic," he says gruffly, scowling at himself. "I swear to you, no harm will befall you within my walls."

Despite the story of that fateful party, you believe him. There's a fierce conviction to his voice—he sounds like a man who would tear through anything to protect his own, and at least for tonight, he's decided you count as one of them. His eyes are bright in the firelight, his hands curled tight on the arms of the chair.

He makes a frustrated noise in his throat, and then his hybrid accent—perhaps part French and part Arabic, judging by his books—settles into something calmer, smoothing out the rough edges of emotion. "Would you allow me to try the conversation again? Ask me a question and I shall endeavor to answer."

◆ If you have the marker **FULL OF WINE . . . TURN STRAIGHT TO PAGE 74.**

◆ Otherwise . . . your mind lingers on the paintings. Ask about the man named Casimir in the portraits. **TURN TO PAGE 78.**

SORRY, I DON'T FOLLOW

The full force of the strange wine has been seeping into your blood like a massive hammer very slowly hitting you over the head. Now that Casimir has actually started speaking, you've been having to focus all your effort to understand what he's saying. What did he want? Another question? You ask where he grew up and try to make it seem like the delay was a thoughtful silence, not a bewildered one.

He says something you don't quite catch that you're sure includes living in Cairo and the Empire—the Ottoman Empire? You can't ask, in case he already said. That was a long time ago, right? You try to figure out how old he is, but your thoughts coagulate, wondering whether the furniture was named after the empire or the other way around.

Casimir is saying something gravely, and you're still thinking about whether you could ever afford a sofa. When did he go quiet? He's looking up at you as if waiting for an answer, and you know whatever he just said, it was something really serious.

"I've never told anyone that before," he says in a quiet voice. You have no idea what to say, and you're suddenly very aware of how awful it is that you weren't listening—so aware that you accidentally let out a panicked laugh.

His face goes stony. He stands, his large form looming over you, then grabs the front of your clothes, lifting you effortlessly out of the chair and right off your feet. "Don't make me sorry I saved you," he says in a quiet snarl that's way more threatening than a shout.

Your tongue feels heavy and stupid as you try to explain you weren't laughing at him.

He lets go of you with a noise of disgust, and you stumble back into the chair. After a moment, he sits back down in his own, but his expression remains stormy, challenging, waiting for you to speak.

- Explain you're just too drunk to listen properly and apologize. **TURN TO PAGE 80.**
- Explain you're just tipsy—but not too drunk to have a good time. Ask if you can make it up to him and try to climb into his lap. **TURN TO PAGE 70.**
- Ask whether he has more to drink, actually, and start opening cupboards to find out. **TURN TO PAGE 76.**

SIT CONFIDENTLY IN ONE OF THE ARMCHAIRS

You confidently sit down on a chair angled toward the fire. On the other side of the room, you hear Casimir drop some of the books he's moved off the floor onto a table with a soft thump. He moves slowly back into view, placing another volume down on the mantelpiece.

As he turns to look at you, he raises one eyebrow, his eyes slowly sweeping over your body before settling on your face.

"You're sitting in my chair," he says coolly.

Something about the note of authority in his voice makes you feel as if the wind's been knocked out of you, and you find you've sprung up before you realize what's happened. He seems calm—but every nerve in your body feels taut. You try to be normal, mumbling something about how you didn't know as you move over to the other chair and sit there instead.

He draws in a breath, watching you, eyebrow still raised. For a moment you have no idea what he's going to do, and you're filled with the wild idea that he might be about to pounce. Then he settles himself in the chair you just vacated.

"Somebody," he says, running a finger up the spine of a thick leather book in his hands, then looking smoothly up at you, "ought to teach you some manners." It sounds like a threat—or a promise.

- Apologize about the chair and talk to him to find out more about him. (If that was an offer, it seems it will stay open.) **TURN TO PAGE 72.**
- You're not interested in talking. Tell him yes, actually—you've been very bad, and maybe you deserve to be punished. **TURN TO PAGE 100.**

A TERRIBLE GUEST

You open cupboards at random, find bottles and glasses, and help yourself. Casimir just stares at your audacity, not actually stopping you. So you unstopper a crystal decanter, pour a healthy measure—only slopping a little over your hand—and drain the glass, letting it burn down your throat. You're on holiday, and you're a guest—what's he going to do?

You pour another, bigger glass and sit heavily back down by the fire, head spinning.

It takes you a couple of tries to find your mouth to sip at your drink.

The room is lovely and indistinct, and it takes you a minute to notice Casimir still watching you with undisguised disgust. You start the conversation again to lighten the mood, but you find yourself dizzy, the flickering shadows on the wall unnerving. Your words come out muddled, and you forget what you were trying to say. Casting around for a subject, you tell him about vampire powers you've seen in films and ask whether he can do that, too, and see his jaw tighten. Your head swims, and your mouth just keeps on talking despite your brain telling it to please stop, actually. As you make a final little joke about whether he sparkles, he stands.

Casimir looms over you, and in a slow, controlled snarl, he bares his white pointed teeth.

Something in your wine-slow body finally trips over into raw, primal panic. It builds in your chest until you can hear every heartbeat frantic below your clammy skin.

Casimir steps into your space. His cold fury lights something in his face. It reminds you you're looking at a dead thing, a creature beyond the concerns of human rules. His eyes are on your neck, where you feel your pulse beating in spasmodic fear.

You have a sudden strong impression of being a very small creature in the lair of an apex predator. This is the last thing you'll ever see, you think wildly. You think about the wine at dinner—was the vampires' plan to eat you all along?

He seems to be barely holding himself back, flexing his jaw. "Get out," he growls. You stumble gratefully toward the door without looking back and open it to the very cold and very dark stairway. Your shaky legs are already carrying you downward with your feet fumbling every few steps, every fiber of your being screaming to get as far away as possible. You realize you have no idea where you're going, but your body is moving without you, stumbling as the world whirls around. You feel your body overbalancing, hitting off walls without feeling the pain of the impact. You see pinpricks of eyes watching you from dark corridors and hear noises thumping above that spur you on as you stagger around dark corners—something ancient-wired into your lizard brain howls: *Escape, escape, escape.*

Finally you see a dim light over a door and wrench it open.

The air is cold as you lurch out into the forest, tripping and falling and picking yourself up to continue doggedly onward, putting as many steps as you can between you and the castle. The wine-fuzz is sour in your stomach, and you've pushed your body too far—you find yourself slowing, stumbling to your knees, retching helplessly into the bushes.

Why did you do this? Is it that you didn't want to make it home?

You latch on to the idea of home. You're in absolutely no state to drive, but what if you could reach the terrible car to shelter until morning?

After a long moment you're able to straighten up, panting. You're still unsteady but feel instantly much better, sharper in the cold air. The dark shapes of trees loom around you on all sides.

You've just started to move again, treading carefully onward through the forest, when there's a noise far behind you. With your mind slowly clearing, it's only now you remember Casimir telling you not to leave the castle.

The noise comes again, and your unsteady limbs are seized with the adrenaline of a prey animal.

Before you can think about it, you've picked up the pace, moving desperately, starting to run downhill as fast as you can manage while avoiding the trees in the rain and the night. You're suddenly wide awake, increasingly sober as your whole mind propels you determinedly forward.

After what might be a terrified minute or twenty—no way to tell—you emerge out of the forest and into what seems like fields, the sky open above you. This isn't the way you came, you realize—you're out on the other side of the hill.

TURN TO PAGE 52.

THE OTHER CASIMIR

Casimir lets out a long sigh—you're not sure he needs to breathe, but it conveys the feeling. He shifts in the chair, consciously relaxing his hands.

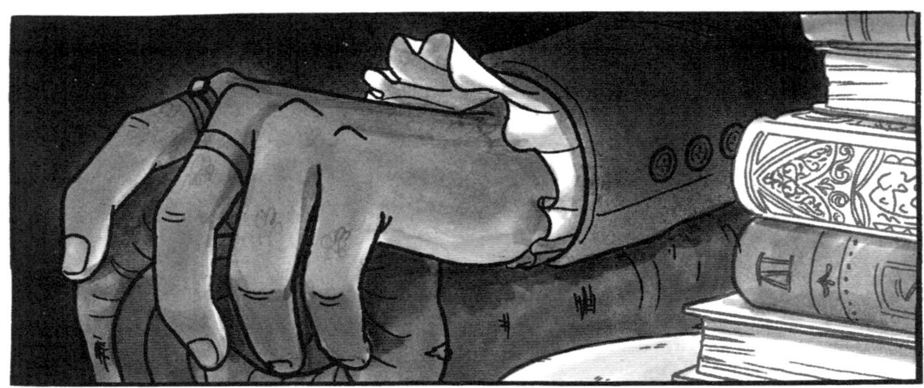

"The truth is, the man in the paintings was the count who owned this castle," he says in a quiet voice. "He is the man whose name I took for myself."

He glances into the dancing flames and begins to speak as if telling a story. "I met the count when I was not yet thirty—too young to exercise caution at the scent of danger. He told me he had come to Cairo to see the pyramids.

"He was from the northernmost territories of the Empire—places I had never even heard of."

The Ottoman Empire, you recall from the guidebook, last reached Romania more than a hundred years ago—another age. You adjust his possible age in your mind as he goes on.

"The count had sailed out of Konstantiniyye and down the coast of Anatolia to see the classical ruins, apparently unconcerned with the dangerous waters full of pirates and slavers. At the time, I romantically thought it was because the world called to him, as it did to me.

"I was working in the caravanserai on the outskirts of the city where he came to stay. I had run away from my family to live as a man, and for many years I took any work I could get. I had been raised as a girl, you see," he says, to make himself absolutely clear, "and could not return home." He meets your eyes in a level gaze, waiting for your reaction.

You explain that his gender not matching what his parents expected is actually way more familiar ground than him being hundreds of years old. His mouth crooks in amusement, and he goes on.

"I didn't know what the count was at first—or perhaps I noticed small, strange things but denied it to myself.

"He hid from the sun on shaded balconies or in covered litters—but then, he was the palest white man I had ever seen, skin almost colorless, so it seemed to make sense. He was unusual, of course, but it was a city full of foreigners, and he was not much noticed.

"It was part of what I loved about Cairo. There were soldiers, bureaucrats, merchants in the coffee trade from all around the Mediterranean; scholars who came great distances to the mosque-university of Al-Azhar; a great wave of pilgrims on their way to Mecca each year. It was a perfect place for me to meet new people, learn Turkish, French, and English—and to pass as a man or find new work when I could not.

"And so, too, it was the perfect place for the count to find victims who could go missing and not be much missed."

He rubs his thumb along the stubble at his jaw. "I was not missed, either, when I left with him."

> Ask about traveling with the count. **TURN TO PAGE 90.**

> First, ask about his childhood and leaving his family. **TURN TO PAGE 81.**

APOLOGIES

Casimir regards you coolly. "That much is obvious," he says quietly, but he seems to accept your apology and make an effort to swallow his anger.

"It's been so long since we've had guests, I'd forgotten how August likes to *provoke* them," he mutters, eyebrows drawn. He looks around the room almost bitterly, as if wondering why he invited you up, and seems to make a decision.

"Come," he growls, standing and sweeping out of the room and down the steps. You stumble dizzily, trying to keep up without falling down after him. Down in the hall, he calls for August, and a few minutes later, their pale figure slips from a shadowy arch.

"Our guest," he says flatly, "appears to have drunk too much wine."

August barely looks apologetic. "How *embarrassing*," they say with a slow smile, eyes on you. Casimir instructs August to show you to a guest room in a warning murmur. Then without looking back at you, he turns and disappears back into the dark—back to sit alone in his empty room and to keep his silence once again.

August leads the way through the winding corridors. They carry a candle in a small pewter holder that flickers as they glide along, red skirts billowing in their wake. You notice missing stones and wall hangings that have turned to gray scraps as they take you into a cold, dark, disused part of the castle. Dark doorways loom around you, and there are occasional howls of wind from the storm outside. You jump at a sudden loud rattle from an ancient windowpane, and August glances back archly. They seem to be enjoying leading you through the most desolate, ghostly corridors, daring you to be frightened in your disoriented state.

You climb echoing stairs and emerge onto a long stone corridor on an upper floor. You pass a few doors in the dark stillness before August opens one, the wood creaking as it moves.

"Here we are," they say smoothly, drifting in ahead of you and placing the candle on a plain, dark side table. In the flickering light, you can make out a large bed in the gloom, a carpet on the floor, the shapes of furniture along the walls. "I expect Caz means for you to sleep it off. But it's *early* yet." Their finger brushes the doorframe, and their silky voice drips with menace. "Won't you join me for another drink?"

› Go with August. **TURN TO PAGE 144.**

› Go into the guest room. **TURN TO PAGE 47.**

THE WHITE NILE

He looks at you for a moment as if he didn't expect the question, but he seems pleased by your interest, as if glad to have someone to speak to about his past.

"I grew up by the banks of the White Nile. Today the land is south of Khartoum in Sudan, but there was no Khartoum then. This was the time of the old kingdoms, long before British control—before the occupation by Ottoman Egypt and the rise of the slave trade.

"My mother was the daughter of traders and traveled the Nile in her youth. She would tell us stories of what she had seen: the Kushite pyramids, the great mosque at Sennar, the lands nearby. She was proud of her ancient people and of her unusual education. Usually Arabic was spoken by traders and officials and not women, but she taught it to all her children, along with her native Nobiin and phrases in many other tongues.

"When I grew older, she would tell us of peoples in the hills where some men lived as women, where that was the ordinary, unremarkable way of things. She told us tales she'd heard of peoples farther west, where some women's husbands were women, too. I think she spoke of these things because she suspected the truth about me. I think she knew one day I would leave to live my true life. I hope she wished me well and loved me from afar.

"But the version of Islam in my father's head had no room for such a way of living.

"If he had traveled farther, seen more, he may have learned that his was not the only version. No matter how I felt, he expected me to marry and bear children.

"I could have borne remaining home if I could live as a man, but he made it clear there was no question of that. So I watched the boats on the Nile and dreamed of travel, and when I was old enough, I ran. I traveled a long way over many years, moving slowly north along the river, beginning anew as a man."

Casimir frowns into the fire. "I never went back while I was alive. And only once after—many years after my family had passed. I found half the languages my mother spoke changed or extinct, our lands flooded and gone. Even Cairo felt unbearable—I felt each change too keenly. Each symbolized to me the loss of all I'd had, the home I'd once made for myself: all lost after the unwilling end to my life."

› You ask about how the count came to make him a vampire. **TURN TO PAGE 90.**

AUGUST SHOWS YOU TO YOUR ROOM

As the others disperse, August lights a candle in a small pewter holder and gestures for you to follow. "We have guest rooms, of course," they tell you, leading you through a door and through the winding corridors into the dark.

You hurry to keep up as they glide along, red skirts billowing in their wake, lit only by the small, flickering flame. You notice missing stones and wall hangings that have turned to gray scraps as they take you into a cold, dark, disused part of the castle. Dark doorways loom around you, and there are occasional howls of wind from the storm outside. You jump at a sudden loud rattle from an ancient windowpane, and August glances back archly. They seem to be enjoying leading you through the most desolate, ghostly corridors, daring you to be frightened.

You climb echoing stairs and emerge onto a long stone corridor on an upper floor. You pass a few doors in the dark stillness before August opens one, the wood creaking as it moves.

"Here we are," they say smoothly, drifting in ahead of you and placing the candle on a plain, dark side table. In the flickering light, you can make out a large bed in the gloom, a carpet on the floor, the shapes of furniture along the walls.

› Go into the guest room. **TURN TO PAGE 47.**

◆ If you have the marker **FULL OF WINE ...**

Whatever was in the strange wine has started to hit you, and you stumble as you enter the room, drawing August's attention. They turn to you with a beautiful spreading smile that slightly reminds you of a child pulling the wings off a fly. "But it's still so early," they say silkily. "Won't you join me for a while—for a drink?"

With this marker, you can also choose to go with August. **TURN TO PAGE 144.**

HOW MUCH DID I GET DRUNK OUT OF LAST NIGHT?

Looking around, you notice that in the night, the frames and cabinets lining the walls have been covered with sheets, so you can't see what's beneath. You wonder whether August has something to hide and think it safer not to snoop around.

You try to get yourself as clean as you can using the reflection of the window. You're able to rub off the last of the dried blood with a bit of effort, and rearrange your clothes so the stains can't be seen without peeling back layers.

You leave the mysterious room to look for a proper mirror but never find one—and then can't find your way back.

In the light, the castle seems cold and ordinary and, as far as you can tell, entirely empty of people. You call out, but there's nobody around—at least not anyone who wants to speak to you.

You spend what feels like a long time looking around, until you try a door and find yourself unexpectedly blinded by daylight. You stumble out the side door and see a path leading down the hill back toward the road.

TURN TO PAGE 265.

UNAFRAID OF GHOSTS

August steps aside as you walk back to the door, looking shocked and fascinated.

They gesture you indoors with the lamp they're holding, making sure to avoid any chance of contact with your wet clothes. "I heard an awful noise from some part of the castle we never even go to, and when I arrived, the door was shut fast, and I couldn't even break it down," they say. Their tone is very curious but somewhat detached, like they're telling you about a plot development in an interesting book.

"But I saw what happened from the window—the end, anyway. I got the *gist*," they say with a smirk. "Unexpected, I have to say."

Feeling slightly off-balance, you explain that you heard noises and your door closed behind you. You followed the light, then this seemed like all you could do.

"Hmm," they muse. "There were a lot of old ghosts here when we moved in—but I thought we'd got them all." Their nose wrinkles, and they shiver dramatically. "Casimir found an unspeakably awful basement full of remains in various states of decay when we arrived in the '40s, and he grimly buried them all out there by the old mausoleum. But then, he had my help, and he's a very *determined* sort of person."

You nod, trying to process this new information about the number of previously deceased creatures kicking about near your gran's house. August is looking you up and down appraisingly, like you've suddenly become more interesting.

"You'd better change back into your old clothes," they say, voice with a hint of apology under the imperious tone, beginning to lead you back into the maze of corridors. "I'm not sure we've anything else suitable."

Back at your guest room, they manage to shove your door back open with an unnatural, fluid strength. "I ought to fix that," they say absent-mindedly.

As you go inside, they hover in the doorway. "Would you like to join me?" they say. "I've a fire lit; I expect it's warmer." Their sharp smile looks more sheepish than dangerous for a moment. "I didn't mean to leave you so bored that you felt the need to *wander off*."

> Accept August's invitation and join them downstairs. **TURN TO PAGE 64.**

> Decline. You are done with the supernatural and want to go home. **TURN TO PAGE 49.**

THE MAUSOLEUM

You hurry through the rain, into the open door of the mausoleum and down the steps. You pause just inside, catching your breath, and take stock of your surroundings.

You're standing in a stone chamber that at first looks mostly empty and mostly lifeless in the dim light. It's quiet and bone-dry: nothing dripping or growing and only your own heavy breathing breaking the stillness.

A grimy round window in the roof lets a few faint wisps of moonlight through, and as your eyes adjust, you can make out what the room was built for: the huge stone sarcophagus on the dais at the center. The heavy lid is missing, and with a lurch in your stomach, you realize what you're seeing: looming in the cold stillness ahead of you is a figure standing in the coffin itself.

She steps out and descends with a regal, deliberate slowness. Her heels click and echo on the stone steps, and for a moment, you find yourself frozen.

She looks dressed for a funeral, but lushly—immodestly. The lace of her black hat shadows her eyes in only a cursory veil, the long slit of her immaculate black dress exposing stockings and skin. She was white when she was alive, and now she is *white*, the sickly color of bleached bone—but as you stare, your mind shifts: perhaps she's the color of thick, indulgent cream instead. You find your eyes tracing down her throat, over the deep V in her dress. Your terror softens. You have no urge to move.

Her face is utterly cold, devoid of pity or kindness. Her voice is rich and imperious—perhaps a little disgusted—when she asks whether you've come to give yourself to her. In the beautiful stillness, under her pitiless gaze, you feel unnaturally calm.

› Of course you're here to give yourself to her. You want to thank her for deigning to address you at all. **TURN TO PAGE 86.**

› Weird calm or no, you're still aware this woman may want to eat you—better try to run for it, while you still can, and find some other way out of the courtyard. **TURN TO PAGE 42.**

A GIFT TO THE CRYPT

You nod fervently. You're hit with the urge to sink to your knees and ask for forgiveness—or punishment. Would she step on you if you begged for it? You're not sure if this is a vampire powers thing or if she just has a presence that brings "yes, ma'am" naturally and enthusiastically to the tip of your tongue.

You find you've taken a step closer, lingering over the swell of her white chest where it strains the fabric taught, where the black skirt pulls against belly and hips. The thin black stockings at her thighs would tear gorgeously under your fingers. And what would she do to you if you ruined her stockings?

She steps forward and with cold, unflinching fingers takes hold of your face. There is no gentleness to the gesture, and you shiver deliciously as she drags your chin up hard to expose your throat.

Her mouth hinges wide like a snake, and you see her long fangs before you feel their soft scrape along your skin. She pauses, and you can feel your rabbit heartbeat pounding in your neck. Her hand tightens on your face, body pressing against yours. Your blood has rushed downward as heat pools in your stomach and between your legs, leaving your head weak and spinning. She observes your involuntary twitches and squirming with placid disinterest as her teeth press your skin gently, like a wolf playing with its food.

And then she snaps your head up and sinks into you, sharp and terrible. You writhe in blissful agony as she feeds.

The hot, joyful feeling in your throat climbs and climbs as she sucks the life out of you. Just as it feels as if you can bear no more, your shivering ecstasy peaks, shuddering into the nothing of the end as your nerves spasm and give out. The skin of your now-empty body wrinkles, dry and leathery, and your emaciated husk eventually crumbles to dust on the floor of the crypt.

The creature, flushed pink and panting but ever composed, now beautifully swollen like a satiated leech, descends gracefully into her stone sarcophagus, warm and satisfied, returning to the sweetness of slumber.

YOUR NIGHT ENDS, AND SO DO YOU.

You didn't survive the castle, but you did have an extremely good time in your final moments—and hey, at least you don't have to go back to work next week. To restart from dinner, **GO TO PAGE 28.** To go back to the start of the section, **GO TO PAGE 46.**

WHAT DID I TELL YOU?

Something weird is going on here. You don't move toward the tea.

The chained man's face suddenly becomes a mask of rage, and he leaps up, pulling against his restraints. He forcefully tugs one of his arms forward, and his foot slams to the floor—a loud thump echoes through the room and down through the castle, and you recognize the sounds you heard downstairs. "Please," he snarls, "you don't know what you're doing—"

But before you can say any more, you notice a faint light streaming from one of the windows set into the roof.

The thick rain clouds have parted, and in the sky above, you can see the full moon. You hear a crack as the thick chains snap.

In the place of the small man grows something else, expanding rapidly outward as his features elongate with a horrible wet cracking noise. Thick fur appears in waves over his body, his eyes bulge and stretch as his face contorts, his arms balloon with thick muscle and slam down onto the floor ahead of him so he crouches like a beast ready to spring. The creature reminds you of a wolf, but wrong—it's bigger and uncanny looking, with something awful about the way it fits together, skin too loose and sagging around the eyes, which swivel with a rabid frenzy.

The huge jaws crunch over your head before you have much time to scream, and it's over mercifully quickly. Your last, slightly hysterical thoughts are that your gran can get pretty grumpy when she doesn't have her tea, too.

YOUR NIGHT ENDS, AND SO DO YOU.

You've met your end.
To restart from dinner, **GO TO PAGE 28.**
To go back to the start of the section, **GO TO PAGE 53.**

NO WAY OUT

She shifts uncomfortably. "I . . . closed the door to keep you here. I lose shape outside this courtyard, and I *must* speak to you. There is a latch on the other side; I can move through the walls to open it again—but only if you help me first."

Her eyes look desperate, and when you turn to look back at the door, her hand shoots out to grab your arm with a fierce strength. Her grip shifts strangely, like you're being held by something made of flowing sand—or like maggots moving beneath the surface of her skin.

"Don't leave. *Help me*," she says, her hoarse voice tearing jarringly out of her throat. She drags down her collar, ripping at the material. Underneath there's a gaping wound at her neck, surrounded by bruises and the puncture marks of teeth. Her expression is grim, almost skull-like, and the wound starts to bleed, dark liquid seeping out onto the soft blue glow of her dress. She does not let go of your arm, only moves closer, her hair drifting around her.

"I was killed here in the castle, my body thrown in a disused well. I lived as a Christian and asked for a Christian burial, and it was denied to me. There is no marker for my grave. My death was not mourned. No living soul remembers me."

Her grip tightens. Her hand no longer looks like that of a living creature, her pale fingers turning black where blood pools like it would in a corpse. She drags you out into the rain and you stumble behind helplessly, clothes catching and tearing on a wet tangle of bracken. Beyond the hallowed ground of the graves, in a dirty, hidden-away corner of the courtyard, a low circular wall huddles beside a gnarled black tree, its spidery branches bare and leafless. There are still the rotting remains of a cover over the well, and tied around the black tree is a thick rope with regular knots.

In another burst of lightning, you see the spirit at your side, her light, wet dress sticking to the skeletal remains of her body, expression grim and hopeless. "Please," she rasps again, her form growing more decayed and ghoulish by the minute, her grip on your arm weakening as her hand loses shape. "*Please*. My bones are forgotten in the dark. Let me die. Let me rest."

- › Go down the rope into the well to find her bones and bury them. **TURN TO PAGE 39.**
- › The ghost seems to be disintegrating, and the open door of the mausoleum is close enough to reach. To escape inside, **TURN TO PAGE 85.**

A GUEST IN CAIRO

He looks past you as the start of a frown creases between his eyebrows again. "At first, the count hired me as a personal servant. He had taken up residence in the largest rooms in the establishment, and I was the attendant he liked best. I delivered his meals and took his strange requests for almost-raw meat and tools I could not devise the use of. He paid so well that nobody mentioned it further, and I was urged to keep him happy. He seemed to like me, almost to court me. He would invite me to sit and drink with him on warm evenings and recount stories of the sights he'd seen in rapturous detail.

"Well, his seduction was a success," says Casimir darkly. Fleetingly, his face had been animated with descriptions of his old home. Now his expression is closed off again. Any traces of boyishness are lost deep under a great wave of suppressed emotion.

"The count told me how earnestly he desired me as a traveling companion. I had no family and few friends to tie me to Cairo. And besides, I had come to the city with dreams of traveling farther one day." His voice lowers bitterly. "What reason did I have to refuse?

"Of course, I would learn later why he lingered in each place for only a week or so. There are only so many bloodless corpses that can be pulled from a river before arousing suspicion." Thunder cracks outside the window. You feel yourself shiver as he continues.

"He would allow me carefully closer to him, rationing his affections so it felt like a heady honor. He wanted me, and made that clear—he told me my body made me no less of a man, and must have known that was exactly what I'd always longed to hear. I was not only powerless to refuse but eager to follow him," he says, frowning in disgust.

"He grew quickly bored and reckless and showed his true cruelty. I began to panic and suspect him of twisted murders. Eventually, one night, he fed me opium and turned me in my sleep."

Casimir looks out at the rain beating on the window for a long moment. The story seems to pain him, but the telling seems cathartic, like it's a release to let the words free.

- Wait for him to go on. Listen to whatever he wants to say. **TURN TO PAGE 91.**
- His tragic backstory is killing the mood. If you were more interested in him when he seemed sexily threatening, tell him you have some ideas of how to take his mind off the past. **TURN TO PAGE 100.**

PAST SINS

Your quiet patience seems to encourage him to continue as he frowns out at the storm: "What can I say of the years that followed? There is little I wish to detail. I was newly formed, ravening. I was not told I could feed without killing," he says, voice heavy and grieved. "Even in the frenzy of feeding, I spent every moment hating myself.

"I traveled with the count for many years—long enough that the world changed around us, that the cities we revisited grew up, fell, and were made new. But I had no joy for them at that time. My existence was a stupor of misery, willed on only by survival. Everyone I had known was gone. I had gone so far into the darkness, impossibly far—beyond all I had been taught forbidden and profane, into an undiscovered land where all symbols were meaningless."

He goes on slowly, eyes not meeting yours as the growl of his voice builds back to a place of smooth, powerful authority. "But slowly, I learned control. I realized I could feed on those already on the brink of death—and on animals, too. I weaned myself off healthy human blood until I was able to sustain myself without taking life. I clawed meaning back into my world. And in my clearing mind, I realized that this meant the count had never taken the care to learn this discipline. When I told him, I found he knew feeding without killing was possible, but he'd kept it from me. He didn't care.

"I returned to myself with a driving purpose. It gave me the strength to leave his side—but first, I teased information from the few vampires he associated with: how to end a deathless life. I vowed one day I would strike the count down for good." Casimir looks up, eyes intent, and an electric thrill runs unbidden up your spine. You're frozen in your seat, breathless.

"And, eventually, I did," he says calmly. "I had already adopted a new name once, hoping to live a life as my true self. Now I had been taken so far from myself that I hardly grieved at taking another. I ended the count and took everything from him. Even his name." You watch the grip of the man's powerful hands.

You have the sense of him, then, as something beyond human—something coiled and deadly. You are breathing and alive because he has chosen not to strike. He's invited you into his space and offered you his story.

◆ Gain the marker **CONFESSION.**

You ask the name he chose for himself before he took Casimir's. **TURN TO PAGE 94.**

LOST TO SENSATION

August's smile seems a little sad. But then the traces of vulnerability in the expression are subsumed into a more polished, glamorous performance.

Their lips press to your neck, their fingers sliding down to touch you, and you respond in kind, moving breathlessly against them in the dark. There's no kissing, no hesitation, only your body thrumming with anticipation as their head dips toward your collarbone.

You feel their teeth sink into your neck—a slow, deliberate bite, drawing it out as their hands knead at your back, your thigh.

The sharp pain is followed by slow, giddy relaxation as something spreads through your veins, a venom that goes shuddering through your body. Your body relaxes in August's jaws and into their arms.

You feel *good*.

August moans deep in their throat and sucks harder, pulling your clothes impatiently aside. Mouth still at your neck, you both stumble back to the cabinet, to lean against it and give in to your bodies' need for friction. You feel heavy with arousal that's only sharper for the edge of fear in your mind.

Blood still pulses from your neck as you move together, and August licks it hungrily from your skin. They suck again, and the giddy sensation spins through you, building to something almost unpleasant before they pull their head away with obvious effort.

They replace their mouth with a practiced hand to your throat, holding the slippery wound closed. Their mouth is red and wet, pupils blown wide with an uninhibited thrill of indulgence, back arching into the pleasure.

Afterward, they extricate themself neatly and slowly stagger a couple of steps away from you in a blood-drunk haze. They seem to notice the mess of red smeared over your neck and look down at their own bloody hands. You don't feel hurt or unusual, only loose and satisfied, the strange relaxation already ebbed away. Feeling your neck, you find the wound has already sewn itself over—some strange trick of August's tongue.

August, satisfied you're not about to die, continues retreating into the shadows, looking away from you. "I ought to clean up," you hear them say in a strangely hollow voice.

Before you can say anything, the darkness is still. August has slipped away, and you don't see them again.

You sit back down by the embers of the fire, sinking into the warm cushions of the settee, suddenly worn out. You listen to the rain hammering against the windows and let your eyes slowly start to close.

The next thing you know, you're coming stickily awake, dried blood flaking away from your neck, and the gray light of morning is seeping through the windows.

TURN TO PAGE 83.

TRUE NAME

The fire has burned low. You've been speaking for a while, you realize—the amount you talked about yourself at dinner evened out. His untouchably stiff posture has softened a little. He stands up, as if restless, and leans on the mantelpiece as he looks into the fire.

"Khalil," he says quietly. He shakes his head and lets out a sound of frustration, muttering a curse in a language you don't know—you're not sure which, given his tongue's wide repertoire.

"It's strange to say it after so long. My name—not the one my parents gave me, but Khalil, my true name—was so precious to me. When I was young, it felt like one of the only things I had power over. I adopted 'Casimir' almost as a penance."

He goes on, speaking deliberately. You have the sense that this is something he's been wanting to tell someone for a long time. "As a boy I thought I was the only person in the world like myself. And in Cairo, just as I was starting to learn more and meet others, the count took me away and turned me into a monster. For years I thought I would never have another friend.

"So when I met August, and they were eager to be turned, their company was a revelation. It was a relief to be around someone who understood me. Even though we are very different, of course—we felt our difference in gender in our own ways. For one thing, they had no desire to change their body."

He lingers over this—opens his mouth, closes it again.

You tell him that if he wants to go on, you'll listen. He regards you, dark skin edged with gold in the firelight, and seems to make the decision to trust you. "In truth, there were some parts of my body that I lived with peaceably—and other parts I couldn't, and wished I could change. August always had an interest in the medical treatments being developed—for others' sakes—and had heard of hormone therapy. But it was so difficult to get information back then, and when we learned the Nazis had burned the libraries at the Institute of Sexual Research, I lost hope of medical treatment as a real possibility and stopped looking."

Still leaning at the fireplace, you see him crumple for a moment, turning his face away into the shadows. "For so long, I forced myself into an uneasy truce with the body I had."

He turns and moves to the window, where the rain patters against the cold glass. "Thirty years ago, a youth from the village came to the castle. He had heard we were demons and begged to sell his soul for a man's body." His rueful smile flashes at you from the shadows. "How eagerly would I have joined the count if that had been within a vampire's powers.

"But I could see how he burned for relief. It was so much simpler to recognize the need in another—to send Raisa to investigate what could be done, when it was a service to somebody else. This was before the treatment was widespread, but I was able to organize a way to source the medication for him from the West. The town doctor took a little convincing, but he agreed and knew what to monitor to keep the boy safe." His voice holds no warmth for the doctor. You wonder which of the three of them did the "convincing."

When he goes on, his voice is distant, as if recounting a fable. "And he gradually changed. Half the town thought it a possession, others a miracle." The embers of the fire are a soft red glow. It's just his voice carrying you in the dark now, low tones building in a swell of restrained emotion.

"I watched from afar and saw him grow into himself. I could see a new peace in him. I realized I'd been hungry for that relief all my life, and all my years after."

You feel his body draw closer to you, intent as he speaks the heart of the truth, words that feel more intimate than touch. His voice is still controlled but with a raw scrape—just contained, a cup full to the brim. "When I finally began the treatment myself, I found my body's chemistry was not so altered by my age or the great change of death—the medicine still took. Something still moved in my veins. Enough to change me."

In the last firelight, you see his hand unthinkingly rub the hard-won stubble along his jaw. It's a gesture of comfort. As he shifts his broad shoulders, you're full of the impression that this is a man who knows his body and what to do with it. The air between you seems to burn with his closeness.

"For the first time in my life, my voice became my own. It was like becoming whole. My body felt like I belonged in it."

› Run your hand along his jaw, too, and kiss him. **TURN TO PAGE 101.**

PARTY GRAN

That winter, you do sit around doing nothing and playing cards and watching the snow outside the window—but you also help your gran fix up the house. There's plenty to do, and you end the days pleasantly tired, sleeping well and feeling a fond satisfaction at getting to know her better.

You slowly learn the language and do get on well with some of the slightly embarrassed grandchildren of your gran's werewolf friends who come to visit.

In the spring, you learn how to grow herbs and vegetables as your gran sits in a deck chair shouting instructions and telling you you're doing it wrong. She teaches you all her recipes and how to make the strong plum liquor she likes, then insists on throwing a party where everyone can try your first batch, and you find yourself strangely at ease being teased ruthlessly by old ladies—it means you've been accepted as part of the family and fabric of the town.

In the summer, you finally get to see some of the castles and sights in your guidebook. You and your gran take road trips, driving slowly through the mountains with stops for incredible meals and wine, and staying over with the people she seems to know in every town. You go to parties held by vampires with huge villas and pools and spare rooms with absurd picture-book vistas over the mountains. You send photos home to friends who excitedly make plans to come visit, and your gran enthusiastically figures out whose spare rooms they can all stay in.

You grow to understand the townspeople's squabbles and grievances as well as their history of dark times. You realize the split between the people who love the vampires and the others who tolerate them, and you see the things they all come together for and enlist the vampires' help with anyway: improving the trains, stopping illegal logging, and making sure the government thoroughly rejects another idea for a *Dracula* theme park. In the New Year, you start to hear your grandmother's friends complain about tourists, and you realize it's because they're not including you as one of them—they've firmly and fiercely decided that this is your home, for as long as you want it to be.

THE END

Want another adventure? See what else there is to do: **GO TO PAGE 266.**

KISSES BY CANDLELIGHT

You slide Casimir's hand away from your thigh and press your lips to his without heat. He kisses back, drawing you lazily over to the bed, where he guides you down with a powerful hand at your back. He leans over you, but his hands go no further.

Pulling away from your mouth, he opens his eyes and gives you a long, slow smile with a flash of sharp white teeth. Braced above you on strong arms, he seems in no hurry to do anything or go anywhere. His grin closes into a fond and serious smile as he regards you admiringly, like the cat that got the cream.

He adjusts his shoulders, as if used to holding himself tense and unsure how to move in this loosened state. Then he rolls to lie beside you, still in contact at your side, angled toward you like a new green branch toward warmth.

You run a hand slowly down from his cheek, down the deep V of exposed dark skin to the hair scattered over his heart. On either side of your hand, his chest swells out under the shirt where the muscle gives way to a heavy curve. He lies at ease, perfectly comfortable in his body, and it suits him, every part. Your fingers brush across his belly, and he gathers them up slowly to kiss them in the candlelight.

You stay like that for a long time, lying close together on the bed. He covers your face slowly with kisses, without pushing for anything else. His touch is casually intimate, firm but achingly careful.

You ask inconsequential questions about the castle, about parts of his life he's told you about, and listen to the sound of his low, murmured replies—happy to answer, pleased when you remember a detail or tell him something of yourself in return.

Nestled beside him in the soft bedclothes, you fall into a contented doze.

TURN TO PAGE 104.

VAMPIRE'S BRAT

Casimir's eyes glitter in the firelight. Leaning forward, he moves an unnaturally strong hand to hold you under the chin, fingers digging into your cheeks with a firm but steady pressure. His dark eyes look liquid where they reflect the fire, intent and hungry. "If you're bad," he breathes, voice very low, "I'll have to teach you a lesson."

You do not follow orders. You find being handled roughly does not teach you the lesson at all; in fact, it rather inspires more disobedience. Casimir could definitely murder you instantly, but his strength stays leashed under his control. Instead of just breaking all your bones, his touch smarts and bruises in a way that makes you ache with want.

As you fail to follow his instructions, the orders come out in an increasingly rough voice. Your reactions cause flashes of undisguised need in his eyes as you feel his impatience build deliciously and he seems to unravel. He pulls off his immaculate jacket and tosses it aside to roll up his sleeves and attend to you properly. You find he likes to pause, leaving you gasping and desperate on the bed as he demands you beg for more. With his strong hands holding you down, you find yourself acquiescing, your slightly strangled voice muffled by the pillow.

He drags you over and makes you watch as he goes through a drawer where you glimpse leather and glass. He waits until you're trembling with anticipation before he roughly takes hold of you. Then he spends the rest of the night indulging you—more than once—until he's taken you completely to pieces. By the end, his control has unwound a little, his fingers tight enough to bruise, the noises in his throat ragged. You feel a sharp pain in your neck and feel his moan hum through you as he bites down.

Your body relaxes strangely into it, and your pleasure unspools in a rapturous haze.

◆ Gain the marker **BLOOD BANK.**

Afterward, you lie trying to catch your breath, sprawled on the luxurious bed. Your body is exhausted and completely satisfied, every nerve tingling. Casimir untangles you, runs a warm wet cloth over your body, and lays you down on clean sheets, your body boneless and your mind pleasantly blank. You hear him moving around the room as you fall into a doze.

◆ If you have the marker **CONFESSION . . . TURN TO PAGE 104.**

◆ Otherwise . . . **TURN TO PAGE 120.**

DADDY?

Casimir's expression changes but just minutely. He looks back at you—calm but not disinterested.

"Is that so?" he says, leaning back in the chair to spread out. The firelight turns the edge of his face golden brown, his dark eyes glimmering. He rubs one hand slowly down his thigh to rest on his knee. He looks poised, ready to strike. His tone of voice feels like it's melting an important part of your brain into soup, and when he speaks again, it's even quieter, almost a purr.

"If I asked you to kneel, would you do it?"

Your legs twitch forward as you start to move from the chair almost without thinking, and he makes a disapproving noise low in his throat.

"I only asked a question. I wanted an answer, not an action."

He looks you up and down very slowly, like he's enjoying himself. You slide back to sitting in the seat. You wonder whether you're sweating. His dark eyes take a leisurely route over you before they lock back on yours.

"But I see you're very eager to obey."

He leans forward until his elbows are on his spread knees, gaze still on yours.

"I like that. If you're good, we could enjoy ourselves tonight." His eyes flick over to a table, where you think you see what might be restraints in the shadows. "But you'll act only when I give you permission."

- Sit still and tell him you'll be so good and so obedient. You're willing to be instructed and restrained. **TURN TO PAGE 102.**
- Slide to the floor to kneel in front of him without his permission. Ask him what happens if you're bad. **TURN TO PAGE 99.**

EMBERS

You move to him, running your fingers along his jawline, up to the curls of hair by his ear and back down to his lips.

Before you've finished, he's kissing you. His hands slide up your hips to your shoulders, and he pushes you up against the side of the fireplace. You feel the warm stone along your back as you sigh into his mouth. He responds to the gentle touch you began with, matching his pace to it, powerful body under perfect control.

After a slow indulgence of kisses, he draws back. His body looks looser, his eyes bright in the last embers of the fire. Without the frown, he looks younger suddenly—someone who could lose himself in touch, in a book, or in a thought.

He pauses deliberately, inviting you to sit back down as he lights a nearby candle on the last of the fire. It blooms into light, and he carries it—very steadily around the books—to the table dripping with wax, and easily lights the candles anchored there in a long arc. They flare to life like constellations, bright warm points of light, throwing shadows that make the drapes of the bed look like a baroque painting.

He returns and bends down to kiss you, his hand full of unnatural strength at your back. The other brushes along your jaw and then down your neck. He moves close to your ear, and his mouth is close enough for you to feel the low rumble when he speaks again.

"I said I know how to keep control of myself, and I mean it," he says, softly. One hand strokes your neck. The other moves to rest on your thigh but goes no further than an unspoken question. "But if you want pleasure, I know how to take the reins—hold the whip hand." His mouth twists in a playful smile as his voice lowers to a purr. "Or perhaps if you're very good, I'll have no need to use it."

You get the sense he'd be pleased with whatever direction you give him.

- You want to kiss him, but nothing physical. **TURN TO PAGE 98.**
- You want him but tell him you have no intention of being good—you like the sound of a whip in his hand. **TURN TO PAGE 99.**
- You want him and to give yourself over completely. Tell him you'll be so good and obedient for him. **TURN TO PAGE 102.**

YES, SIR

You tell him how good you'll be, and a dazzling smile spreads across his face that lets you see his fangs. You wonder how often he gets to entertain up here. "Come here," he demands in a firm, low voice that seems to flow through you—and you obey.

He watches with cool confidence, broad shoulders still and calm as you fall easily into the comfortable rhythm of following instructions, the burden of choice removed from your shoulders, ready to be shaped in his hands. "Stay still," he orders. You sit back, waiting on the bed, body tight with anticipation, unable to see him beyond the fall of the curtain. Then the mattress shifts as he slowly sits beside you. He comes into view, hair brushing over his shoulder as he leans over you, commanding. His firm, cool hand slides over your hip to hold you still.

"Tell me: Do you want to be touched?" His voice is rough in the low light. You find you're nodding. He leans over until you can see the glint of flames in his dark eyes. "Good. You're going to take what I give you. Stay quiet for me."

Over the evening, you find he enjoys making you wait. When you stray out of line, a noise sounding in your throat against his orders, he pulls away, leaving you wanting, his smile white in the dark. He asks things of you in the same hard, irresistible voice, then steps back to watch, fully dressed. His gaze follows your movements, and you feel hot shame along with a thrill at the controlled hunger in his dark eyes.

He strips his jacket off and tosses it aside, then rolls up his sleeves slowly like he knows you're watching. You can see the muscles in his forearms ripple with the movement. "Lie down," he demands, and you move without question. You hear drawers move in a cabinet, objects lifted out that you're not allowed to see. When he returns to your field of vision, kneeling over you on the bed, he has a look of intent and a rope in his hands. You find heat pooling in your stomach, aching for his touch to return.

He ties you up with deliberation, swift hands betraying their eagerness. He instructs you on where to move your arms and purrs "Good" when you do, neat patterns crossing over your body until you're held tight. The pressure feels like his strong hands holding you down, at the ankles, across your chest. "You'll speak if you want to stop," he tells you, no room for argument, arms flexing as he tugs the last knot into place.

Piece by piece he commands your total submission, enjoying his power over your gratification—the cruelty of denying it, the care of granting it in small increments. He uses your body, explores it almost clinically as he finds exactly how to make you gasp and strain against your ties. But behind the controlled expression, his dark eyes watch your reactions with increasing hungry relish, unraveling until he seems unable to hold himself back.

He drags your head up to look into your eyes. "There's something I want," he says, voice rough and wanton. In the candlelight his now-rumpled shirt is open, revealing the dark skin and hair scattered over his heart, the heavy curves of his chest on either side. It looks right on him—the soft shapes and the powerful muscle together, his powerful hands and perfect control.

You're panting, mind blissfully blank from its complete absorption in following his will. He watches for a moment, drinking you in, then slowly moves his mouth down to your throat. You feel the scrape of sharp points, grazing along your jugular. Even now his control seems absolute, his hands willful on your body, but the pressure of his teeth feather-light as he waits for you to deny him. You tell him yes in a voice that comes out shaking.

◆ Gain the marker **BLOOD BANK.**

His hand moves firmly over you as he bites down hard. Sharp pain gives way into a heady pleasure. Blood pulses in your throat and his mouth. He teases until you want to scream and thrash and can't take it anymore, his mouth still at your neck. Then he relents, and sensation pours in as the friction of the ropes hold you rough and firm. He pulls away, licking the red from his mouth in an expression of pure indulgence as the end of the wave surges through you.

Afterward, he unwraps you slowly. Your whole body still feels achingly good, and you move boneless in his hands. When your hands are freed, you find the wound at your neck has healed unnaturally fast. He cleans you and lays you down on soft sheets. You hear him moving around the room as you fall into a heavy doze.

◆ If you have the marker **CONFESSION . . . TURN TO PAGE 104.**

◆ Otherwise . . . **TURN TO PAGE 120.**

AWAKE IN THE NIGHT

You wake up shivering.

Gradually you remember where you are and notice you're alone in the large bed, covers only half pulled up. One candle flickers on the table beside you that's covered in wax, throwing an orange light over the folds of the rumpled bedclothes. On the other side of the bed, a book rests on pulled-back sheets, left with a careful bookmark placed partway through.

You realize you must have been woken by Casimir stirring, and can still see his solid form in the dim light from where you lie. He's thrown on a plush, velvety robe and is looking out the window, contemplative, as if thinking about something out in the dark.

You can see the very edge of his face, brow a little furrowed. He looks restless.

Seeming to make up his mind about something, he moves almost silently out of the room and down the stairs.

He leaves the door ajar.

Does part of him hope you'll go after him? You can see your clothes scattered nearby and could easily dress and follow.

- Dress and follow him.
  TURN TO PAGE 105.
- You want nothing to do with his secrets. Go back to sleep.
  TURN TO PAGE 115.

THE BLACKENED ROOM

You take the candle and move down the stairs behind him. He seems to be walking at a mostly human pace—slow and wandering, lost in his thoughts—so you can make out where he's going, even if you can't catch up.

You retrace the way down the stairs and around a corner where you thought you saw a flutter of his robe disappear. Past the portraits of the count, you find yourself in a long gallery with a dusty, once-expensive carpet. As you move forward, your candle illuminates a grand set of doors that have been left slightly open.

You follow inside into what must be a huge, dark room—but something about it seems wrong. You find yourself on edge, gooseflesh shivering over you in the still air. You think you notice the very faint smell of burned hair.

"Did I wake you?" You jump at Casimir's voice, low in the shadows and strangely calm. You wonder how well he can see in the dark. You tell him he did.

"Hm. I sometimes find myself down here lately, on sleepless nights." When he doesn't emerge out of the dark, you move toward the sound of his voice until you can make out his silhouette staring fixedly at something tall in the center of the room—it looks like the remains of a bed. In the candle glow, you realize he is only calm the way the sea seems calm before the waves break on the rocks: unbroken above, roiling beneath.

"What do you see?" he asks.

You draw closer, full of a sick dread, but the flickering candle reveals nothing living and nothing dead. There was a fire here, you realize. Now there are only the blackened remains of the bed frame and the last scraps of the sheets sunken into ash. And there—a glimmer. Each of the corners has the remnants of a jagged bedpost, and as your eyes strain in the candlelight, you think you see a glint of metal in each of them.

A clap of thunder booms through the roof as the room flashes bright with lightning. You start and stumble back, and find the broad man right behind you, his solid arm at your back, keeping you upright—or close enough to strike? The flash of light made it clear what you were looking at: shackles, hammered tightly into each post, chains long enough to fix to wrists and ankles—to keep a person from escaping.

> Tell him you see chains, and ask whether the count died here. **TURN TO PAGE 106.**

> Say you're not sure what you see. **TURN TO PAGE 107.**

ETERNAL CHAINS

The man who calls himself Casimir nods, slowly. "The count was far more powerful than August and I put together. He was older and stronger than any vampire I had met at that time. All his life he had fed without scruples or any sense of shame, which he believed enhanced his powers."

He glances at you sidelong in the dark. "I believe the vampire hunting us has an even greater power—it is why we have not yet tried to confront him.

"It was not only in Egypt that the count had gorged himself. Only in his absence did I discern the pattern: For a thousand years, as empires rose and fell, he followed in their wake and toured their 'conquests.' He found he could feed on the colonized with nigh impunity. The country's rulers would invite him into their homes, eyes turned away from the suffering of the native people. The count told me we killed the poor to save them from their miserable lives—all the while accepting the hospitality of the very people in charge who'd caused that misery. Some even knew what he was. Slowly, I discovered this all because—"

Casimir's voice sinks to a bitter growl. "Because I was usually there, with him. I have taken too many lives and done many things that are unforgivable. But this"—he gestures at the charred shell of a bed—"this, at least, is a death I will never regret."

You let the silence stretch out between you. The rain drums the windows. In the dark room, you do not flinch away from the ruined bed.

The quiet is strangely comfortable between you, even here at the preserved site of the murder. You wonder whom he last let see this room.

Casimir speaks slowly. "I wanted revenge, but I was caught up in my own melancholy, with no plans to act. It was only when I met August that they sharpened my purpose. They had . . . grand ideas. A great crusade. And when I saw the count again, we both saw his true colors."

› Ask about the night of the fire right away. **TURN TO PAGE 108.**

› Ask about August's great crusade first. **TURN TO PAGE 110.**

CAUTION IN THE RUINS

You feel Casimir's hand tighten, then the absence of his body behind you as he steps away.

"Are you afraid of me, little mouse?" he says. His white smile is rueful as it flashes in the candlelight. "And here I was thinking we were getting *comfortable*."

He looks toward the bed in the darkness. "Only reasonable when confronted with a predator, I suppose." You hear him take a long, slow breath into his dead lungs. "I have done many unforgivable things. I have fed on innocents before I knew I had a choice. But this"—he gestures at the charred shell of a bed—"this is a death I will never regret.

"The count was old and powerful, had spent long years gorging himself with no sense of shame—and not only in Egypt. Gradually, I discerned his pattern: For a thousand years, as empires rose and fell, he followed in their wake and toured their 'conquests.' He found he could feed on the colonized with nigh impunity. The country's rulers would invite him into their homes, eyes turned away from the suffering of the native people. He told me we killed the poor to save them from their miserable lives, all the while accepting the hospitality of the ones in charge who'd caused that misery. Some even knew what he was. Slowly, I discovered this because"—Casimir's voice sinks to a bitter growl—"because I was usually there, with him."

You let the silence stretch out between you. The rain drums the windows. You wonder whom he last let see this room—this murder scene.

Casimir's expression is complicated. "I wanted revenge, but I was caught up in my own melancholy, with no plans to act, until I met August. They sharpened my purpose. They had grand ideas, a great crusade. And when I saw the count again, we both saw his true colors."

He looks at you, frowning in real concern. "I am sorry to have led you here. I understand if you wish to hear no more of the dark deeds surrounding this castle. But know this: I suspect the vampire hunting us out in the night is just as powerful as the count. You may return to the tower room, if you wish, but I beg you: Do not wander in the dark again."

- Ask about the night of the fire right away. **TURN TO PAGE 108.**
- Ask about August's great crusade first. **TURN TO PAGE 110.**
- Return to the tower room and go back to sleep. **TURN TO PAGE 115.**

THE NIGHT OF THE FIRE

Casimir lets out a long breath. "We came to the castle unsure of what to expect.

"August, expecting danger, made a pretense of being only a man. But to our surprise, the count welcomed us in like old friends. It became clear that much of the town that once respected him held him in disdain and disgust, and perhaps he was lonely.

"He crowed about powerful friends: The Hungarian princes and old king had given way to a new order, whom he told us he supported, smiling while he did it.

"I wanted to rip his throat out right away. I hated to be in his presence. But August is better at wearing a smile over their rage. While I fumed, they drew out the full story: The count had welcomed the new fascist government and its representatives. He knew about the death camps. They meant nothing to him.

"August and I killed him that night.

"He had terrified human servants bring us slabs of raw meat. I felt sick to my stomach, but August played along, eating quietly with knife and fork and drinking as much wine with the count as they could, pretending conviviality and keeping him busy. Eventually, his senses slowed, as far as is possible for one of us to slow. August drew him away, making a bet with him about who could drink the most from a slaughtered cow, and by the time I had found shackles in a basement and filled his bed with oil and kindling, he was swollen with blood like a bloated corpse. August had retched it all up in private but looked gruesome, grimly determined as they played at the same languor.

"I think the truth is that the count never truly considered me a threat. He still thought me under his spell—he saw the same boy, eager to see the world: a servant he had shaped and charmed. But most of all, he trusted August's smiling white face and polished English manners." You see his hands tighten at his sides, still speaking calmly, as if in a trance.

"He followed us upstairs easily, though it came to a struggle in the end. It was a mess. Before the last shackle was in place, he gave me wounds that took a very long time to heal. But we subdued him together. I won't forget the sounds he made as he burned. But he was gone."

Casimir takes a shuddering breath into a body that no longer needs it. "Reality caught up to me after that. There are no laws among vampires, no rulers—but most think badly of ending another vampire's life. Most think we ought to have an unspoken kinship. I was unashamed of our actions but wary of how others may react.

"August went through the count's papers, writing desperate appeals to other vampires to help in the war, making no mention of the count's death. But the few replies we received told of many casualties among our own kind. A new, awful class of firebombs made our final deaths ever easier, and instead of fighting, most vampires had retreated to hide themselves away in distant wild places. No appeal could win them to our side.

"The real situation became clear: The horrors of the second war were too vast for us. The small acts we had undertaken ourselves had been fighting a Hydra—one head struck down, many returned in their place, worse than ever."

As he spills out the last of his story, anguish is creeping into his features. "To survive, we, too, had to hide. We remained in the castle, feeding on forest animals and avoiding suspicion. I took good care of the castle servants, who did not dare question my taking Casimir's name and position, using quiet bribes and threats to keep the estate running and unnoticed. We hid those who fled the camps and the front, and in the aftermath of the war, when the surrounding towns were half ruined and hungry under the new Soviet occupation, we sent what aid we could. We could not change the world, but at least we could help a few. A sticking plaster on great wounds.

"August went on without me, going among the locals like a shadow. They found allies to assist, enemies to threaten and terrorize, removing any they thought irredeemable.

"And I retreated to my rooms. The least I can do with my wretched existence is watch over others. But whether the town sees us now as tormentors or protectors, I do not know." Casimir's face twists in misery, and he walks a few steps away into the darkness, shrouding the emotion he's allowed himself to show. "I have taken so many human lives, done so much that cannot be undone."

> Tell him to forgive himself for the people he hurt in the past: He had no choice or knowledge of how to avoid it. What matters is he changed and did what he could. **TURN TO PAGE 111.**

> Tell him he didn't do anything wrong—the people he originally fed off were tragic deaths but not his fault at all. Also, killing fascists and the count was actually cool and good. **TURN TO PAGE 112.**

> Tell him it's not a big deal and you like his dangerous side. What does it matter if he killed a few people? Everyone dies; it barely matters. **TURN TO PAGE 114.**

THE COLLABORATOR

Casimir looks a little calmer when you ask about August, grateful to change the subject. "When I finally fled from the count, he remained calm. He said I'd become a burden to him anyway. In a fit of anger, I took all the money from him that I could, and it eased my way forward.

"I traveled across Europe from city to city: melancholy, but finally free. It was more dangerous than traveling together—my complexion meant I was greeted with instant suspicion, and the scrutiny often led to the danger of being revealed. I had to move often to evade escape. Over the years I moved slowly west from Budapest, and at the start of the Great War, I fled Paris for London, where I met August.

"August's friendship revitalized me. They've always had a keen sensitivity, vicious passions for the rightness of things—and as fascism grew across Europe, August was hungry to flex their newfound strength. We planned their chosen targets carefully: violent bigots, key officials, fathers and bosses with decades of known, cruel abuse. Their impulse was to carnage, but I persuaded them to keep to secret assassinations, feeling a responsibility to control the damage. August was sure of each murder's moral rightness, even where I was not—though with what followed, I wonder whether they were keener than I credited them.

"Their trail of death could not stay hidden forever. Soon we had to flee England, and as the '30s ended, we traveled south through France and beyond, avoiding bombs and authorities, until I realized we were not far from the count's ancestral castle.

"Things had been growing worse for some time. August was dogged, seeking out information in each new town, trying to set things to rights with blood. But I could see the despair growing in their actions as we watched the war erupt around us. We could not reach the halls of power. Officials we struck down were replaced, villages we freed recaptured. We were in danger constantly—though strong, we were not invulnerable—only two people against the great grinding of the war machine across Europe.

"August was still convinced we could prevent bloodshed if only we could remove the right figures and make others join us. And I still thought of the count as amoral in the way of a wild animal—bloodthirsty only for the thrill for death. I thought perhaps if we provided the targets, there was a chance he would join our side, even bring other vampires to our cause."

TURN TO PAGE 108.

FORGIVENESS

In the dark, Casimir remains still for a moment, turned away from you.

You hear an exhalation and a rough noise in his throat that might be a sob. You think about the young man in Cairo who wanted to learn all the languages he could and see the world—but not like this.

You wait patiently. You let him come to you. Casimir has composed himself when he steps toward you out of the gloom.

"I can't forgive myself," he says in a low, flat voice. "But to hear someone else ask it of me—a human ask it of me . . ." He swallows. "To not be judged a monster is a greater kindness than you can imagine. Thank you."

◆ Gain the marker **ABSOLUTION.**

He draws you by the hand out of the room, shutting the door behind.

You follow him back up to his study in the tower. He kisses you for a long, tender moment, hand cupping your jaw protectively, before blowing out the last candle.

In the dark, you feel him holding you as you fall asleep, and it feels different—like with his history spoken aloud, something in his body has finally been able to relax.

TURN TO PAGE 115.

SOME OF THOSE MURDERS WERE COOL AND GOOD

Casimir lets out a small, surprised laugh.

He hesitates for a moment, perhaps getting his emotions under control, before he speaks again. "There was, I suppose, a grim satisfaction to using the power the count forced upon me to bring about his own end—to do at least that small good in the world."

He shifts in the shadows, as if reluctant to come back toward the light. "I'm not sure I can forgive myself for being his instrument of death," he murmurs. "But to hear a human not judge me as a monster is . . . it's a greater kindness than you can imagine. Thank you."

◆ Gain the marker **ABSOLUTION.**

Casimir seems to stir himself and moves toward you. "Your . . . *open-mindedness* is admirable, but so is your patience. Thank you for letting an old man talk for so long." His teeth flash white in the dark, a self-effacing smile that looks tired. But something in his dark eyes looks bright where they reflect the candle flame, and for a moment he looks younger than he has all night.

He moves his hand gently to your back. "Come. Let's not linger here. No need for me to dwell on the past any longer than you've already borne."

He leads you out of the room and shuts the door hard behind, shoulders seeming to sink in relief as the door closes.

You follow him back up to the tower room, and as you fall asleep, you think you feel him drawing close beside you in the dark, a body relaxing as if unburdened after a long time.

TURN TO PAGE 115.

THE CONFRONTATION

Casimir agrees with you, seeming almost eager to take on the most risk.

On the night of the planned attack, Casimir kisses you possessively. "No matter what you hear, you will stay *inside*," he commands seriously before leaving you in tense anticipation by the fire in the dining room. You don't ask what happens if the three vampires don't survive this fight—whether the rogue vampire will still need to be invited in when there's no host left.

When the noises begin, they are awful. Far off in the forest, you hear visceral screeches and shouts ripped from the throat like wild animals. A thump seems to shake the outer walls. The lamps all go out as something cuts off the gas line.

When the noises stop, the waiting is even worse.

Your whole body seizes with terror when the door to the room finally opens with no warning. Across the long room, you hear Casimir's voice from the unlit gloom of the corridor beyond, not moving into the light. "You're all right?" he asks, voice low and intense, like he's struggling to get the words out.

You tell him yes, standing uncertainly. The murky shape of his shoulders relaxes in the shadows. Something drips from a hand you realize he's cradling. You ask what happened.

"He's dead," he says firmly. "But it was . . . messy."

You try not to imagine what a vampire considers "messy" might look like. You step toward him unconsciously, and he moves reluctantly forward into the firelight.

His clothes are torn and bloody, and so is his face. There's a long gash across his nose, ripping his handsome features, slowly dripping a strange thick, dark blood. The tear runs through one eye, the whites flooded purple-black, and you can't help flinching away.

"Is my appearance very fearsome?" he says with a sad smile, then winces slowly as the expression pulls at the wound. "Vampires heal," he says simply. "Even if this one will take some time." In the weeks that follow, you find yourself running your fingers over the thin, ragged scars still just visible across his cheek, remembering his determination.

For now, he looks up at you seriously. "I would much rather it was me who was injured," he says fiercely. His eyes burn, and you think of how he only went to confront this terror once you arrived. He would rip a man to pieces if it meant keeping you safe.

TURN TO PAGE 124.

NO BIG DEAL

Casimir frowns at you, as if looking at you more clearly for the first time. The rain hammers outside as he remains in the shadows.

"If one individual's life being cut short—their experiences, memories, comforts, every small moment of kindness—if all that no longer matters, then nothing matters. I'm not sure I can bear seeing the world in such a way."

He's quiet for a moment. "We . . . create our own meaning," he finally murmurs from the darkness. "I hope you find yours."

He moves to the door, out of reach of your candlelight, and you move to follow. "It's late," he tells you, waiting for you to leave the room, then closing the door firmly behind.

He leads you up to the tower again—but as you fall asleep in his bed, you think you hear him slip from the room once more to wander the castle in the dark.

TURN TO PAGE 115.

BRUISES IN THE MORNING

You wake to a thin light streaking through the windows, the bed empty beside you.

You dress and pad downstairs, trying to retrace your steps, and find the dining room below. The fire is lit, filling the room with a glow of warmth against the overcast day. On the table you see a steaming pot of coffee next to a teapot, teacups, and a handful of random teabags—realizing it's an attempt at hosting from a man who does not need to eat or drink.

"I wasn't sure what you wanted." Casimir leans in a far doorway, where steps must lead down to a kitchen. His clothes look crisp and carefully chosen. He stands slightly stiffly, as if covering his nerves with formality. You have the feeling he's not talking about the drinks.

You pour a cup anyway and sit down, which seems to make him more at ease. He comes and sits at the head of the table—that's what he's used to, you think. Sat alone, apart, and in charge: a man who's learned iron discipline, wrested the power and hunger of his body under control. Given a ravenous bloodlust against his desires, he was made to serve, misled into tearing through people, violent and wild—then clawed back control through sheer force of will and took his revenge.

But he also considers it an unspoken necessity to offer drinks to a guest in his house. There's a warmth and quiet humanity to him that death couldn't scour away.

◆ If you have the marker **ABSOLUTION** . . .

He tells you softly that he enjoyed your company and you'd be welcome to stay a while longer. His casual words can't hide the feeling in his eyes. To accept, **TURN TO PAGE 118.**

◆ If you have the marker **BLOOD BANK** . . .

In a low voice, he tells you he found your night together stimulating. He suggests leaving your contact details before you return home, if you want a repeat. To accept, **TURN TO PAGE 130.**

◆ If you have both markers . . . both offers are on the table–it's your choice.

◆ If you have neither marker . . .

He sits politely while you drink, then leads you back to the entrance, giving you a nod before closing the door. You step out into the sun, leaving him in shadows. **TURN TO PAGE 265.**

GOOD-NIGHT KISS

Andrei's eyes widen a little as you speak—but when you move closer, he bends toward you as if not having to think at all and presses his lips to yours. The tension in his broad shoulders releases and softens, and he sinks into the kiss like it's a relief.

He lets out a breath, rough fingers brushing tentatively against yours, then moving to rest at your jaw. He pulls back and opens his eyes slowly, gentle hands stroking down your shoulders, almost reverent as he looks at you.

He gives you a shy smile. "When I saw you came to visit your grandmother, I wanted to talk to you, but"—he spreads his hands with a slightly embarrassed shrug—"I did not know how. I thought I . . . missed the chance. I was, you know, cursing myself."

You tell him he didn't miss his chance. As the rain hammers outside, you sit together on the soft bed, and you talk. He seems earnestly interested—and distressed—at everything you tell him about your life back home. He tells you about his sister and friends in the village and a cake recipe he wants to try. He tells you about the farm, both small tasks and big projects—"*Agricultura regenerativă?*" he says uncertainly, looking up words on his phone to explain sustainable farming grants and the wildlife in the hedgerows.

Time passes quickly, and when he notices his phone clock creeping into the early hours, he apologizes seriously. He kisses you soft and warm once more before gently closing the door, leaving you to fall into a deep, satisfied sleep.

You wake late to a knock at the door. Andrei brings in a tray laden with pots of honey and several homemade jams, a pat of butter in an old-fashioned dish, and what looks like still-warm fresh bread.

He's brought tea and coffee—he offers you both and takes the one you don't. In the light of day, he seems a little nervous and gruff again, but when you ask about the jams, his voice warms and grows more confident. There are some that seem to have no translation: "Rosehip and plum, but not jam. A little

different," he says, describing the process of how he made it and telling you the names. "It's about, uh, how much sugar?"

He points out a kind of fruit jelly, and when you ask about it, you discover there seems to be old customs around it: "Just for honored guests," he says with a quiet blush.

He offers to pick up your things from the terrible car, then take you on to the station. But as you're getting ready, you make an offhand comment about how your horrible flat is not very appealing compared to being brought breakfast in the big, soft bed, and he pauses.

"If you must go back, I understand. But . . . I have many rooms, always lots of work . . ." he trails off. His dark eyes are earnest—serious and hopeful about inviting you to stay.

> Stay with Andrei. **TURN TO PAGE 242.**

> Go back to London. **TURN TO PAGE 265.**

PARAMOUR

Casimir tries not to alter his expression when you accept, but he doesn't quite manage.

His eyes are bright, his shoulders settled more easily, like your company is a prize he didn't expect to win.

You find some phone signal on a hilltop, tell your boss you'll be gone a bit longer to look after your sickly grandmother, tell your friends you're on holiday, and breathe a sigh of relief.

You spend another week with many nights like the last one, beside the candles lit like constellations in his tower room. Before you fall asleep, Casimir sometimes leans up on an elbow to look at you or brushes a hand down your side, reverent and satisfied. Sometimes he repeats long-memorized lines almost unconsciously. "*You breathe; new shapes appear,*" he murmurs, fingers tracing the shell of your ear.

Casimir disappears in the daytime. When he comes to find you in the evenings, he gives evasive explanations about running the castle, not quite letting you in.

He leaves his massive, haphazard library at your disposal—though only some books are in languages you understand. He gives you permission to read whatever you like, as if this is a considerable gift and gesture of trust. Once, you run into August in a corridor and mention it—their eyes widen, and they give you a strange look, as if reevaluating your importance.

In the light of day, you start to learn the corridors, and when you find a broom, you make some of the places you use most look a bit less like a haunted house. Casimir assures you the forest is safe in the daytime, too, and you wander the tall trees, relieved to have nothing pressing that needs to be done.

The food in the castle gets much better, and one day you discover Raisa with bags of shopping heading down to the medieval kitchen, where she tells you proudly she's wired up a fridge to the generator for Casimir's "*friend*." She chats with you happily and asks about your favorite meals, which then start arriving in the evenings.

The other vampires seem to be growing more comfortable around you. One night you're sitting with them at the long dinner table—slowly demolishing a plate of stuffed peppers and *sarmale* that are so good, you're sure they're paying someone in the village to make them—when Casimir arrives looking stormy, sweeping in and slamming the door behind. Raisa pauses from stealing the few bites of food she can safely digest, and August, a more unusual presence, pauses and looks up from their notebook.

Feeling the tension in the air, you ask directly what he's been doing as he sits down.

Frustrated, Casimir grits out the real answer: "We've been discussing how to deal with the rogue vampire that lurks in the forest at night. We need a *careful plan* before taking any action," he growls pointedly at the others. Raisa makes a noise of disagreement; August scoffs.

August lists off a few plans that seem wildly risky. "And if a human won't *volunteer* as bait, I'm *sure* I can find someone suitable," they say with a sharp smile. Casimir is giving August a stony look, like he's already categorically refused all these suggestions.

"Or why not simply attack head-on?" August says. "You last faced him alone. We'd be three against one. How old and powerful can he really *be*?"

"If we were killed or wounded, what would happen to"—you're sure he's about to say your name but his eyes stay deliberately on August—"the humans in the village? There's no telling what further havoc he could cause. We must be sure of ourselves."

August's loyalty seems to prevent them from arguing their case much further, and the conversation goes nowhere.

"It doesn't matter!" Raisa exclaims, throwing her hands up. "It has been too long. Just choose. The town is in danger *now*. Now he does not come and go; he is here *all the time*. You both have lived too long. You don't know how to do things fast anymore."

Casimir's brow is furrowed. He looks over at you and raises an eyebrow, as if asking what you think.

- Ask more about the rogue vampire hunting them. **TURN TO PAGE 121.**
- Suggest using your own blood to lure the rogue vampire to a good location to strike, even if it's risky for you. **TURN TO PAGE 122.**
- Tell them they need to team up to take out the rogue vampire, even if it's risky for them. **TURN TO PAGE 113.**

A MYSTERIOUS NIGHT

You wake to thin light streaking through the windows, the bed empty beside you.

You dress and pad downstairs, trying to retrace your steps, and find the dining room below. The fire is lit, filling the room with warmth and a glow. On the table you see a steaming pot of coffee next to a teapot, teacups, and a handful of random teabags: an attempt at hosting from someone you suspect does not need to eat or drink.

"I wasn't sure what you wanted." Casimir's voice makes you jump as he appears silently in a far doorway, where steps must lead down to a kitchen. His clothes are clean but rumpled, and he leans in the doorway wearing the hint of an amused smile.

You have the feeling his words are not just about the tea and coffee, but you pour a cup anyway and sit down. He comes into the room and settles into his chair at the head of the table—apparently the mysterious head of this strange household.

There's so much you don't know about him and haven't asked—but the moment to talk to him seems to have passed by. His face is calm and amused but back under perfect control—and unwilling to give anything further away. In the cold light of morning, his eyes now deny any possibility of further conversation.

You consider what you do know: This is a man who knows what he wants. He's learned enough discipline to hold himself back—to wrest the hunger of his body under control, to give pleasure and take his own without much harm, even full of bloodlust and inhuman powers. You sip slowly at your drink, looking at the teacups. This is a man who likes to take care of people.

◆ If you have the marker **BLOOD BANK** . . .

He tells you in a low voice that he found your night together stimulating. He suggests you leave your contact details before you return home, if you want a repeat. If you choose to accept, **TURN TO PAGE 130.**

◆ Otherwise . . .

He sits politely while you drink, then leads you back to the entrance, giving you a nod before closing the door. You step out into the sun, leaving him in shadows. **TURN TO PAGE 265.**

THE ROGUE VAMPIRE

"Over the years, vampires who had known the count would occasionally come to the castle and find him gone," Casimir says, leaning back in his chair.

August smiles. "I'd tell them the count simply went missing one night while we were staying with him. Probably some *awful* accident," they say innocently.

"I suspect most of our visitors guessed the truth," Casimir continues, "but were happy to let matters lie. Even vampires who accepted the count's cruelties disliked how much attention he drew to our kind. He barely covered his tracks—bragging of his exploits to powerful humans. Some visitors were happy to spread the idea that the count went missing, likely killed in the chaos of war—others told us outright they were glad to be rid of him."

"And those," says August, "are the ones we invited back. After the revolution, travel became easier, and by then we thought ourselves safe. We began the Hallowe'en ball."

Casimir still looks bitter. "The parties grew larger, and we grew less cautious with time. Word of the count's death spread among our kind—whether they forgave us or not, none challenged us. The world was changing, and many thought we could not afford further infighting. I, too, thought we were safe.

"But there was still one last associate of the count's we had never heard from. I suspect he is the man who made the count a vampire to begin with." Casimir scowls, as if this was all his own fault. "He turned the count in the lands controlled by ancient Rome—he is disconnected from humanity by thousands of years of blood. I suspect that is why he is so powerful and so vicious.

"Finally, he arrived at our door and attacked. When I faced him after the ball, he had become almost feral—impossible to reason with. He overpowered me easily, and he may have ended me if the others had not managed to get me back within the walls. And now he appears periodically to terrorize the forest, waiting for his revenge on us."

The room falls into a grim silence. You see more clearly how much this rogue vampire has disturbed their peace. While he remains, travelers will keep going missing on the forbidden road, and Casimir will remain plagued by guilt and fear.

> Suggest finding the safest way to use your own blood to lure the rogue vampire to a good location to strike, even if it's risky for you. **TURN TO PAGE 122.**

> Tell them it sounds like they need to just team up to take out the rogue vampire, even if it's risky for them. **TURN TO PAGE 113.**

THE LURE

It takes some argument, but eventually Casimir agrees. "He'll be able to sense your heartbeat. It's not enough to smear your blood on the outer walls and keep you safely inside. You'll have to be out there yourself, in the path of danger," he says grimly. His clenched hand flexes where it rests on the table. "But we can wait nearby—choose the location. We can plan."

In the days of preparation that follow, Casimir grows increasingly protective—and occasionally wretched—at you putting yourself in harm's way. But he seems quietly proud of your bravery. When he draws you into bed the night before the attack, he pulls you close and lets his look give away his open admiration. "You'll be careful," he says, and it's an order.

With you as a lure to guide the rogue vampire's path, the plan is to set a trap. On the day itself, August, Raisa, and a group of friends you think might be werewolves enlarge a ditch to make a huge pit trap in the shadow of the castle wall, safely clear of the trees. The top is covered in leaf litter and a net, the bottom filled with stakes and an odorless oil.

As evening falls in the forest, Casimir gives you a last, urgent kiss in the shadows. His expression is complex, but he gives you a nod of confidence. "I'll see you soon," he commands, then leaves you standing seemingly alone. You move into position.

When the last rays of sun sink below the horizon, you take a deep breath and prick the back of a finger with a knife as agreed—then you wait. You start to shiver in the evening cold.

Eventually you hear it. The slight shifting in the trees, cracks of disturbed branches, drawing nearer and nearer. You move around beside a tree, making a half-hearted, terrified show of having caught your hand on a twig. Your heart thuds. The noise is close now. Then, from the corner of your eye, you see the creature's shadow, driven forward by the scent of blood and thrill of ending one of the castle's guests. It's only a split second of blur in the moonlight, and he's almost upon you—

The leaf-covered net gives way beneath his feet. He careens down into the pit at a speed, but you see him twist out of the way of the stakes. His legs are caught, but he's still moving feverishly toward you, starting to tear himself free.

The world seems to slow as you see a trailing arc of flame soar down from the castle wall. The bottle and its burning rag smash into the oil-filled trap in a burst of explosion.

The rogue vampire is still lunging toward you from the pit as fire sears to life around him. You throw yourself back against the wall as his sharpened-claw nails tear through the fabric and flesh of your leg—but in an instant, Casimir's in front of you, out from his hiding place. His face is a mask of cold fury as he sends the creature back into the flames with a kick to its head. The thing's corpse-like features crack backward, illuminated for a moment in the fire that blooms to life around it, wide once-human eyes reflecting the light—and then he's swallowed by the consuming fire that fills the pit. The creature's guttural, inhuman screeches are muffled by Casimir as he pulls you tight against him, shielding you from the flames and horror.

The noises strangle and choke to an end. You feel suddenly faint and exhausted, and Casimir half carries you through a whirl of dark corridors to the nearest room indoors, prepared that day with a bed and supplies and bucket of water.

He lays you down on the bed looking wild and strange, then moves with unnatural speed and force to slam and lock the door. You hear a strange rasping on the other side that your woozy mind can't understand for a moment—because surely the danger is over. You saw the rogue vampire char and fall apart, the same way the count must have done long ago. Then you realize: You're faint from blood loss. Your leg is slick with red. The scratching at the door is the other two vampires.

In the lamplight you see Casimir flex his jaw, his dark eyes wide and locked onto your injury. Your nerves are alight in the face of the barely controlled threat: one powerful creature only a few steps away, two more locked behind the door—

But Casimir forces himself under control. Eyes still on your leg, he removes his jacket and rolls up his sleeves. Then—without a word, as if the effort takes all his focus—he cleans and wraps the wound with shaking hands. It's only after he's staunched the flow of blood and assured your safety that he lets himself buckle, falling to his knees to lick the excess clean, sucking the soaked fabric and making a mess of his shirt.

The bloodlust abates, and he gathers himself bitterly, standing to wash his hands and face with the bucket of water. Then he sinks down beside you to cup your face. He looks undone, wrecked with emotion. When you try to sit up to reach him, he lets out a noise that's almost a growl, pushing you carefully back down to rest as your head spins. He dips down to kiss you possessively, like you belong to him. As you lose consciousness, you're aware of him holding you in his arms—almost painfully tight, like he'd rip the world apart for you.

TURN TO PAGE 124.

AFTER THE MURDER

By the time the wounds have healed, you find yourself feeling almost at home in the castle.

With the rogue vampire gone, there's no one left who cares to remember the old count. You pass by the old portraits in the gallery, the painted man's eyes still seeming to follow you. When you reach Casimir's rooms, something in your expression makes him rise from his armchair. You ask why he keeps the old relics of a dead man who hurt him—the portraits, the blackened room, the name.

Casimir—Khalil—seems genuinely surprised at this question—as if without you, he'd never have considered ending his self-imposed punishment. He looks away from you in a way you're becoming familiar with, to hide a swell of emotion.

"I suppose the last person who cared about the count is gone now . . . With his death no longer a secret, I can find no reason not to use my old name," Khalil says slowly, brow furrowed. "My true name."

You notice him growing contemplative several times over the next few days, staring into space with the book in his hands forgotten. He says no more about it, but one night, you hear Raisa yell "Khalil!" down from an upper floor, and he goes to find her without comment. When you use his real, chosen name for him in private, he's sometimes unable to fight down a smile.

The next week, you find Khalil burning the portraits.

He stands in a stone courtyard, staring into the fire, as you come to join him.

You stand together in silence, but after a moment his hand rubs across your back. He glances at you as if quietly pleased to have you present.

You ask whether this is all of them.

"Almost," he says in a murmur. "The old countess still sleeps here. I've put one painting of them together down in her mausoleum, for her to keep or destroy as she wishes." He looks at you wryly. "We found her a while after the count's death, to our surprise. We were prepared for another fight if she wanted revenge—but she seemed delighted to be rid of him. I wonder whether she, too, was turned against her will. She sleeps quietly now, as long as she is not disturbed."

He looks philosophically into the dancing flames, where the frames fizzle and pop.

The count's painted face distorts as it melts and chars, just as his body did.

"Long lives do strange things to our kind. The countess can sleep contentedly for centuries, barely needing to feed or leave her chamber, slowly forgetting her human life.

But the count and the rogue grew more cruel and bloodthirsty the further removed they were from their humanity."

The reflected flames dance in the dark pools of his eyes, which seem to be looking somewhere distant as he goes on, somewhere beyond the fire and beyond the castle. "Undying—but slowly unraveling, too.

"Will my memories fade to nothing as the time passes and I sink deeper and deeper into fugue? '*In that sleep of death what dreams may come . . .*' Do I have a core that will remain? Are all minds Theseus's ship?"

You're not sure whether he's expecting you to reply, but you move closer to him in front of the fire. August and Raisa have been making plans to go traveling. You, too, are still expected back home, an unspoken but obvious fact between you.

Khalil's life is changing around him after a long time standing still—old things ending, creating space for something new.

"When I was younger," Khalil says in a low voice, "wretched at having been made a monster, I dreamed that one day, when I was free of the count, I would find my own companion with whom to live out the long days of my death. A human whose brief candle I could keep burning.

"But the longer I live, the more I think it a terrible cruelty to turn even a willing victim into a deathless thing"—he glances over toward you—"even if I were to find such a willing companion."

He leaves the sentence open like a question. Behind him, the bonfire crumples into a dark red glow in the courtyard. Soon it will burn out. But the night feels alive with possibility for what may come next.

- › Tell Khalil you'd like to stay as a companion, even if the time you have together is limited. **TURN TO PAGE 140.**
- › Tell Khalil you'd like to stay—and ask him to make you a vampire. **TURN TO PAGE 127.**

AN OBEDIENT MEAL

He moves toward you, smiling. "Did you enjoy your meal?" he asks quietly, his eyes hungry and glittering as he pulls out a chair beside you.

You nod, and he draws slowly closer. "Pleased to see me?" he says, voice so rough with want that you find it hard to stay still.

When you nod again, he makes a low "hmm" in his throat that your body reacts to. He moves his mouth to your ear, one strong hand cradling your neck, pressed close. He moves a hand to the back of your thigh. "Hands behind your back. *Good.*"

Casimir orders you exactly as he pleases, and you find yourself eager to obey. He instructs you to unbutton his shirt while making you gasp, holds you down and tells you how well you're doing. He pushes you down to bite the inside of your thigh as your want tips over the edge. The puncture wounds heal unnaturally quickly under his tongue, but not before a spray of blood turns the delicate leftover plates into a sordid mess.

He makes you fold your clothes before ordering you into the huge bath, his voice thick with desire. His eyes stay fixed on you as he unbuttons his cuffs and shrugs out of his shirt. He buries his face into your panting neck as he grazes it with his teeth, and you can *feel* how easily he could drain the rest of the life from you, stop your rabbit-fast heart. He stays poised on the tightrope, teeth not quite sinking down, rocking together until you both fall apart.

You lie warm and content, clean in a plush robe on a very large bed. Casimir emerges from the next room and sinks down beside you in the dark.

After a moment, he asks what you want from your trip. He's regarding you carefully, and you think you understand. He wants you, hungrily—but he also likes to please you: to have everything ready and perfect without you having to really think about it.

- Tell him you want to see the sights and explore the cafés and art galleries—and maybe you can see some of them together. **TURN TO PAGE 134.**
- Tell him you want to stay in the hotel, to go to the spa and try the bar and be ready for whenever he wants you. **TURN TO PAGE 137.**

CREATURE OF THE NIGHT

Over the next few days, Khalil asks several times if you're sure, not quite promising to do it.

But when the others leave on their travels, promising to visit, you think he's told them. Raisa gives you a big hug and a wink before revving her motorbike and screeching off down the overgrown road. August gives you a searching, knowing sort of look as they stand in the doorway, pulling on their gloves. "I hope you know what you're getting yourself into," they say warily. "Take care of him." Then they slip out the door into the night.

You only speak vaguely about what's to come, but Khalil sees that the road is cleared so new furniture can arrive to make the castle more hospitable for you. He seems full of restless energy: eager for your company, eyes bright like he wants to devour you—but nervous, too. He disappears "to think," and you find him occasionally in odd corners of the castle, absentmindedly staring out a window with a forgotten book of poetry in his hand.

One night you come upstairs to find the tower room has been carefully cleaned, the books filed unusually away to their rightful places, as if for an honored guest or a formal funeral. The wax-landscape table is bathed in light, all its flickering candles lit. The night outside is the dark stillness of winter, cold stars scattered glittering across the sky and everything snow-silent, as if the whole forest is holding its breath.

Khalil rises from his chair, as if he'd been waiting. "You're sure?" he asks for a serious, final time, rubbing a thumb across your hand.

You nod back.

You haven't agreed what life will look like afterward—or death, you correct yourself. You haven't decided whether to tell your family and friends you're alive, after it happens: That would be a comforting lie that would have to be corrected at some point. It might be easier for them to know part of the truth: that you died on the forbidden road.

You'll decide as it comes—it's impossible to tell how you'll feel on the other side, no matter how much you discuss the experience with him beforehand. You only know the immediate future: At first you'll be here at the castle, learning to control your urges and feed on the animals in a safe haven away from the world. After that, you could do anything. You and Khalil have talked about traveling—going to see all his old haunts across Europe and North Africa and out beyond to places unknown to him, past or present. You only know one thing for sure: You'll be together.

He nods at you seriously, eyes bright. "Together, then."

He dips to your neck and drinks, the points of pain giving way to giddiness, and he catches you before you fall.

Khalil slices at his palm, the knife's flash of silver kissing across the skin and parting it neatly in two. His strange purple-dark blood spills from it slowly, and he holds his hand up to your lips like an offering.

You taste his blood, lick and swallow. Your mouth is full of it, thick and metallic, and for a moment you feel like gagging. What might be a shout or scream builds in your throat—but it burbles and cuts off as you force it back down.

The process is messy, the pain worse than you'd expected. You feel your muscles flex and twitch, your nerve endings alive and raw. Your stomach clenches and contorts, your bones sear and shiver as your body pulls itself loose to reconfigure anew.

You register Khalil looking down where he still holds you, one hand to your mouth. His eyes are wild, melancholy, and slightly frantic as you're remade in his arms. But you don't need to know whether he regrets his decision—you feel *perfect.*

You drink deep. You suck at his hand until he has to restrain you, thrashing, to pull it away.

The whole world changes around you. Far outside, beyond the castle walls and deep below snow-covered boughs, you hear the shuffling of birds and their fluttering heartbeats, vigorous and warm. From your distant vantage, you can feel life all around you: the burrowing, wriggling things under the soil, juices writhing through them; the tangle of roots and fungus as it pulses, alive beneath the frozen ground; spiders in dusty corners, crawling and forgotten things that move in the dark. You are hungry for them all.

Your life ends, and a new creature emerges from its ruins: terrible and vibrant and perfectly made. The living world closes its doors to you, and a new one forms in its place: yours for the taking.

THE END(?)

Want another adventure? See what else there is to do: **GO TO PAGE 266.**

SUGAR BABY

The terrible car just makes it to the station without falling apart—but you barely notice, because you spend the whole drive and the whole plane ride thinking about last night. The forest had looked ordinary in the daytime, but the shadows between the trees made you think of the darkness the night before—and Casimir at the door, shutting it out.

For two weeks, you don't hear from him, and your life seems to go back to its usual state. You're kicking yourself for not getting some way to contact him—wondering whether he has a mobile phone or whether it would be crazy to go and visit your gran again soon—when a letter arrives.

You're eating a plasticky-tasting microwave meal in the 4 p.m. darkness of winter on a Saturday—because you were too exhausted to cook again and forgot to eat lunch—when you notice the envelope on your doormat.

It's weird that someone had bothered to come up instead of leaving it in the downstairs mailboxes or just vaguely throwing it over a nearby fence somewhere in the vicinity and not letting you get a refund, as with most parcel deliveries.

There's a thick, creamy texture to the paper. You don't recognize the courier stamps and stickers, but your name and address are written clearly in a slanted copperplate hand, like something out of a fountain pen and the distant past.

Inside is less an invitation than a summons.

The letter tells you what train you'll be catching, where a driver will meet you, and the hotel you'll be taken to. It also heavily implies your job has been informed and won't miss you—and that you should dress nice.

In the envelope there are also first-class Eurostar tickets to Paris and a matte-black gift card for a boutique you've not heard of. When you look it up, you find the shop has clothes in exactly the style you would like—if you were a bit more adventurous and could afford to "dress nice." Even the website looks luxurious, and you notice it also has a list of ethical credentials alongside the beautifully styled photos of expensive fabrics. This guy's really done his research.

At the boutique, you're ushered into a bright, quiet space and offered tea or Prosecco before a stylist unobtrusively helps pick a selection of clothes that are actually comfortable and look amazing. You're told they'll be tailored for you and delivered tomorrow. When you ask how much money's on the card, expecting enough for one outfit at most, they tell you everything's been taken care of: All of it's being paid for, whatever you want.

You get on the train feeling vaguely self-conscious in a warm, perfectly fitted new coat from the boutique, but it helps you feel like less of an impostor in first class. You accept a drink and settle back in the seat as the gray, flat countryside whips by. You take satisfaction in your secret: None of the few scattered passengers know you're a regular person with a hot benefactor, one who's paying for the luxury tickets so he can tie you up and drink you like a smoothie.

The hotel is on one of the roads leading away from the Arc de Triomphe, and it looks old and grand—art deco balconies, awning and red carpet at the entrance. You wonder if it's an old haunt of Casimir's or if he chose it just for you. A deferential staff member at the front desk gives you keys to a presidential suite, and you go up by private lift to the absurd rooms. You leave your coat and bag by the door, where they look very small in the grand apartments, and stand for a moment, overwhelmed in the large space. Your body sings with anticipation.

There's no sign of Casimir, but an ice bucket of champagne and a huge spread of dishes are spread out on the dining room table, timed for your arrival. The literal real-life butler uncovers the plates, tells you your "friend" has left a message for you to begin without him, then gives you an actual fucking bow before leaving you alone in the rooms.

The food is arranged beautifully on the plates, each carefully labeled by someone in the kitchens with the name and ingredients in English. There's more than you can eat, but you try several things and savor each mouthful. It's so good that you find yourself enjoying it easily despite your nerves, almost forgetting you're trespassing strangely in another world.

You're licking a drop of sauce from a fingertip without really thinking about it when you notice a figure out on the balcony in the dark. Did he just arrive by some mysterious means, or has he been watching you all along? You're not sure which idea thrills you more.

"I . . . heard the food was good here," comes Casimir's low voice.

> Expose your neck and tell him he should come and try for himself. You want to push him and misbehave. **TURN TO PAGE 132.**

> Stay quiet and obedient until he gives you permission to speak. You want to be good for him. **TURN TO PAGE 126.**

A DELECTABLE MOUTHFUL

As he comes into the light, you can see he looks hungry, barely restrained. In a moment, he's at your side, hand at your collarbone, lifting and pushing you like a ragdoll until you're lying flat on the table.

He's rough as he seeks your satisfaction, and as your want tips over the edge, he bites down hard, crumpling your new clothes and spraying blood over the shining table below you.

Afterward, you both doze on a sofa until he gently carries you to a warm bath, then attends to you much less gently all over again.

Before sunrise, he slips out of the mess of sheets in the palatial bed. "In daylight, I shall be sleeping in the next room and am not to be disturbed until sunset," he commands as he does up his cuffs. His eyes are drawn back to you, over your body. He growls, "You're to behave yourself. I shall know if you misbehave"—which very much encourages you to do so.

After sleeping through the morning, you spend the next afternoon at the bar trying the most expensive drinks you can on Casimir's tab.

His imposing figure appears, looming, alongside you late in the evening, and you pretend not to notice as you ostentatiously order the most expensive bottle of champagne they have.

You think he enjoys the act of collecting you sternly, dragging you upstairs, and punishing you thoroughly in every room in the suite. The "punishment" is not much of a deterrent.

The next night, you spend the evening in the pool, then stay at the spa flirting with whomever you can find.

Casimir finds you, arriving all in black with a stormy expression that has the other guests making excuses to hurry away. For a moment, he just watches you from across the room, jaw tight—like he finds your behavior maddening but is aching to get closer, like he can't believe he likes it. His perfectly tailored suit looks as if he put it on in a hurry, and in the private lift on the way up, he bites you hard enough for bruises to blossom across your neck the next day, as if he can't wait to get you closer.

"You like to play games," he says as you're laid out panting on a plush rug in the suite, feeling extremely good. You roll your head to look up at him where he sits leaning back in a chair, watching you—he's fully dressed, you notice, where you are decidedly not.

You tell him you're pretty sure he enjoys it.

A smile spreads over his face, wide enough to see the points of his canines, deadly in the low light. "If I didn't enjoy games, you wouldn't still be alive.

"But I want to make sure you're *fully satisfied* with your trip." He looks serious for a moment, and you think you understand—this guy's whole thing isn't just being in control: He likes to do things for you. He likes the rooms ready to every last detail, full of good food he can't really eat, for your pleasure. He doesn't bite you to sate his own hunger and leave you bleeding: He wants you, and he wants you to feel good, too, whatever that takes.

› Tell him you do enjoy games but you'd love to see the sights, cafés, and art galleries. Ask to see them together. **TURN TO PAGE 134.**

› Tell him you're very thoroughly satisfied like this. You want to stay in the hotel, trying every single luxury they have on offer, and be ready for whenever he wants you. **TURN TO PAGE 137.**

PATRON OF THE ARTS

He gives you a slow smile that you don't know what to make of—curious, maybe. He describes some of the places in Paris you might like to see, and he seems to gauge your reaction and file away your preferences carefully. The winter's long nights make it easy for him to take you out after sunset each evening.

You walk around the Louvre in the hour before it closes—he quietly takes you to his favorite pieces instead of the famous ones, slowly showing you parts of himself. You wander gardens in the darkness, head down hidden staircases to out-of-the-way cafés or basements where a jazz band in the corner plays long past midnight. And after the bars and cafés close, you return to the absurd hotel, and he tells you what to do.

He bites with deliberation, reveling in your reaction. He enjoys pushing you to the point of desperation, stretching your pleasure out for hours before he lets you finish, taking his own hungry and slow. The sensation is more than what you've ever experienced before, your whole body left deliciously sated afterward.

You return to London from the first trip to discover someone has made a legal threat to your boss at your terrible job. There's no longer any unpaid overtime, and everyone suddenly gets paid in full and exactly when they're supposed to. It makes you realize you probably could have done that yourself, and that spurs you into going to a citizen's advice place to ask how to do the same with your landlord, too.

The second letter comes a month later. This time your train changes in Paris and goes on to Vienna. You're shown to a private carriage that makes you feel as if you've stepped into the past, where everything is inlaid with gold and dark wood. Velvet seats frame a small table at a window, and at the far end, a double bed takes up most of the width of the space. The lights are off, but you see the shape of Casimir sitting in the dark on the bed, the teeth of his white smile. The noises he draws out of you all night are lost to the rattle of the train in the dark.

In the New Year, you see Venice "before it entirely sinks," Casimir says darkly before telling you what it was like two hundred years ago. In the spring, the train takes you on to Budapest, and instead of a faceless luxurious hotel, your cab arrives at an unusual one full of strange old furniture and locals who tell you their authoritative opinions about the food. This is what Casimir prefers, you realize—he's letting you know him. He takes you to parts of the city you would never have visited alone, and you find they're his old haunts.

When you go back to London—only a little faint from the blood loss—it always feels like a dream, a delicious secret. You return each time a little braver and more able to do difficult things. You call old friends, volunteer some Saturdays, and try reading some of the books Casimir talked about. You save things up to tell him about next time. Perhaps, one day, there won't be a next time—but for now you live in delicious anticipation, fingers brushing over the bruises at your wrists as they slowly heal.

One summer night, you're looking out over Prague from the top-floor balcony of a boutique hotel nestled away near the old town square. Casimir appears through the night, eyes lingering on you as he strips off his coat and throws it over the back of a chair, as if he wants as much time as possible to drink you in. "How was the trip?" he asks in a low voice, then breaks into a dazzling smile when you tell him, of course, that everything he organized was perfect.

He leans down to kiss you, slow and deliberate, letting his teeth scrape along your lower lip until you're gasping. Just as you're thrumming with anticipation, he draws back, amusement playing at his mouth.

"Tell me about London," he says, leaning back on the rail as the lights of the city glitter below, laughter sounding up from the bars in the street. You think he's making you wait, drawing out the pleasure, and you reply without really thinking—you're now used to responding to his instructions like a devoted subject. His hands slide over your shoulders as he gently draws out answers about where your friends live; his mouth grazes your ear as you tell him what sort of place you'd dream of living in, if you could. His attentions build giddy want within you until he relents, biting you up against the railings and then pulling you inside.

You've forgotten about the questions by the time a thick, creamy envelope arrives on your doormat next month with a key inside. Written in fountain pen is an address in an area you've dreamed of being able to live and the words *A reward for being good.*

You go to your new flat for the first time after dark, and he is waiting for you.

He sits sprawled on the sofa in the low light, like he owns the place—which he must—and like he owns you. The blood pulses in your neck, eager and willing. When he asks you to kneel, his voice is low and pleased, like it's a pleasure to give you what you deserve.

THE END

There are more secrets to discover in the vampire castle.

See what else there is to do: **GO TO PAGE 266.**

BLOOD BANK

You spend your mornings in bed being brought food you could never afford, your days in the spa, and your nights panting and desperate, pushed up against every surface in the suite. You're treated roughly, pleasured thoroughly, and treated like Casimir's own personal blood bank.

And it feels good to be used.

You sleep blissfully and wake lazily. By the end of the week you feel almost painfully good—bruised and tender and a little giddy, your whole body left deliciously sated.

You return to London dreamy. Your coworkers can't figure out what's gotten into you, and you decide not to go into too much detail. But through them, you discover someone has made a legal threat to your terrible boss. Suddenly there's no more unpaid overtime, and everyone gets paid in full and exactly when they're supposed to. It makes you realize you probably could have done that yourself—it spurs you into going to a citizen's advice place to ask about how to do the same with your landlord, too.

The second letter is a month later, and this time your train changes in Paris and goes on into the Alps.

You're shown to a private carriage that makes you feel as if you've stepped into the past, where everything is inlaid with gold and dark wood. There are velvet seats by a small table at a window, and at the end a double bed takes up most of the width of the space. There's champagne on the bedside table, new clothes laid on the bed for you—fitted to your measurements from the boutique—and you eat alone in a private dining car specially arranged just for you. In the large window that looks over the fields that roll by, the sun sets, and Casimir arrives to watch you eat dessert and orders you to bed. The noises he draws out of you all night are lost to the rattle of the train in the dark.

In the New Year, you're flown to a luxury villa in the Caribbean, where you eat looking out over an ocean sunset and wonder what will happen to the palm trees when the seas rise further. The pink sky stretches out above, and you savor each mouthful as you eat—you'll see the beauty in the last of the world before it goes. Casimir spatters the poolside with blood as you lose yourselves in each other, the thrill of danger sharpening your pleasure. You wake up to find you've been carefully bandaged, hooked up to an IV in the night. He does care, you think woozily before falling back to sleep.

Each time you go back to London—only a little faint from the blood loss—the previous trip feels like a dream, a delicious secret. You find yourself living in delighted anticipation, fingers brushing over the bruises at your wrists as they slowly heal. Maybe one day there won't be a next time, but for now, letters keep arriving every few months. While you wait, you fantasize about the way he demands things of you, about his body and his teeth.

On a hotel balcony overlooking an Italian mountain vista in the setting sun, Casimir's eyes flicker down over your body. "If you're good, I'll reward you," he says in a low voice, and you assume it's all part of the usual game, the murmur of conversation that escalates to the usual rush, to the escape of giddy sensation.

But back in London—not long after your wounds from the trip have healed—a thick, creamy envelope arrives on your doormat with a key inside.

Written in fountain pen is an address and the word *Tonight.*

You go to your new flat for the first time after dark, and he is waiting for you.

The flat is the entire top floor of a building made of glass in the middle of London.

You drop your bag by the door and run your hands along marble countertops in the huge kitchen. The place has an industrial feel to the luxury—gray walls rough, surfaces polished and sterile. You think how easy it would be to clean blood off every plane of this place. You think how hard you could be forced onto the cold stone floors. You like the idea of ruining its unsullied monotony—wrecking the place together.

Casimir sits sprawled on an angular sofa that probably cost more than anything you own. The room's lights are set low, and he sits like royalty, like he owns the place—you assume he does. He sits like he owns you. The idea sends a shiver up your spine. You feel the blood pulsing in your neck, eager and willing.

"Kneel," he commands from the shadows, and his voice is firm; he's entirely sure he can give you exactly what you want.

THE END

There are more secrets to discover in the vampire castle.

See what else there is to do: **GO TO PAGE 266.**

A BRIEF CANDLE IS STILL A LIGHT IN THE DARK

Khalil watches you for a moment, a small smile curving his lips despite himself. Then he leads you back inside, away from the dying fire. He closes the door against the cold courtyard and draws you into his arms, kissing you with feeling, one cool hand against your cheek. "You're right. We're both here now, and I wish to make the most of it"—he flashes his white, roguish smile—"at least, for as long as you'll have me."

Finding the spot of signal, you tell your friends and family you'll be staying and to come and visit sometime—and you finally tell your boss to fuck off.

Over the next few weeks, Khalil gradually lets his guard down, until one night he admits feeling lost. During the repressive regimes of the twentieth century, there'd been clear, accessible goals to protect the town and occupy his time: local officials to threaten and terrify, necessary supplies to smuggle. Then in the years since the revolution, he'd busied himself distributing the old count's amassed fortune. He acted on Raisa's ideas and August's insistence: selling the castle's land cheaply to locals and investing in schemes to protect the Carpathians' ancient forests. But now the treasures are all sold, and there's only enough left in the old accounts to maintain the three of them, the crumbling castle, and a few small projects.

"I feel purposeless, adrift in this new age," he murmurs beside you after the last candle's flickered out. He tells you he's seen the region of his long-ago childhood home torn apart, horrifying pictures that load slowly on an old computer Raisa set up. New technology has granted him an overwhelming flood of awful global news, a constant bombardment that leaves him daunted and frustrated.

"Sometimes it feels as if trying to help anyone is only a vain attempt to ease my guilt," he says. "Whatever I do, it's only a drop in the ocean." You tell him an ocean is made up of drops, and he watches you thoughtfully as the first embers of dawn start to light the horizon beyond the mountains.

In the spring, he shows you around the outer walls, pointing out the names of towns below and offering a formal hand over muddy hollows without thinking. He explains his intentions to fix up the castle, replant trees, and clear the way to the road. As you listen and offer suggestions, he seems to animate, standing taller. His plans gain form and dates, a clear way ahead. Now that it's for you, making the castle livable seems important. There's work to do, and it seems to tether him, to connect him to the world outside.

One day, August returns abruptly from their travels after you see a dead billionaire plastered across the news, his surprising new will distributing his assets charitably to August's chosen causes. "I show up as an unreadable smudge on the security footage," August says blithely. "Hiding out is just a precaution." Khalil puts on a show of gruffness, but he has the manner of a proud and slightly indulgent parent.

Not long after, an old friend of August's arrives, too. She brings wild stories and a handful of books for Khalil, admitting she's lying low after being caught feeding on a deer in the highlands. "Their other natural predators have been killed off. They damage protected habitats," she says defensively in a broad accent. "Nature agencies do culls, but *I* eat a wee deer now and again, suddenly it's a problem."

Khalil steps into his role as host, seeming to enjoy taking charge—and when Raisa brings a werewolf who lost her job when someone found out, he barely pretends to grumble as you both make up another guest room.

Soon word spreads, and desperate people with nowhere to go come to the forbidding castle—never many at once but always a mix of creatures you'd never heard of and, more and more, humans turned out of their family homes.

"You can stay as long as you need, for no charge. And when you're ready, we can help you find your own living situation. But . . . you understand that not everyone here is human?" Khalil gravely asks a trans boy with a black eye who can't be more than twenty.

"I don't mind," he replies shyly in a thick Romanian accent. "I kind of like it."

August regrows a garden, and when Raisa returns, she shows anyone interested how to work the generator and fix up old cars. Khalil—once, long ago, a servant in a guesthouse—is wryly amused to be running something like his own. You clear out rooms and set up electricity and bring in a cook who knows your gran. "Oh, we all like the vampires," she says. "Old people in town, we remember."

It changes Khalil to see the people he's helping in front of his eyes—people like himself, given a small space to call their own. His brooding moods become less frequent; his cynicism softens. There's laughter in the corridors now, practical work to be done each day. He sits at the head of the busy dinner table, quiet but satisfied—he makes small exhalations of laughter when someone makes a joke or tells an old story, and he watches you fondly when he thinks you're not looking. He likes the company, you realize—hundreds of years ago, he grew up with siblings and lived happily in the bustle of the city, before his imposed isolation. He's feared by new residents seeking refuge, but he's trusted and loved by the ones who stay long enough to get to know him.

The following Hallowe'en, Khalil hosts the masquerade ball once again. You walk into the tower room on the day to find a tailored outfit in your favorite style draped across the bed, with a mask that will match his. He slips quietly into the room behind you and runs his powerful hands over your sides as he murmurs "Do you like it?" into your ear in a languorous, confident tone. He already knows it's perfect.

That night, the newly comfortable castle fills with current residents and old friends. Werewolves from town greet Raisa with loud excitement; refined, ethereal vampires give formal bows to Khalil before launching into discussions about books and philosophy and inviting you both to stay in their grand apartments in Budapest and villas in Italy. Khalil welcomes them all with easy confidence and introduces you reverently like you're a guest of honor.

When visiting your gran in town, you discovered she was fully aware of the various supernatural presences in the neighborhood. She arrives at the party in style, flanked by a group of old ladies in a mix of outrageous costumes, old-fashioned shawls, and combat boots. She gets in as many free drinks as possible and makes a *lot* of dirty jokes about vampires. But a few beers in, she also looks at you warmly, promising to reassure the rest of your family you met a "nice young man." "And it's true—you know he is like vampire king here!" she says, waving her drink at Khalil. "*Very* handsome, powerful.

"And you are always very strange. So for you, a strange man"—she points at her teeth, indicating his canines—"is good. A nice boy," she says, nodding to herself as she sips at her drink, apparently satisfied with your life choices.

Later, as some guests retire upstairs, the party unravels comfortably into something smaller and more intimate. An old record plays in a newly restored living room full of old, elegant furniture, fire smoldering in the ancient hearth against the autumn chill.

Khalil's dinner jacket is draped over a sofa somewhere, his mask discarded and creamy shirt open at the collar, casually rolled-up sleeves showing off the muscle on his dark forearms. He's spread out on the sofa at the edge of a murmured conversation, but a slow smile spreads over his face as you enter the room. He stands to greet you, holding out a hand.

"May I have the next dance?" he says in a low voice, pointed teeth flashing in a roguish smile. He draws you close, one hand at the small of your back, and leads you easily around through the steps of a dance, unhurried and patient, charmed when you go wrong. He tells you about the club in Paris where he learned it, bringing up the past without the anguish that once accompanied it.

With the stubble at his jaw grazing your cheek, he murmurs promises—the places he'll take you, the things he wants to do with you. And before dawn breaks over the mountains, he abandons his hosting to draw you upstairs, as if he can't wait to have you to himself again.

THE END

Want another adventure? See what else there is to do: **GO TO PAGE 266.**

A DRINK WITH AUGUST

Head swimming slightly, you agree, following as August leads you farther along the corridor—farther inside.

You follow down more pitch-dark corridors, through cobwebs and dust, directing all your slow, woolly thoughts on keeping up and trying not to stumble again. Then all of a sudden, August opens a creaking door into a large room with a fire already crackling. A faded settee and a couple of mismatched chairs have been drawn into a disorderly circle in front the fireplace. Flames dance and send long shadows over what looks like a large, once-luxurious room, crowded with things along the far walls that you can't quite make out. Among the dark shapes, you think you see vases of dried flowers, insects and fern fronds laid out in glass picture frames, a stuffed crow.

But the room is now unsteady around you, and you can't take in the details—what was in that wine? August draws you over to the settee by the fire, and you sink down into it.

Compared to the rest of the cluttered room, the part around the fireplace is clear. Under your feet is a rug so worn you can't make out the pattern. As you look woozily around, you see the cabinet and the tables nearby hold only a notebook and old-fashioned ink bottles near the far chair where August is now sitting. The furniture looks like it was expensive long ago—now it's just a forgotten echo of opulence.

August reaches into a cabinet and pours a golden liquid into two elegant little glasses, sliding one toward you on the table at your elbow. You sip it before you've really thought about it, tasting something heady and cloyingly sweet before putting the glass back down, wondering vaguely whether it's a good idea to have another drink yet.

August watches you like a cat, curling their legs up underneath them. Eyes glinting in the firelight, they begin to ask you probing questions that increasingly verge on the uncomfortable. They're particularly interested in whether you have someone waiting for you at home, in a voice that sounds sweet but words that cut sharp: "A boyfriend, girlfriend, or sweetheart of some other kind? There must be someone." They smile beautifully at you.

> Make something up about having an incredible partner waiting for you back home. **TURN TO PAGE 146.**

> Tell them the truth; admit that you're single. **TURN TO PAGE 148.**

HOW DO YOU MAKE A VAMPIRE?

August lets out a little scoff of a laugh, wrinkling their nose at your audacity. "You're *wonderfully* direct," they say, still smiling alarmingly.

They stretch out like a big cat eyeing its prey. "But since you've been so very direct and truthful with me, I only owe you a similar sort of answer in return. I'll tell you *exactly* how you make a vampire."

August gives you a long, mocking answer with cruel, theatrical delight.

"The mystic incantations really are a bore, but they're necessary for the whole thing to go off smoothly. And it involves an *awful* lot of virgin sacrifice," they're saying, "but of course, we have to deflower them all *very* thoroughly as part of the ritual." You blink, and August has slipped over so they're sitting next to you on the settee, leaning a long way forward, a hand resting on your leg. You think you'd be able to feel their warmth—if their body were less unnaturally cool. Your limbs feel heavy but very aware of August's fingers, any slight movement on your thigh sending an unthinking sensation prickling through you.

Their lilting voice drops to a husky tone. "The bite itself can send humans *wild* with lust. Some say it's the most intense experience a person can have. Many are *desperate* to try it . . ."

Your head spins with wine; your body feels slow, your tongue reckless.

- › Ask August to bite you. **TURN TO PAGE 147.**
- › Ask August whether they can be killed. **TURN TO PAGE 154.**

YOUR INCREDIBLE IMAGINARY PARTNER

You tell August about your fictitious partner, who is *so* overwhelmingly physically attractive that it actually sort of stuns strangers on the street, but who is also so kind and emotionally sensitive to your needs, you know? And who just *happens* to have a very well-paid job that's also ethically wonderful and completely fascinating.

August listens intently, sharp smile slowly widening. "Is that so?" they say. "Tell me more."

Stumbling over your words a bit, you are forced to continue, and find your imaginary partner's virtues growing slightly out of control—August's questions tying you in knots you're unable to adequately explain. You might have been able to pull it off if your head was a bit clearer or you were talking to someone paying less attention, but August's razor-blade smile seems to catch every word and contradiction as they focus on each tipsy misstep.

You try to change the subject, mind grasping at the first topics you can think of.

- Tell them the relationship isn't exclusive and you're extremely sexually available. **TURN TO PAGE 147.**
- Ask August about how you turn someone into a vampire. **TURN TO PAGE 145.**

YOU ARE VERY AVAILABLE, FULL OF WINE, AND FULL OF DELICIOUS BLOOD

August regards you for a moment as you speak, their face in a lethal smile. They fill your glass very full of golden liquid again, enough that it slops over the side and down their fingers.

They slide down to kneel over you on the settee, one leg on either side of your hips as they lift the glass to your mouth. Their other hand is at your neck, tipping your face upward. The drink slips sweetly down your throat, the room a warm blur as August sinks into your lap. They discard the glass and run their fingers down over your torso. Their other hand stays clasped on your jaw, perfect nails making shapes in your cheeks, so that all you see are the dark shadows dancing on the ceiling as your heart thuds in your chest. You're very aware of every place their body is in contact with yours, but it still doesn't feel like enough.

Breathless with anticipation, you feel the tickle of their curls on the side of your face before August dips their head below your ear and sinks their teeth into your neck. There's a sharp pain, then a giddy relaxation as something spreads through you, your limbs growing heavy. The world whirls around you. Are you dying?

August moans deep in their throat and sucks harder, pressing against you in a way that sends electricity through your numbing body. Want pulses through you, but August's hands only move to get better purchase with the efficiency of a well-adapted predator. Their nails dig in deep, and you hear yourself cry out.

August wrenches their head back, face wet and red and terrible. Their pupils are blown wide, eyes locked to the place where you feel hot blood leaking out of your neck with each heartbeat. They tip your head very far back, enthralled, and you feel suddenly aware that they could easily keep pushing, snap your neck with no effort at all. The creature in your lap is not human any longer. But your body strains to push up against them, heavy with arousal despite your mind's quivering dread.

"This is what you want, is it?" they say, voice thick and sticky in their throat, full of blood and malice, playfulness gone. Their mouth twists in vicious disdain, the expression unrelentingly bitter. "You want to be devoured? You want a monster?"

› Tell August they're not a monster. Beg them to spare you. **TURN TO PAGE 149.**

› Tell August they are a monster. Ask them to bite you some more. **TURN TO PAGE 151.**

GRUDGINGLY ADMIT YOU'RE SINGLE

Back in London, you'd swipe endlessly through apps and go on occasional terrible dates to crowded bars where the cheapest drink was more than a tenner. The people you met up with were exhausted and wrung out from work, jaded from everything, and usually spent the evening complaining about online dating or, worse, intensely scrutinizing your suitability. Even the best dates just didn't click, or things slowly fell apart after a week or two until you stopped looking, stopped trying, and spent your evenings mostly alone in your horrible flat with takeaway you couldn't really afford.

You mumble some of the truth back at August, tongue wine-heavy in your mouth.

"Really? *So* hard to believe," teases August in a playful, lilting voice that's definitely designed to hurt. "What a shame."

Something about their shit-eating grin makes you want to get back at them somehow, but August parries every inquiry about their own life and seems to turn it back around on you.

They draw out more details that reveal your flaky friends, unreliable family, and past relationships in a way that really makes it sound pretty resoundingly pathetic. Feeling slow and sticky with wine, you accidentally let slip about your possibly jobless future and shitty flat. At another barbed comment, you find yourself finally snapping back, telling them, yeah, now you're thinking about it, you really do have very little left for you back at home.

August's smile seems to falter at this, their face dropping into something more open for a second. They regain composure quickly, though, managing to reply, "There's no need to be like *that*; I was only asking," in a way that, to your irritation, makes you feel as if you did something wrong.

The room falls quiet for a minute, shadows flickering over the barely discernible shapes of stacked boxes and frames leaning against the far walls of the room.

August looks down at their glass, a long, elegant finger tracing over the rim, head tilted as if considering what to do with you—you wonder what they'd intended from your private audience.

› Tell them that, being single, you're also very sexually available. **TURN TO PAGE 147.**

› Ask August about the mysterious room. **TURN TO PAGE 157.**

BEG FOR YOUR LIFE

Your pleading voice is hoarse, almost unfamiliar to you. You feel weak and floaty, and the sound comes out broken.

August quickly pulls back their hand, and your head lolls forward onto your chest. You reach shakily up to your neck, and you make an involuntary noise when you feel the blood. *Please*, you hear yourself say again.

When you look up, August's eyes are wide above their wet red mouth. After a moment of hesitation, you watch them lick their palm, then move forward to press a hand against the wound on your neck. "Shh, shh," they croon, almost to themself, manner calm but eyes slightly frantic. "Everything's all right. I wouldn't have— I wouldn't." *They fucking would have,* you think, but you don't say anything, just concentrate on slowing your breathing and being alive.

August moves a bloody hand away—you realize your neck has stopped bleeding—but they still look mesmerized by the red slippery mess on your throat and hand. They sway forward and you flinch, involuntarily—but they move deliberately and carefully, without the frenzy of before. You feel their tongue, rather than their teeth. They lick you clean, slow and hungry.

Your body responds, and you run your hands up their cool thigh to touch them, mind still giddy and strange. August corrects your motions efficiently and unselfconsciously until you're doing exactly what they want. They hum toward pleasure with animal instinct, mouth still at your neck, deep in their own senses. They move as if in a trance, sending sensation shuddering through you as they lick the blood from their fingers.

You pass out—or you assume you do—because the next thing you know you're coming stickily awake, smeared in dark dried red that's flaking off you, half-undressed on a settee splattered with blood. The gray light of morning seeps through the windows.

Your head feels fucking awful. You try to sit up too quickly and find your head spinning, and wonder how much blood you lost. You pull your clothes back on and try to sit very still for a while until you feel more human.

TURN TO PAGE 83.

INDIVIDUALISM

"*Oh*," says August with feeling, smile suddenly fixed and bitter at this answer. "Just out for *yourself*? Oh, I *see*." They put the lamp down with a deliberate "clack" on the cabinet beside them and slide down to the floor with the soft landing of a predatory cat. It's hard to breathe, suddenly. The night air feels cold. The light seems very small in the huge, dark room.

"That's certainly a philosophy," they say, and suddenly they're right in front of you, wearing their awful smile. "Perhaps it's one I ought to employ in turn . . ."

They reach out a hand so fast you barely see it. You realize they've given you a hard shove only as you're falling backward over a box to sprawl on the floor. August steps unconcernedly forward to stand over you, one neat shoe clicking deliberately down between your legs. They're silhouetted against the lamp behind them, all shadow, but you see the angle of their chin as they regard you coldly.

"If you were the one with the power—if you were wearing the *boot*—you'd make sure to crush others under it, would you?" Their other foot comes forward to press gently down on your windpipe. You struggle and try to move away, but they're flexing their inhuman strength and don't have to exert any effort to keep you pinned beneath.

August shifts lightning-fast, and now they're crouching over you, a cool hand replacing their foot at your neck. Your body flounders, and you hear yourself thrashing involuntarily in panic. "So if you had powers like mine, you wouldn't hesitate to do whatever you wanted?" You gasp in tiny breaths through the pressure on your throat, unable to respond. "Hmm," they muse. "I ought to try that."

You feel your head wrenched to one side and searing pain at your throat as August punctures your carotid artery.

The room full of bones swims as your consciousness sputters out—in your last moments, you wonder whether yours will join them.

YOUR NIGHT ENDS.

You've met your end. To restart from dinner, **GO TO PAGE 28.**

To go back to the start of the section, **GO TO PAGE 155.**

THE MONSTER

There's something hard and miserable in August's expression as they pull your head forward again to look you in the eye—as if they're suddenly not having fun any longer. You see a flicker of anger pass over their features, real anger, revulsion from some tormented core.

"*Fine.*" You hear the word escape their lips and drift out into the air, where it hangs for a moment in the darkness. Their voice is wretched.

And then August moves faster than you can see. You hear the crunch before you feel the pain on the other side of your neck. Something has broken inside you—a collarbone? You find you can't move your arms, and your vision is starting to fade. They push you down sideways onto the settee, and you feel something else crack before their limbs crawl back over you, animal and merciless, toward their feast. You feel the cushions wet under you and realize it's all blood—your own blood.

You feel your wine-slow mind lose track of your body as August pulls all the life out of you.

The last thing you think before everything's over is *Well, at least I don't have to go back to work.*

YOUR NIGHT ENDS.

You've met your end. To restart from dinner, **GO TO PAGE 28.**

To go back to the start of the section, **GO TO PAGE 144.**

CLEAR YOUR HEAD

You tell August levelly that you'd like a glass of water.

Their eyes narrow, but then you feel their nails slowly relax their grip on you, like you've passed a test. After a moment, they step back from your chair.

"I . . . apologize," they say slightly uncertainly, as if this is a sequence of words they're not familiar with, and then more firmly, "A moment."

Before you can say anything else, August has slipped into the dark. The far door stands open onto the dark corridor.

You stand up and carefully walk toward the unlit parts of the large room, trying to get a better look. Now unpleasantly conscious of your tipsiness, you try to focus on being extremely careful. As you move very, very slowly, your foot hits something in the shadows—thankfully soft enough that you don't hear anything crash or spill or break. As your eyes adjust, you realize you're standing in front of a cabinet with a row of something on top. The shapes are just visible in the black as something round, going from the size of a tennis ball near your left-hand end to a football at the other. Tentatively, you reach out toward one of the shapes and feel something cool and smooth. And then your fingers touch the point of a sharp tooth.

Suddenly there's a light, and August is right behind you, nails tight on your arm.

The lamp in their other hand illuminates the shapes ahead of you clearly, and you realize with horror that your outstretched fingers rest on the jaw of a canine skull mounted on a stick, its mouth open hungrily toward you.

The whole row of objects on the long cabinet are creamy, carefully polished skulls.

They're organized in order of size, starting with rodents far away to your left, up to what must be wolves in front of you, and maybe bears toward your right elbow. The skulls are all posed dramatically in their place, held up on a metal spike—some facing each other as if in conversation, others with dried flower stems threaded into the eye sockets, exploding with bouquets. Your eyes struggle to adjust to the light as you take in the macabre diorama laid out before you, body tense in shock, half waiting for August to close in.

But as you recover your breath, you realize August's clamped hold on your arm is steadying you, preventing you tumbling forward into the meticulous display as you reel a little in woozy surprise.

"First, water," they say with some disdain and maybe some amusement. Before you can see any more of the room, they've steered you unsteadily back to the fireplace, where a jug and glass are set out next to the settee.

As you start to drink, you realize how thirsty you are. The water is cold and clean, and you wonder if there's something medicinal in it, because as you finish it, you already feel slightly better. August pours you another glass of water after you finish the first, then drops languidly onto the settee next to you, curling their legs fluidly underneath. You realize they've pulled on a knitted V-neck over the red dress and ask, without thinking, whether they get cold.

August gives you a withering look but replies anyway. "I can enjoy wearing clothes even if I don't need to." Then they seem to consider for a moment and say, almost reluctantly, "It's a habit, I suppose. I like the feel of it."

August fishes out a pen from a drawer, picks up a notebook, and leafs through, balancing it on their knees so you can't see the pages. Pushing their sleeves up their pale arms, they carefully open the ink pot, dip the pen, and begin to scratch something out on the page.

As their hand moves, they ask musingly why you don't leave your job and flat when you dislike them so much. You're not sure if they're really interested—it sounds more like an offer of less aggressive conversation after their probing earlier—but you try to answer anyway. You sip at your water and try to tell them why it's not that easy to just "get a really good job" or buy your own place. From their somewhat abstract replies, you get the distinct sense that they've not had a normal job in a very, very long time.

The fire burns lower as August draws in the lamplight. They point you to a bathroom with ancient plumbing and no mirrors, and you feel a bit less unsteady on the way back. After sitting back down and talking idly for a while as the wind howls out beyond the windows, you realize your head feels clearer and less like soggy cardboard.

Eventually, August looks up and seems to scrutinize you for a moment. Apparently satisfied, they put the notebook down for the ink to dry, standing in a fluid motion.

They take the lamp and move deeper into the room, making an offhanded gesture with their fingers that you think is probably a demand you join them.

TURN TO PAGE 155.

WHAT A QUESTION

August laughs again. There's no joy in it at all.

"I think it very unlikely that I could be killed by *you* at all," they say musingly. "You really are the most incautious creature I've ever seen. I'd have thought all animals have *some* impulse of fear or rationality when faced with danger.

"Not you, though," August says, leaning over to pour another glass of the amber liquid and putting it threateningly gently into your hand. "Won't you have another drink?"

You feel woozy, some primal part of your body wanting desperately to bolt, and you try to refuse.

But August moves lightning-fast. "That's very bad manners," they say in a quiet, level voice, teeth close to your ear. Even your blurry mind can recognize the threat in their stance, and you drain the glass, feeling instantly disorientated. You realize your hand is shaking.

"Anything can be killed," August says, slightly hollow.

One of their hands moves faster than you can see, and now it's holding your face, nails digging in, wrenching your neck painfully back so that all you see are the dark shadows dancing on the ceiling. August dips their head, and you feel a sharp pain in your neck and hear yourself cry out—you try to wriggle free, but August is holding you firmly still with the efficiency of a well-adapted predator.

August draws their head back, face wet and red. Their eyes are strangely blank, pupils blown wide.

"Am I satisfying your curiosity, little tourist?" they hiss, voice thick and sticky in their throat, full of blood and malice. They push your head farther back, and you're very aware that they could easily keep pushing, snap your neck with no effort at all.

"Isn't this what you wanted?" Their mouth twists in disdain, and the expression is vicious, unrelentingly bitter. "To see a monster up close?"

TURN TO PAGE 151.

THE COLLECTOR'S ROOM

August stands in front of the row of skulls.

They take a deep breath—probably an affectation for dramatic impact since you don't think they were breathing before—preparing themself to speak. "When we first arrived here, we ate only animals from the forest, to avoid having to feed on humans," they say in their offhand, lilting voice, as if talking about the weather. "Animals can't speak to you, so it can be harder to know when to *stop*."

They run a white finger along the jaw of a cat skull, artistically nestled in a burst of dried leaves and flowers. "I'd never mean to do it. I'd lose myself for just a moment and feel their little hearts give out under the fur, the rhythm seize and stop. And then I'd come to."

August hesitates, holding themself very still, fingertips poised on what was once the cat's cheek. "Nothing makes you feel more like a monster than finding your wet, red hands holding a corpse."

Their slow touch on the bone is gentle, almost a caress. "I wanted to honor them somehow. I'm not sure any animal can deserve such a violent death.

"Not like humans," they say, voice dark and sweet, flicking their eyes up toward you with a wicked razor-blade smile.

Despite the smile, you notice their hand pull quickly away from the long display of skulls. You think they're trying to draw your attention away from the thought of them crouched, bloody and bereft, realizing they've killed a cat.

› Be serious. Tell them the display they've made does honor the animals, a beautiful memorial. **TURN TO PAGE 165.**

› Play along. Indulge August's murderous subject change. Ask about the humans who deserve a violent death. **TURN TO PAGE 156.**

VIOLENT DELIGHTS

"Oh, I'm *sure* you can think of people who deserve unhappy deaths," August says, seeming to recover themself. They turn to glide away deeper into the room, taking the circle of lamplight with them, and you hurry to keep up.

The lamp illuminates the cabinets and walls and their strange adornments. You see a stuffed crow, perfectly preserved and arranged as if in flight; more bones arranged in patterns on a dark table; glass jars variously full of dried thistles, colorless amphibians suspended in liquid, gleaming teeth.

August keeps talking as they move slowly through the room ahead, looking over each object as if bored by them. "There are people who do nothing but harm. Becoming meat to be eaten is the most good they ever do in their lives." Their shadow stretches huge and terrible behind them, jagged where it hits all the dried, dead, and pickled things lining the walls. They turn and raise a perfect eyebrow. "Vampires are animals, just like you. We're just a step above on the food chain."

They slide themself up to sit on one of the dark cabinets nearby and watch you curiously, as if sizing up what they know about you. "I mean no *offense*," says August, obviously about to say something offensive, "but most humans' lives are full of little *miseries*, all piled up together. Unnecessary, cruel ones. And if England's anything like it was in my day, they're careless cruelties, caused by people with power who don't give a fuck about anyone but themselves.

"Doesn't it make you angry?" they say in a quiet, merciless voice. "If you had to eat a person, aren't there some you'd rather rip apart?"

- Ask them more about their past—who made them so angry? **TURN TO PAGE 162.**
- Indulge their anger. Tell them there are definitely people who deserve it and ask for more details about their victims. **TURN TO PAGE 163.**
- Contradict them. Tell them the rich having more is the natural order of the world and you'd behave the same without hesitation if you had money. **TURN TO PAGE 150.**

THE ROOM FULL OF BOXES

August looks surprised at the question. Hesitantly, they tell you it's a sort of collection, then fall silent.

You ask what the collection is of and whether you can see it.

August eyes the remaining golden liquid in the glass at your elbow with a strange expression, as if doubting themself. "If you really *would* like to talk," they say slowly, "perhaps I ought to get you a glass of water?"

Their face looks softer for a moment, and you wonder suddenly what they were like before they were a vampire. Treacle-slow, you realize they asked a question, but as soon as you don't immediately reply, August's face closes off into a bitter smile, like an oncoming cataclysm.

"Or maybe you don't *want* to talk. Why did you come down this road—to this room? Do you *like* the idea of being alone with a monster who cannot control their urges?"

They stand like a snake uncurling to strike, and the fire casts a jagged shadow huge on the wall behind them. In one step, they seem to be right in front of you, leaning forward, perfect nails digging into your thigh, sharp teeth right above you.

August looks down at you, lip curling in derision. "Perhaps you'd like another drink," they say in a very quiet, dangerous voice. Their face has gone very still. "Perhaps you don't want to speak to a person, only to lose yourself to sensation." Their leg presses between your thighs.

> Ask for the water and clear your head. **TURN TO PAGE 152.**

> Accept another drink. **TURN TO PAGE 147.**

BUTTERFLY KISS

August has drawn very close, and closing the gap to kiss them is simple. August . . . laughs.

It's a low, breathy exhalation into your mouth. Then they kiss back, smoothly slipping the drawer and its precious creature into the cabinet. They drape their arms around your neck, pressing their cool lips to yours.

You stand twined together in the lamp glow, an island of warm light in the huge room full of shadows and all the dead things that August lives with.

> Deepen the kiss, heavy and burning. Seek their touch. **TURN TO PAGE 161.**

> Kiss them again, slow and sweet. This is all you need. **TURN TO PAGE 184.**

VAMPIRE SNACK

At the next full moon, you find Luka with August, hand-pollinating the row of plants growing in the little indoor greenhouse. As soon as August notices you, they're quick to delightedly suggest you all spend the evening together.

Luka is obviously a good friend and laughs and jokes with August easily. He switches into English whenever you're around, explaining he often works with tourists or at conferences where English is the common language—though around August, he's mostly talking about plants in enough detail that it's hard to follow in any language.

He grows shy whenever August's teasing strays into the suggestive. He blushes prettily and makes excuses to clean his glasses so he doesn't have to make eye contact when August says things like "We won't need chains if I'm there, but how do you feel about a leash?"

When you go up to the attic, Luka seems slightly overwhelmed by the situation, excited long before the moon is out or anyone touches anyone else. August finds Luka likes being discussed like he's not there and ruthlessly exploits the discovery. "How much can he take, do you think?" they ask as Luka practically whimpers, and then they give you a deep, lingering kiss right in front of him. Luka looks like he might be about to have a heart attack—which you can understand, since that's how August makes you feel a lot of the time, too.

He chats and grins bashfully, all excitement and half embarrassment until the point at which he transforms, groaning and bulging into his bigger, hairier form. His body seems to take over, and he pants and struggles, still half-restrained with a collar. August delightedly takes your lead, kissing and touching you just out of Luka's reach until you both take mercy and move closer.

Before the night is over, you and Luka get to see August's aloof manner disintegrate between you until they turn needy and frantic and bite you wildly in more than one place.

Luka is lovely the next day but keeps a friendly distance. Both of you seem to implicitly understand August's desire to be your main partner—even if you doubt August would ever express it directly. "But maybe I can visit again," he grins, slightly pink under his mop of dark hair, before he waves and heads off.

TURN TO PAGE 181.

CONSCIENTIOUS

"Despite very strongly objecting to joining the war effort, I was not recorded as a conscientious objector," they say, bitterness flaring. "Rather, I was given an exemption from conscription on 'medical' grounds. The doctor they made me speak to thought being queer an *affliction*. My family was told, and they were ashamed enough to cut ties without ever trying to have me 'cured,' which I suppose I ought to be grateful for." Their hand runs over the reeds in the vase, voice tight with a long-distant horror.

"The tribunal was awful, but they weren't sure what to do with me, I think. I was a public embarrassment they wanted covered up, out of the way, so I walked free. People already treated me like dirt when I dressed as I liked, so the fact I wasn't fighting hardly set me apart much further. I was grateful to have avoided prison, really. Avoiding disgust was too much to hope for." Their hand brushes over the cotton fluff of a bud, whisper-soft. "It wasn't much of a life, I suppose, but it was my own."

August resettles their shoulders, returning their tone to its usual lilting cadence, storytelling. "After Casimir saved me—after I died, I mean—that's when my life really began.

"He had money and a story about being a dignitary from abroad, and we lived together in London. He liked the company and looking after me like a responsible parent. But most often he would brood at home while I used the night to explore.

"I found the places men meet other men, and there I met other people like myself. We clung to each other in the dark of the world, only for me to slowly watch them all break. The ones who survived the virulent family, the public shame or private asylum, the hard labor sentences, they all had some vital spark in them extinguished. They'd return, dead-eyed, to the world. Respectable shells who would marry and look at me with disappointed faces I hardly recognized." August's face is cold in the low light. "It made me furious. It made me want to shout until it woke them up, until it called back their playfulness and they told me it was all a joke. But it *wasn't*. The friends I didn't lose in the war I lost to 'respectable' society."

They look up at you with a tight, humorless smile. "But I knew the perpetrators. I followed the newspapers. I knew the names of the lawmakers, protected by money and titles, the heads of companies who had chosen to line their pockets with others' suffering. I remembered their names."

TURN TO PAGE 163.

SOMETHING HEAVY

You kiss August, deep and open.

Your bodies move slowly together, and you feel August make an involuntary satisfied noise against your mouth.

You are strangers to each other, but strangers sharing a moment of closeness, a pleasure sheltered in the dark from the storm outside.

Their hands flutter over you, body pressing forward. You kiss them slow, your mouth hot on their cool neck, your hands slipping up under the wool of their jumper, across the silk of their dress, down over their angular hips.

August responds in kind with a slowly building fervor. They make breathy, impatient noises pressed against your cheek, into your ear, along your neck. They are eager for you—hungry.

In the faint glow of the lamp, you see the row of skulls a little ways off.

› Let them bite you. **TURN TO PAGE 168.**

› Continue, but move their mouth away from your neck. **TURN TO PAGE 170.**

A LOSS OF MERCY

August's shoulders sink down, and some of the fight drains out of them.

They give a mournful sigh—breathing deliberately to do so. Their feet dangle idly over the edge of the cabinet in a way that makes them look suddenly youthful. They run a finger over the rim of a stoneware vase next to them, full of dried cattails and cotton buds.

"I don't know," they say thoughtfully, idly rearranging the stems. "I grew up before the Great War. So many of the boys I went to school with died pointlessly in the trenches. There was such a mess of muddled orders and incompetent superiors, nepotism all the way up. Of course I was angry about it all. You'd have to bury your head in the sand not to be."

They draw a long cattail out of the vase to inspect it, rubbing a thumb along the reed as they speak.

"I avoided the war but not the Great Influenza. Governments all over Europe lied about it furiously to avoid hurting 'morale' or saying anything unpopular. They delayed the panic by letting the disease sweep through civilians and war camps alike, unimpeded. And after the war, authorities deemed it appropriate to open the bars and street fairs, knowing full well the sickness traveled through the air." They wrinkle their nose delicately as they turn the reed in their long fingers. "I caught it in a later wave, when everyone had stopped keeping the windows open. Over the past few years, it's been difficult not to get a sense of déjà vu.

"It's how I died," they say dryly, looking up at you. "So I've always found it rather difficult to forgive."

The words spill easily out of them now, as if they don't get the chance to talk very often and have deemed you an acceptable confidant. They talk as if recalling strands of distant memory—another life—but seem glad to have an interested audience.

- Ask about how they avoided the war. **TURN TO PAGE 160.**
- Ask about how they avoided dying. **TURN TO PAGE 178.**

REVENGE

"In the years after I was first turned, I used to love going out in London at night—not just to the queer places but going out alone, to *hunt*." August slides carefully off the cabinet and lands light on their feet, watching you as they go on.

"It was so easy, moving unseen in the dark, finding ways in through unlocked windows on an upper floor. I would make my way into the fashionable places in London—dressed appropriately, in whatever way I thought would work best—and blend into the crowds. I went to the best restaurants, the most expensive hotel bars, even sometimes wore a suit to infiltrate the gentlemen's clubs." They move slowly toward you, and their sharp smile stretches wide and dazzling.

"'Heart attack' is how they usually recorded the cause of death. I was very neat, avoided a struggle, and usually made sure the targets were older. I'd done my research.

"I knew what they'd done. When you look like a woman who might pick up men in the most expensive hotel in town, it's easy to get them alone and bite where no coroner will look."

Their hand extends out to brush along your shoulder, slowly up toward your throat. You shiver involuntarily.

"But it doesn't always have to be lethal, you know. I'm perfectly capable of stopping.

"It can be fun. It can feel *good*." After some moments of honesty, their armor seems up again. You think about drained corpses in London hotel rooms, heart pounding.

Their pointed smile looks like a shipwreck, a catastrophe—a natural disaster ready to swallow you whole.

Their thumb rubs slowly along your jaw in the huge, dark room among its strange collections. In the lamp glow, shadows dance over bones in the corner of your eye, over dried flowers and distant corners you haven't seen. You've seen glimpses of an August beyond the murder-sharp smile. There's more to the person before you, more than the night of pleasure they're offering, if you wanted to go looking.

- Tell them you'd like to know more about the things in the room—you get the sense the offer of "feeling good" will still remain on the table later. **TURN TO PAGE 165.**
- Tell them all you want is to get bitten and feel amazing. **TURN TO PAGE 92.**

GO TO SLEEP

August nods at you slowly with a sad smile, something closing off in their face. Their eyelashes flicker down, and your eye contact is broken, the moment fading away, something to tuck away in your memories but not follow.

You feel very aware you're in a dark room full of dead things, and you're suddenly so tired.

They look down at the butterfly in their hand and go to slide it back to its place in the drawer. "Preserved in death . . ." they muse. "I sometimes feel as if I've been pinned and left to gather dust."

They pick up the lamp and lead you the long, slow way up to the guest room. In the doorway, they hover for a moment, as if about to say something. The rain beats relentlessly on the windows. But then they slip away into the dark, and that's the last time you see them.

In the morning, the castle is cold and ordinary and, as far as you can tell, entirely empty of people. You couldn't find your way back to the room with August's collection if you tried, and so you don't.

TURN TO PAGE 265.

BONES THAT HONOR THEIR OWNERS

August's predator-smile slowly falls from their face. For a moment they just look at you, face unreadable.

And then they turn and walk away, past the cabinet of skulls full of flowers, picking their way over boxes and picture frames wrapped with paper and twine. You move to follow—and realize they're letting you see more of their collection. As you pass by more bones, they say, "I don't kill animals any longer. I've learned how much is too much." Their voice is almost gentle.

In a hidden-away part of the room, behind a row of cabinets, they show you a wall tightly packed with hanging wooden picture frames, each one containing a different plant. There are seaweeds and ferns carefully teased out to lie beautifully fanned, dried and pressed against the glass in an elegant sweep. There are delicate flowers and huge hothouse leaves, and beside each there are two sets of notes in a tight, scrawled hand.

August explains the first notes describe the type of plant along with the time and place of the specimen's origin. You notice the dates go back more than seventy years. The second notes are their thoughts from that day: what the weather was like, what they were thinking about, what else was happening. These parts are often long, sometimes written in contours that frame the leaves and take up most of the page. Here and there you can make out people's names, mentions of emotions and the clouds. These aren't the notes of someone recording with sterile professionalism—they're the marks of a devotee or a poet.

You listen, and when they lapse into silence, you ask small questions—what's this one, which is their favorite—and they begin to give you longer answers. They describe a garden they once kept here in a courtyard now long overgrown, a greenhouse long abandoned. They tell you about a very dry summer where all they wanted was to examine a rare kind of flower in the mountains—and their disappointment that the right weather conditions never materialized for it to bloom. The August in the stories does not sound cold and derisive—you wonder whether that's a face they reserve for when other people are around.

Farther along the wall there's a place where the frames crowded into a corner are full of dead butterflies, pinned in place, many with broken parts and torn, ragged wings. "My father had a collection like this when I was a child," August tells you. "He had drawers and drawers of the things, all neatly labeled. He loved to put things in order.

"When I was young, we both liked the idea that I would follow in his footsteps . . ." August trails off, holding the light up to the butterflies, whose iridescent wings glint behind the glass.

You ask what happened when they grew up.

August's lip curls as they talk, absentmindedly pulling out a small drawer from a cabinet made up of hundreds of them, revealing a shining green beetle on a dark felt bed.

"I grew up colorful in a way that was unwanted. I grew into myself like an unusual insect, a pest that didn't fit his categorization—the wrong thing out of the cocoon." And then, both the venom and music dropping entirely out of their voice, they say bluntly, "He'd expected a son."

August closes a drawer and opens another, going through the chest methodically as they continue to talk. "When I first arrived here, I had an idea of making my own collection, including all the faulty specimens, the ones I found crawling with cankers and broken legs. I spiked them through. I thought I'd build a catalogue of messy lives.

"But one day I walked in and saw them all together and couldn't fathom what I'd done. Why couldn't I just leave them be?"

They open another drawer and seem to find what they're looking for, putting down the lamp and sliding the entire piece of wood out until it sits neatly on their pale hand. "I found this one after I stopped killing things to collect. It was already dead." They smile at you with a wry amusement. "Like me, I suppose."

You lean toward them to see the butterfly laid out in the drawer. On the left side, the wing is a pure, velvety black. On the other, the black has spots of red and orange, a swipe of pale gray over the tip.

"It's a bilateral gynandromorph. It's a perfect split: male wings on one side, female on the other. The phenomenon has been written about in Europe for hundreds of years—though it's more common to find butterflies that are a patchwork of male and female parts."

Your heads draw close together to see it in the lamplight. August tilts the drawer a little so the colors catch the light, and both of you just look at it for a moment, watching a green iridescence flash across one wing.

August speaks softly, conspiratorially. "I read about them as a youth, before I'd met anyone like myself. I found knowing they existed a great comfort, somehow. Something in nature that showed on the outside how I felt within. Rare and interesting, no matter how much my father might have thought them faulty specimens."

August looks up at you, pale eyelashes lit up in the glow of the lamp, hair like a halo as they show you something precious to them. Their sharp, bright eyes slip down toward your mouth.

- Kiss them. **TURN TO PAGE 158.**
- Pull away. Tell them you're tired and want to go and sleep. **TURN TO PAGE 164.**

SOFT AND HUNGRY

"Please," they say, cut-glass accent blurring a little as they press into your neck. You tell them yes, and a moan escapes their lips as their mouth opens against your skin.

They bite, slow and deliberate, as if trying to hold themself back, hands grasping at your back, your thigh. You feel a well of pain and something cold slip into your bloodstream, like the feel of an injection, a venom that spreads from those two points of contact and goes shuddering through your body.

You feel *good*.

Your body relaxes in August's jaws, and the pain fades to nothing as they suck. The moment stretches, long and dazzling, the giddy sensation spinning through you. Mouth still at your neck, August moves their hands lazily, pushing clothes aside. You unconsciously press toward their touch, and they move, enraptured, against you, lost to the feeling of building pleasure.

Your giddiness builds along with it, and you find it just beginning to tip over into something unpleasant—when August pulls their head away with obvious effort.

They replace their mouth with a practiced hand to your throat that prevents any blood spilling from the wound. Their mouth is red and wet, pupils blown wide with an uninhibited thrill of indulgence as their back arches, and they move until you slowly brim over with pleasure.

Afterward, August lets out a breath they'd apparently taken in without thinking.

Carefully they pull back the hand at your neck, where the wound has already sewn itself over—some other strange trick of August's tongue.

As you pull your clothes to rights, August seems to come back to themself slowly, blood-drunk like a sated predator.

They pull away from you and take a few uncertain steps back, a finger brushing over their lips and coming back red.

"You're—all right?" they ask, their nonchalant lilt not quite concealing the note of dismay.

You nod, and you see their shoulders relax in the half dark. You feel satisfied down to your bones but not unusual—the strange relaxation all ebbed away. You can see they're looking away from you.

"I ought to clean up," you hear, and before you can say anything or try to stop them, they've slipped off into the shadows.

You sit by the embers of the fire, sinking down into the warm cushions of the settee, suddenly worn out. You listen to the rain hammering against the windows and let your eyes slowly start to close.

In the last moments before sleep overtakes you, you think you see a shape moving closer in the last red glow of the fire. Someone sits beside you, leans hesitantly forward, and cool lips brush your cheek in a kiss.

TURN TO PAGE 172.

DELAYED GRATIFICATION

You gently wind your hand through August's hair and tug them away from your neck. They let you do it, closing their eyes as a fleeting look of frustration passes over their elegant features.

They seem to be wrestling themself under control and take a few steps back to lean against a cabinet. "I can hear your heartbeat," they say in a soft, low voice, looking away from your throat.

You follow them forward and take the opportunity to touch them. You move, slow and deliberate, until they demand more, and you get to watch the last of their disdainful manner falling apart under your hands.

They pull you down among the boxes. You move a frame out from under them, making sure not to damage any of their careful work. August watches you do it, looking slightly struck, then kisses you, deep and feeling.

They follow what you enjoy and pursue it ruthlessly, but they angle their face away as you make them gasp and unravel in return. You see one of August's sharp teeth bite down on their own lip and suck, their pleasure desperate, edged agonizingly with want. They try not to cry out and don't quite manage.

Afterward, they pull away from you to crouch in the dark. They watch you like you're the most maddening, enticing meal they've ever seen. They look pleasingly ruffled and wrong-footed—debauched but still heavy with hunger.

"I need to eat," they say, crisp accent slightly off-balance, and before you can say anything or try to stop them, they slip off into the shadows.

You put your clothes to rights and go back over to fire, red embers glowing in the remains of the logs. Sinking down into the warm cushions of the settee, you feel suddenly worn out. You listen to the rain hammering against the windows and let your eyes slowly start to close.

In the last moments before sleep overtakes you, you think you see the lamp wink out and a shape moving in the last red glow of the fire. Someone sits beside you on the settee and hesitantly leans toward you, cool lips brushing your cheek in a kiss.

TURN TO PAGE 172.

AUGUST IN BED

You kiss August and guide them back toward the bed. They make a soft noise into your mouth as you push them down, and they drag you with them onto the soft covers.

They look less playful than usual, eyes intent even as their hands travel over your body, like they want to remember each part of you, savor each touch. You kiss them again, trailing your own hand up their thigh, and find there's nothing under the shirt.

August smiles at something in your reaction, their expression sharp and wicked.

You kiss the smugness out of them and turn their teasing into desperate, hungry sounds, first with your hands and then your body. They spread languorously on the bed, their back arching, their hands twisting in the sheets. They breathe your name as they come apart.

Afterward August wraps around you like they're furious anyone might dare touch you—or like they can't get you quite close enough—and you fall asleep intertwined.

After that, you don't ever sleep in the guest room again.

TURN TO PAGE 185.

MORNING AMONG THE COLLECTIONS

You wake late to find afternoon light from the tall windows painting the large room gray. Pale sheets still drape some of the far furniture, but other shapes are uncovered now: labeled cabinets and tall dressers in dark wood, intricate shapes of leaves and delicate bones. Soft rain patters on the windows, and you sit up to find yourself alone in the room.

On a table nearby is a paper bag of pastries and a note in August's tight scribble of handwriting inviting you to stay for a proper dinner. You stay without even really making a decision—it's too late to get back to London tonight, and you'll already have to make excuses to your boss.

In the light of day, you walk around to look at the things you couldn't see in the dark: seed pods and moth specimens; coral and shell spirals; clean, dry fish bones with seaweed elegantly spread behind them like a feathery crown. You flip through a book about plant classification you find among the boxes before going to wander a little. The halls of the castle look much less menacing by daylight, though no less romantic and forlorn—dust gathers beneath grand archways, stone crumbles at the edges. You find no one, only views out over the gray day where mist and drizzle coat the forest.

August walks in before the sun sets, wearing a V-neck and slacks, leather gloves, and sunglasses. They carry a bag of still-hot food, which raises questions: Do the locals know them? Can they drive? You ask whether vampires can go out in the daylight.

"As long as the sun's behind the clouds—though I tend to make sure my skin is covered in case," they say with an offhanded gesture as they elegantly peel off the gloves. "It varies. I've never quite determined the relationship exactly, but I suspect it's the more human blood a vampire's ingested, the worse the sensitivity."

They look up at you carefully. "You know, there's a dangerous vampire out in the forest. But he can't stand the daylight at all. So you're safe to leave whenever you like—just as long as the sun's up." You remember the noises in the forest, and a shiver runs unbidden up your spine.

August lays the food out slightly guardedly for you, as if unsure whether they made a mistake in keeping you here. They build the fire and sit down on the settee with a careful and slightly awkward distance. But you thank them, and as you eat and August doesn't, the conversation begins to flow easily and you end up sitting closer, comfortably side by side.

They take off their shoes to curl their feet underneath them and face toward you as you talk. At some point, when teasing you especially acerbically, their legs stretch out so they're draped over your lap. The closeness feels charged but unhurried. August's eyes linger on your lips as they settle more comfortably over you and the cushions before they pick up their large notebook to write something. You see the front has a drawing of a tall stem of bell-like flowers and *A. F.* written in the corner.

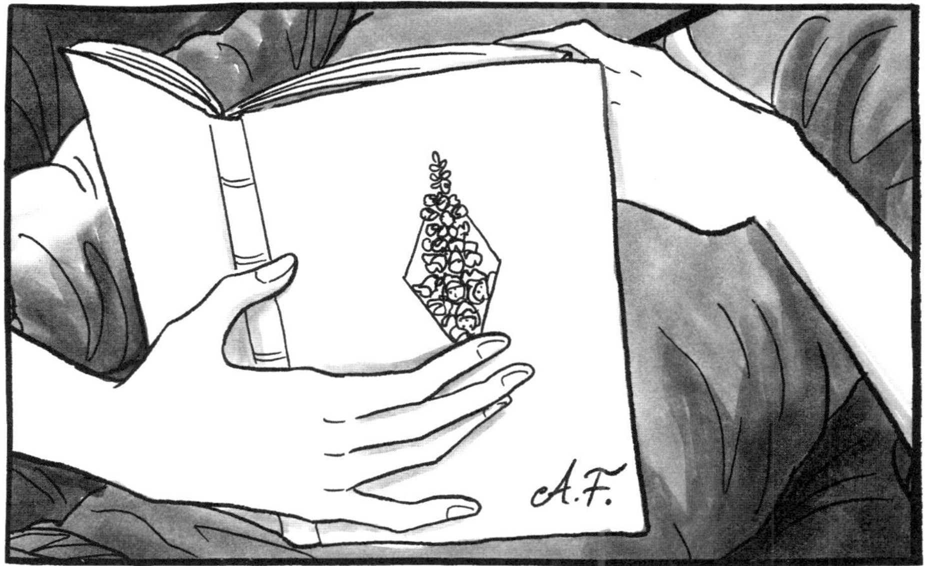

August notices you looking. "It's a foxglove," they say slightly stiffly, like they're self-conscious. "It's the name I used with my friends." You talk about your own full name long enough that they relax, resettling their shoulders with more confidence. Then they lean toward you with an air of showmanship. "The idea was, I'm August Foxglove on account of blooming rather late, and of being lovely but terribly poisonous." A slow smile spreads over their face at their own joke, like they're letting you in on a secret. A curl of hair has come loose over an angular cheek, and you have the impulse to tuck it behind their ear.

"Once I met Caz, I thought, why not jolly well keep it?" they say resolutely, as if they have to justify choosing their own name. "No point in dragging the blasted family name about with me when they'd half thrown me out years ago and I was already dead anyway."

As their fingers leaf through the sketchbook pages, you see glimpses of drawings of ferns, of labeled diagrams of the inside parts of flowers, of teeth in a wolf's mouth. There's so much care in the lines, so much humanity in the slight inexpert wobble of the pen. This journal isn't a scientific tool for slicing nature into controlled categories; it's a love letter.

You realize you've leaned in farther to get a better look, and when you look up, August's eyes are on you. They look caught off-guard for a moment, and you realize suddenly that your human presence is not an ordinary occurrence. This is new ground, and they're not sure how to tread it. It's like they've forgotten to act difficult and menacing, and you kiss them before they can remember again.

"*August.*" You're interrupted by Casimir looming in the doorway. August disentangles themself and slips out into the corridor to have what definitely sounds like an argument.

It's not long before August sweeps back into the room, leaving Casimir skulking in the doorway. They drape their arms over the back of the settee in a sulk that still looks like a fashion pose, leaning down to speak to you. "He thinks your staying is too dangerous at the moment." They flash you the smile that reminds you they've killed people. "But I'm rather of a mind to tackle the danger head-on. And going through the collections has given me an idea. How about this: You can stay as long as you like, if you'll lend a hand."

TURN TO PAGE 176.

AUGUST IN WINTER

You spend the winter in the vampire castle, waiting to be bait for a killer.

It turns out Raisa has a generator set up, and she runs long wires to hook up a fridge "for human food" along with a grow light for the indoor greenhouse where August begins to sprout the plants for the berries. There's also a place you can plug in your phone charger when you retrieve it from the terrible car with your luggage, and you assure your friends and family you're not dead—though you don't tell them all the details of where you're staying.

Your family seems slightly insultingly relieved that you're "seeing someone," though you're not really sure if you are, and you cannot imagine ever letting them meet August.

Your friends are mostly excited. "It's a castle? And the holiday's all-inclusive and free as long as you do a bit of work for them?" one of your friends says incredulously over a crackly phone call. "You lucky bastard. Why wouldn't you stay? So what if you lose your job back here? You've been saying you're about to quit for years." They demand to see pictures, but you're not sure how to tell them August shows up strangely indistinct on camera, a hollow-eyed shadow if anything shows up at all. You tell your friends they're camera-shy.

There are moments when August does seem genuinely fond of you, not just fond of teasing you and appearing suddenly in the dark in a way that makes you slightly afraid for your life. They ask for your help listing and labeling their collections over lazy afternoons. "If there were a proper index, I'd be able to look this sort of thing up," they say sharply, as if reprimanding themself, as you both sit on the floor surrounded by papers and frames one evening. They turn to look at you. "I'd never have realized about the berries if we'd not spoken," they say slowly, as if thinking about this for the first time. And then they kiss you, and you both get too distracted to get any more done that day.

August slides in to spend the nights with you in the guest room, which you clean and make more comfortable, and one day you wake to find they've put a spray of dried flowers in an empty specimen jar by the window. In the back of your mind, you try to remember they're using you as a means to an end. But in the long, dark nights, you feel warm and safe with them and a long way from your problems.

◆ If you have the marker **ANIMAL IMPULSES . . . TURN TO PAGE 159.**

◆ Otherwise . . . **TURN TO PAGE 179.**

AUGUST AND THE ROGUE

"An ancient and powerful vampire is hunting us," Casimir says seriously, hands flat on the dining room table as he looms over it.

He lets the room fall silent. August, curled in a chair at his side, obviously already knew this and fails to react with the drama he commands. You ask what seems like the obvious question: Why?

Casimir gives you a grave look. "Because we killed the count who owned this castle."

August interjects smoothly. "The count really was a frightful piece of work, and the world is inarguably better off without him.

"He—" August's eyes slide to Casimir as they decide how much to say—you have a sense the full story isn't theirs to tell. "He made Caz do awful things; let's leave it at that." The airiness has dropped out of their tone, and their mouth turns grim and set.

"And when we discovered he'd sided with the fascist government in the '40s, there was nothing to do but take him off the board. Most vampires stay neutral in wars, and the count did not. He was a monster, and he deserved a much slower death than we gave him."

Casimir does not speak. His eyes are on the table, fists clenched, unwilling to relive the details.

August continues. "We thought ourselves rather free and clear of the whole thing—but it turns out the count had one last friend who's been holding a grudge. The upshot is, we have a rogue vampire skulking around the forest. He can't come in the walls without an invitation, but he's waiting for us to slip up and go out at night so he can eviscerate us. He means to scare us."

Casimir's voice rumbles from the head of the table. "He *should* scare us. He is very old and very powerful. He has grown almost feral and unthinking. If he killed us, he is likely to wreak havoc on the town—we know he has no qualms about taking human life or revealing himself for what he is." He looks straight at you. "He could easily have killed you last night. He has done it before to any human who wanders too near. When we last faced him, we were lucky to survive at all."

August stands to face Casimir on a level. Their face is a cold and vicious mask, tone ruthless. "Raisa will help. It will be different this time. We'll plan. It's three against one. We only need rip him apart." The way August says it, you fully believe them capable of it.

Then August seems to remember your presence and goes on in a clear, calmer voice. "But showing our guest the collections has given me an idea for the plan. There's a way to do it all very safely."

August lays out a large album with old yellowed pages on the table. It's full of pressed flowers and leaves with their spidery writing filling out notes all around. They start to flip through it.

"In the past, I've stumbled across certain chemicals that are dangerous only to vampires. There's something in our saliva that helps prey blood clot very fast when we finish feeding—it can react with certain substances . . ."

They find the page they're looking for and point at a neat if slightly wobbly lined drawing of a clump of dark berries.

"You know Luka, my friend who's a ranger," they say to Casimir offhandedly, as if sure Casimir will have forgotten. "I spoke to him this morning. He assures me these are entirely harmless to humans. But in a vampire's mouth, the chemical reacts with the one in our saliva to form a soporific. If a vampire feeds on a human who's eaten these, I'm sure it would make them slow and lethargic, especially if we can get enough berries.

"And while this rogue is weakened, we take him out. *Before* he kills the human, I mean," they add hastily, eyes flicking over to you. "We'd make sure to test it first, of course. He'd hardly get his teeth in; the human would be in no danger."

Casimir's tone is wary. "And *how* do we get these berries?"

"They're not common or local—I'd have to grow them to have enough, and it would take several months. But Luka can get me the seeds. Our problem would be solved, and the whole town would be safe."

"What human would agree to such a thing?" Casimir asks dubiously. His eyes flick over to you, too, obviously concerned that August has already come up with an answer.

August gives you a beautiful, dangerous smile.

› Agree to help and stay for the winter. **TURN TO PAGE 175.**

› Play it safe. Go back to your terrible job and London the next day. **TURN TO PAGE 265.**

THE TURNING

"Well," says August, twirling the stem in their fingers and looking up at you, ready to tell the good part of the story. "My parents had sent me packing during the war, so I was staying in cramped little boardinghouses where it was impossible to avoid people who were sick.

"Casimir came to me as I lay dying. He was immune to disease and would wander the hospital wards where they left those they didn't expect to recover—of the flu or anything else they thought infectious. He was always very melancholy. He told me he came to comfort the dying, but I think he was really there punishing himself—as well as giving the furthest gone a quick death that kept his thirst at bay.

"At the time, I'd met a handful of queer friends at university, but that was all. I knew a lot of people who dressed as they were expected to when they went about in the world, and it didn't seem to chafe at them as much as it did me. I think I had hardly met anyone else quite like myself. So when I recognized it in Casimir, all I wanted was to talk.

"We spoke for some time. He was terribly lonely, I think, unable to hold back when we found an easy companionship. As I grew weaker and felt the life ebbing in me, he seemed to be seized with an urgent passion. He asked whether I wanted to live.

"I didn't want to go yet. I still felt so young, only just untethered from my family's control. I was delirious, I think, and not quite sure what he offered, only knew it was unnatural. But then, I'd been called unnatural all my life. I hungered for some power over the chaos of a life where so many had been pointlessly snatched away."

They look up at you with a dangerous, nonchalantly devastating smile. "And power is what I got."

> Ask about how they used their power. **TURN TO PAGE 163.**

> Ask about how they avoided the war first. **TURN TO PAGE 160.**

CONVERSATIONS IN THE COLLECTIONS

You spend a lot of time with August among the collections. You both work without any hurry—you suppose August has no time limit at all—but the act of sorting is satisfying and methodical. Seeing it all logged afterward gives you a sense of achievement you never really got in your job back home. Sometimes August gets bored and starts being coyly threatening or deliberately distracting—usually both—until they lead you up to the guest room and end up dozing curled around you like a cat. But more often, you fall into easy conversation.

One afternoon as the winter sun begins to set over the cluttered room, August has mostly given up. They sit on a cabinet with their legs swinging, watching you work, and the conversation turns to the collection itself.

"We first came here during the Second World War," August says, closing the album they'd been flicking through, looking for some half-remembered note from thirty years ago. "I'd seen a great deal of death, and I had to admit that it was not within my power to end every perpetrator of violence and hatred, no matter how much I wanted to. Later, I learned the language and worked out ways to help the people in town—but at first I was lost, alone for long hours in this tomb of a castle. It was then I began the collection and discovered a piece of myself I'd lost—the child who watched my mother's roses grow and wither back in England, who preferred soil underfoot and watched the slow progress of snails across the garden path."

They often bring up England; now they have someone to talk about it with, dredging up memories of the countryside with a fond longing for the spring blossoms and autumn leaves.

But they also bring up memories of difficult times and people they never forgave, unforgotten political complaints from a hundred years ago. Here in Romania, August understands the situation less. Raisa knows the town best, and Casimir is best positioned to help them—controlling some amount of land and wealth in the neighborhood. August helps, but they're frustrated by their own limitations. They speak restlessly of what they hear happening in England—unfinished business from their unhappy home. You kiss the look of disdain off their face, and they admit with a wry laugh that if you came here from London, they've at least got "one good thing out of that damned country."

TURN TO PAGE 181.

HOLD SOMETHING CLOSE

August curls toward you like a cat and pulls the plush covers over you both.

Their head flumps down on the thick pillows, pale curls spread out around them as they look at you.

Your hand runs through their hair in the lamplight, down over their cool, unnatural skin and to their hip, where you've begun to warm them under the covers.

They pull you tight like they're furious anyone might dare hurt you—or like you can't quite get close and safe enough for their liking.

When you let out a huff of laughter, they make barbed and sarcastic comments as if they're speaking to a rival across a dinner table, not completely intertwined with your limbs. After that, you don't ever sleep in the guest room again.

TURN TO PAGE 185.

MONSTER HUNTERS

Time passes so pleasantly that you hardly notice it go, and by the New Year, the berries are almost ready. August plans a test to make sure it works—a bit more insistent about the safety aspect now than when they'd known you for only two days.

Instead of going to your guest room, they invite you to a door off the collections room you've never seen open before—and stepping inside, you find yourself in their bedroom for the first time. "In case I really conk out," they say with a self-effacing smile. The small room isn't that different in style from the main one—cluttered with the same sorts of notebooks and specimens and strange bone art. But there's something intimate about seeing one of their soft cardigans over a chair, the imprint of their head on the pillow.

"I found a deer in the forest; I've already fed today," August reassures you. "So I'll be able to take just a little." You eat a few berries, and they sink their teeth into your neck for just a moment, able to pull back.

August moves beside the bed to immediately start a big, old-fashioned stopwatch. "Now we only have to—wait to see how—long—" Their words slow like a record player set to the wrong speed, and the watch drops out of their hand. It's like all their usual grace has been switched instantly off, and they sit heavily down on the bed. "Fuck," they say thickly.

You hurry to catch August, making sure they don't hit their head as they flop down onto the mattress. Their hand grasps at the front of your clothes, pulling you with them. Their eyes are hazy, face unhappy and strangely altered from its usual arch expressions, almost childlike. "Don't go," they whisper, pulling you down with them. You lie next to them to try to wipe the distress off their face, and you wonder how unpleasant the chemical lethargy is. Your name is the last thing on their lips before they lose coherence, burying their head in your chest the way a cat nuzzles into someone it trusts.

After about an hour, they seem to gradually regain control of their limbs and tongue. They clear their throat as if they were definitely not just clasped on to you. August shakes their curls out as they sit up, firmly trying to look businesslike despite the physical state of someone waking up from a general anesthetic. "Well," they say, still a little slurred. "I rather think it's ready, then."

TURN TO PAGE 182.

A VICIOUS ATTACK

On the planned night of the attack, August seems jumpy. "*It will work,*" they snap at Casimir at the long table, even though he hadn't said anything.

They tap their perfect nails on the table as you drink the smoothie paste made from the berries. "Finish that," they say sharply, and then, "I mean, you ought to finish that. Please."

They hold your face for a second before you leave, but they don't seem to be able to say anything—not quite able to say good luck or goodbye, not quite able to smile.

You turn and walk out just beyond the walls of the castle as the sun sets, to the place you all agreed on.

The leaves of the forest rustle and whisper in the dark. You watch the last light of day fade, then slice into the back of your hand with a knife.

You spend two dark, terrified minutes shivering with cold and fear, feeling the hot blood pulse over your hand—

And then the noise comes. A few cracks of far-off branches, a hoarse rasp like laughter as the scent of blood draws the creature near.

You're knocked to the ground, sharp pain searing in your neck, world darkening—

And then the dead creature is being dragged off you by the hair, reeling as your blood turns to poison in its mouth. Its usual strength sapped, it lashes out in underwater-slow motions, confused to find itself unable to break free of a thinner, weaker creature.

In the darkness, you see only the faint blur of August's vicious face, but you feel the thud as they slam the stupefied creature's head to the ground. Two more shapes appear at their side, and you're grateful you can't see the details, only August on all fours, holding the thing mercilessly down with Raisa. You hear the sick crack of bone as Casimir removes its head.

August walks beside you as the others carry the body. They don't seem to register their ruined clothes; their eyes stare hollowly forward, catching the light like a cat's. You try to get your heartbeat back under control. You're safe now. You've done it. Later, you see the light of the flames where the body burns in the courtyard, and you try not to think about it.

As soon as you're alone in the collections room, August stalks up to you, pale face cold and furious. They throw their arms around you and talk fiercely into your neck—for a moment you think their tone seems angry. "I was waiting in the doorway for the creature to strike, and I could hear your heartbeat going faster and faster, and—"

They step back to look at you, strangely accusatory, like you've done something wrong. "I thought, what the fuck are we doing? Why did you say yes to being poisoned *bait*?"

You remind August that they were the one who suggested it. Their eyes grow slightly wild.

"I just saw a problem and a solution." Their hands move up to cup your cheeks, like something they're suddenly realizing is precious. "I didn't think about what I was really asking." They lean their face against yours, eyebrows doing something complicated.

"It's only that I'm very glad you're all right," they say, trying to recover themself but still sounding vaguely cross. Then they kiss you with such an earnest intensity that you feel like you'd happily do the mortal peril thing again if this was the result.

August showers for a long time, as if to make sure the feeling of killing is really off them, but tells you not to go anywhere.

They reappear in an oversized shirt, still looking at you with a fiery expression, and tug at your hand, leading you to their bedroom. "You're coming in here," they say in a low, bossy voice, but they pause at their own choice of words as they close the door behind you. "Or—I didn't mean *that*, exactly—we can just go to sleep, if you'd like."

Their debonair manner is all ruffled, eyes slipping down to your neck. They frown and run their fingers over the marks left by the rogue vampire, an unpleasant trespass on something they want safe. Their fingers tighten on the back of your neck, like they want to hold you and not let go.

› Hold them, too. Sleep in August's bed. **TURN TO PAGE 180.**

› You've something else in mind first. Kiss them and push them down to the bed. **TURN TO PAGE 171.**

SOMETHING SWEET

You kiss August, soft and sweet.

August melts into you, long limbs languorous, fitting to your shape with a slow delight and no urgency. They remind you of a cat stretching on a warm day, deliciously content in your arms.

You are strangers to each other, but strangers sharing a golden moment, a kiss sheltered in the dark from the storm outside. The tenderness is fragile, something that could drift away just as easily as root and grow, but those are thoughts for later. For now, your focus closes on your hand in their hair, the feel of their mouth.

After a slow, exquisite interval—which might have been five minutes or fifty but seems to pass a little too fast either way—August pulls away, letting you see their villainous smile. This time it has a playful edge, like they're letting you in on a joke. You're not the prey animal, for now.

With a hand gesture that looks both lazy and slightly imperious at once, they draw you back toward the settee, where the fire glows low and red. You pass stuffed birds and elaborate sprays of desiccated flowers, painstakingly and lovingly made, and wonder how much time August has spent with this mournful assembly their only company.

You sink into the fire-warmed cushions and realize how tired you are.

August is still standing, and you wonder whether they mean to leave you here. "I only rose at dusk," they say in a low, silky voice. "And I should check on Casimir, if he thinks there's danger in the forest tonight. But you can rest here."

They smile with sharp teeth, their eyes sparkling and perhaps a little fond as they say, "I won't bite."

Before they can leave, you pull gently on their arm, drawing them down in another kiss. August's angular limbs soften, and they seem to forget their purpose, returning the kiss and sliding down to sit with you for a moment. They end up draped over you, head on your shoulder, nestled in the wool of their jumper and the loose tangle of both of your limbs.

The rain hammers outside, and you sink into sleep.

TURN TO PAGE 172.

AUGUST IN ENGLAND

The castle is different after the rogue vampire's death. With the woods safe, Raisa spends more time away with humans and werewolves and who knows who else.

Casimir is contemplative, but his mood seems lighter. August tells you he's making plans to go back and visit the place where he grew up and the cities he lived in across Europe.

Over the winter, August learned to use your phone, looking up what's left of the countryside where they grew up and old haunts in London. Your talk of England has stirred something in them, like a sediment they tried to keep settled but always had something waiting beneath. One night, they ask when you'll be going back to London; you know that they want to come with you.

August arrives in England with the furious acrimony of a cat being dunked in a cold bath.

They had read about modern England in newspapers and on an ancient computer Raisa kept in the garage. They knew it in the abstract and were already displeased, unconvinced the place had become as tolerant as it claimed and angry at what was being dismantled and destroyed (the health service, welfare, the arts, the landscapes, the wildlife—but not the old structures of power). But August's hundred-year displeasure does not prepare you for the full force of their quiet vitriol when you arrive.

They seem unfazed by the plane journey, phones, and cars: These are familiar everywhere in Europe. They move through the airport with ease, crowds parting at the cold look on their face as you hurry to catch up. They made sure to feed before being pressed against beating, pulsing human heartbeats on the train into town and seem used to London and its great varied mass of life.

But now for the first time in years, August is faced with injustice up close. You can read the minute changes in their fixed, bored expression: slowly building fury. As your train slides through Blackfriars, their eyes follow the glittering mass across the river: one of the financial centers of the unequal world. Out of their decades-long seclusion, the great wealth divide is painted in vivid reality before their eyes again, tangible—reachable. Huntable.

As you cross a road in the evening dark to descend to the mouth of the Tube, you find August unmoving, eyes lingering on the high street clothes stores. You remember them looking up fast fashion on your phone, reading aloud how much garment workers are paid, how long it takes for polyester to decay, the conditions of people harvesting cotton, and their wide eyes as they scrolled past picture after picture of clothes heaped in landfills. You let the flashing crossing light wink out and stay next to them. The crowds move around you, sending disgruntled glares at August as they dare to look at anything too hard for too long.

August stares up at the security cameras that wink at you from every angle, the doll-smooth models glowing across digital billboards and shop windows. The thin, giant dolls wear cheap plastic-fiber fabrics that were delivered from suffering hands to be worn a few times, then dumped on clogged rising shorelines that used to be people's homes.

Across the street, a security guard forces someone homeless away from the warm arch of an expensive shop, past laughing women advertising disposable plastic razors, banished to wander the cold night.

August turns in disgust and stalks through traffic over the road.

Back at your horrible flat, they run a pale finger along the mold at the window. "It's even worse than you said," they say in a tone so blank, it seems especially dangerous: no bite of venom, no witty observation. Just thinking.

That night, neither of you sleep. With your help, August looks up maps on your laptop and traces the lines of their hometown with miserable, fascinated horror. "The motorway cuts through the old forest," they say in the same flat, dangerous tone. "And what are these?"

You explain they're new housing developments. "So more people can afford houses now?" they say warningly.

They have to excuse themself—Thatcher's Wikipedia page still open on your laptop—to go and tear apart rats in an alleyway. "It makes one consider how value is all made up, doesn't it?" they say coldly, wiping blood off their mouth at your sink when they return. "Houses are valuable because it suits the people who own several houses—while others starve and die and live miserably in cupboards and basements. And people think *I'm* a predator."

But August has one thing left to them in England: Before leaving, they charmed and frightened their way into procuring a false birth certificate for a "daughter" named August, as a way to get documents stamped with an *F*. When August's parents died without a will, their house in the country had passed to the fictional daughter. "If the currency is property nowadays," August says, "let's use it."

You find the right numbers for August to make several phone calls the next morning. Twisting their old-fashioned accent as aristocratic as possible and pretending to be ninety secures them the documents and the key.

As you step out of the train, August's determinedly blank expression falters at the closed-down ticket office. "What about those who can't work the ticket machines?" they say—a threat, not a question. On the village high street, the post office is closed, and most shops are boarded up. "They cut down the trees," August says in a voice that reminds you they're a murderer.

The house itself is dusty, and one of the floors has half fallen through. But the Victorian structure is still solid and rainproof. And surely if you finally told your boss to fuck off instead of going crawling back, you'd have a lot of time to look up DIY videos.

At the back window, you ask August what they want to do with the house.

"It suited me and Caz to live somewhere we were less noticed. And I'd like to have a garden," they say, looking wistfully out over the wide stretch of overgrown land at the back of the house, the bench and rose arch long ago consumed by brambles.

"But apparently this place would sell for an absurd price, even left as a wreck," they say, a dark expression crossing their face. "We could sell it and remain in London. If there were anywhere to make a difference—to make the right people pay—it would be there."

We. They look back at you. You realize their prickly, slightly self-conscious look is looking for your opinion.

August is full of fury about the world, and they're not wrong to be. In London you could do something about it. You could let their old habits reawaken, let their bloodlust and billowing fury loose, and be the arms they return to before the sun rises: You could join them, twin crusaders burning through the night.

But you also see their eyes on the weeds beyond the window. You've seen their collections in the castle, the loving arrangements of pressed ferns, their careful hands sketching the birds in the forest. Away from the whirl of the city, you think something could bloom in them. You can still do good without setting yourself alight.

› Live in the city and close to the powerful doomed. Let things be torn apart. **TURN TO PAGE 192.**

› Live away from the city, close to the trees. Let things grow. **TURN TO PAGE 188.**

A LATE FOXGLOVE

August takes a deep breath into their dead lungs when you suggest keeping the house. They stare out the window for a long time, as if letting you slowly pull them back from the edge, from the full force of their carnage. But when they turn and nod, they seem calm and resolute: ready to fight for the peace they carved out for themself.

You move out to the country and slam the door on the way out of your horrible flat. On your first night, August pulls away from a languid kiss as water starts dripping on your head from the leaks in the ceiling. They point upward, offhandedly. "I was thinking of fixing those, but what do you think?" they say, managing to keep their face deadpan until you start laughing.

They don't complain as much as you'd expected. "It doesn't feel like too great a hardship, after the castle," they say with a casual shrug, halfway through a bottle of wine one evening. "This is luxurious, in comparison. It'll have electricity!"

They glance sideways at you. "And . . . I'm not so alone here," they say quietly, as if admitting to liking your company is a huge secret. "This is ours." They gesture around at the unplastered walls with so much warmth that it stays with you all through the building delays and cold, wet evenings.

Once proper builders have fixed the structure, the two of you work comfortably side by side, stripping wallpaper and sorting through junk. August gets distracted by antique door handles and coat hooks that they carefully chemically clean and bring back to life, putting them back on the doors slightly wonky and bright and beautiful.

When the house is ready, chipped window frames freshly painted, old floorboards clean and waxed, Casimir has August's things sent from the castle, along with a letter with promises to visit. The rooms fill with squashy armchairs and old wooden furniture you sand and clean. The walls fill with butterflies and stuffed birds and strange sculptures, sketchbooks crammed onto shelves and picture frames full of ferns and seaweed.

You get a job in a café in the village where none of the customers are in a hurry and nobody ever shouts at you. August slips by after dark one night and charms the owners, who delightedly hang some of August's pressed ferns on the walls. People occasionally buy them, and August pretends not to be glowing with pride.

You get August a secondhand tablet, and they watch nature documentaries and read articles hungrily—and you help them scour records from town councils and environmental reports as you both make plans.

Local news reports the death of an elderly but tenacious aristocrat who planned to drain the ancient wetlands for golf courses and "luxury holiday homes." His passing conveniently hands over the family estate to an environmentalist granddaughter who quietly reverses it all.

August comes home before sunrise, full and slow, pale skin flushed with blood. They sink down into a chair with a fluid movement, draping an arm over the back. "It was absurd for the aristocracy to still exist in the 1920s," they say casually with a flash of a smile like a knife. "The least one can do is to prune the family trees."

Incriminating documents get leaked online—stolen without tripping the heat sensors or security cameras somehow—and the terrible press gets oil sites in marine conservation areas canceled. An important corporate lawyer dies "of a heart attack," and government money gets funneled abruptly into hydroelectrics instead. A local village will no longer be evicted, a nesting site for terns will survive a little longer. The seabed remains undisturbed, fish glimmering through the kelp beds, fin whales ushering their young up the channels.

But August also refines their tactics. When some problems can't be fixed by tearing someone pitiless limb from limb, they start showing up to local council meetings in gloves and sunglasses, enjoying telling sad stories about their sunlight allergy. Their talent for being terrifying and impossible to ignore convinces committees to pay attention. Their persistence and presentation of details lodges doubts that can't be shifted, a voice in the room that insists preventing harm isn't "pointless red tape" and refuses to be quiet.

You join them at a meeting to preserve a stretch of forest, which you learn will be leveled to build a warehouse for an online retailer famous for mistreating its workers.

August commands the attention of the room when they stand, elegant and unstoppable. "It's an ancient, irreplaceable ecosystem," they begin, and you're surprised to hear how earnest they are—winning people over instead of scaring them into submission.

At the meetings they even make friends, who then come over to help with the house, swap seeds with August, and bring you courgettes when they grow far too many.

Over time, everything blooms. August teases you relentlessly and kisses you slowly and thoroughly in the shade of the old apple trees in the garden. You wander the woods on misty mornings and sunlit evenings. The seeds August planted along roadsides and scattered across abandoned industrial sites in the dark slowly start to grow, and their garden flourishes.

"Look," they say one evening, draping over the sofa behind you and pointing at a video of a distant blurry smudge in the leaves that might be a bird. Their tone fails to disguise their excitement. "It's a nuthatch!"

Your friends love to visit and are only initially terrified by August, eventually becoming fond of their acerbic comments and eager to ask them about vintage clothes. You find yourself fond, too: of August's wicked humor and dramatic dress sense that shocks half the locals, the derisive tone in which they relate news from the meetings, the secret warmth of their eyes on dark nights.

Your family says it seems like something in you is healing—but you think it's more like something growing, something that wasn't there before. You have time to breathe, for hobbies and sleeping late in the mornings, for sitting idly beside August while they look after some rare plant in the garden on cloudy days. August turns the old shed into a studio and makes strange teas and art out of bones. They take the remains of things that are dead and forgotten and build them into the strange and wonderful.

One day, you hear the huge construction project that would ruin the woods has folded. It's all become too expensive and difficult, not helped by the fact that a few of the most unpleasant people involved have met with unfortunate, mysterious accidents and died. Borne along by all the campaigning, council money goes elsewhere, into local businesses and after-school clubs and food co-ops.

In the ancient woods, the moss remains undisturbed. Badgers burrow back to their cubs in their dens, owls hoot in the rustling leaves. A pale figure watches a dormouse sniffling around in the roots of an old oak and then slips away through the night. They, too, have a home to go back to now.

THE END

Want another adventure? See what else there is to do: **GO TO PAGE 266.**

LONDON CALLS

London is a beautiful, sprawling mess full of life that's being slowly smothered: people made to suffer, then considered unsightly—swept out of view and kept out of mind. The vibrant suburbs you grew up around have been turned into eye-wateringly expensive student flats and sandwich chains where you can't afford the sandwiches. Friends are geographically estranged from each other, from their old homes or communities; families are scattered into basement flats and boarded-up high streets on the farthest reaches of the Tube, emigration by the great merciless wave of gentrification.

It's a city owned by empty flats and offshore bank accounts with a great moral void gaping in its seats of power, a wholehearted absence of care. The country makes you feel like you're trapped in a car being driven toward a cliff, the drivers making sure the wheels crush as many of those underneath as possible on the way out.

But you have a monster on your side. And you know the names of the people doing this.

You tell August to sell the house, and they nod slowly, eyes settling into something hard.

You use the vast money from the sale to move to a flat in the middle of London: small but neat and, above all, well suited to your purposes. It's on a quiet street, flanked on all sides by empty properties owned by oligarchs in Russia and investors in Dubai: no witnesses. It has curtains you keep closed, a fire escape that August can slip in through before sunrise, and a good hot shower where August can wash off the blood.

You have a mission, and it devours all your waking hours.

You go from bar to expensive bar, listening to conversations. August finds ways to blend in, sending you on research trails on burner phones under false names whose locations are always moving. You let your family and friends think you're still abroad—it's safer that way. When the authorities catch up to you, they'll find no links between you and the person you used to be.

You're usually the distraction while August acts, charms, and threatens their way behind locked doors. They crawl through air ducts and up drainpipes, and they crouch waiting in cupboards and alleys and filth. They move in the night and break security guards' arms too fast for them to give a good description. They leak information and deliver classified documents to press desks. They terrify the last people who check files before they go to print, to the teleprompter, and to website front pages. They bend the headlines toward more accurate framings, forcibly dragging the path of policy and public opinion in the direction of the truth. The ultrarich media owners search ruthlessly and frantically but can never find the culprit, who seems to disappear inhumanly fast from the crime scenes.

Buoyed by this success, August takes things further. Anyone cruel enough that their replacements will be better becomes a target, and August finds ways to kill without biting, surviving on rats and on you to keep their tracks covered.

Billionaires die on their treadmills full of so much cocaine that it's obviously heart attacks, overdoses. It must be their own doing, cut and dry—nothing else makes sense, because they all die as they lived: locked away alone in extravagant modern palaces, as distant as possible from real, ordinary people.

They live in spotless technological marvels made possible by children coughing in mining pits, constantly monitored workers who are never allowed a seat, prisoners laboring far under any minimum wage. In their glittering smarthomes, they thought themselves safe.

The heat sensors don't trip when something dead moves over the threshold. The cameras can never catch anything, only a few frames that look like a smudge, the smear of a hollow-eyed shadow that moves too fast to see.

August changes tactics regularly and casts their net wide enough that it takes a long time before even the conspiracy message boards suggest connections. Here and there, the drivers of financial crises and oil spills and police brutality wink out of existence. Acts of God, people call them in the pubs and the streets, and when August hears it, they laugh with their murder-weapon teeth in a terrible smile of genuine glee.

August is a force of concentrated fury, absolute determination. They are relentless. The only time their guard slips down is before you sleep, when they hold you tight in arms that tremble only a little. They lose themself in closeness and forget the clamor of the world outside for a while.

August is resolute and passionate—you never see regret in their eyes. If there are flickers of anything, you think it might be fear—not of ending but of not ending: of what more they might do.

The world changes, and it's both of your doing. August slices through London—you both find the path together, and August is the knife.

One day, the absence on the security footage will start looking like a pattern. A trap will close that neither you nor August can fight your way out of. The world spins toward destruction, the road to the end paved with exploitation and casual cruelty. But until then, you'll tear as much down as you can. You'll go down, but you'll go down fighting.

THE END

Want another adventure? See what else there is to do: **GO TO PAGE 266.**

STAY IN BED

You resolutely ignore all the noises. It doesn't stop them.

Outside the wind does not die down, and rain thrashes against the glass. The candle on your bedside table shifts and stutters with no warning—moving hypnotically, as if by an unseen force. You shuffle out of bed toward the dark window to check if there's a draft or shutters you can close—and in the window next to yours, you notice a twinkle of light. The outer wall curves around, and if you press your face up to the glass, you can make out a soft blue glow in the room next door. Through the rain, you can't make out the source—then the glow moves behind some unseen object and disappears.

The thumps above return, growing louder and more frequent until all of a sudden they stop entirely.

As you move back to bed, you hear a gust of wind and splatter of rain against the window behind you, and your bedroom door flies open, hitting the wall and creaking in place, wide open.

Nothing is visible in the pitch-dark corridor beyond.

The wind abates, the room stills. The door yawns open before you.

Curiosity prickles at your mind. The castle beckons. It calls to you in the night, its mysteries waiting to be discovered.

› Take the candle and investigate the noises. **TURN TO PAGE 36.**

› No, seriously—stay in bed. Do nothing and try to avoid encountering anyone or anything happening at all. **TURN TO PAGE 35.**

PREPARATIONS FOR THE PARTY

Raisa whoops when you say you want to go to the party, ushering you enthusiastically after her as Casimir disappears up the stairs and August slinks away into the shadows.

Raisa leads you through the maze of corridors to an out-of-the-way door she bangs open, inviting you inside what must be her room.

Unlike most of the castle, the room is a normal size and actually warm and comfortable. There's a fire burning safely behind a modern grate. A big bed sits in the middle with plush pillows and a thick crochet blanket, and rugs in loud colors overlap on the floor. Old wooden furniture that looks repurposed from the castle has been painted with patterns that remind you of your grandmother's quilts. There are empty beer cans stacked neatly in the corner, a desk that's clean but covered in makeup, cassette tapes, and an empty milk bottle that looks suspiciously like it might have once been filled with blood.

But as you close the door behind you, the thing that strikes you most is the walls. The wall opposite is papered with old band posters, grainy black-and-white photos of basement shows, and what look like record sleeves. You recognize big American rock bands from the '70s and '80s, British punk, and a bunch of names you haven't heard of. There are homemade posters with cutout letters in roman and Cyrillic from some kind of DIY underground scene.

The overall effect is less like a teenage bedroom and more like a massive piece of installation art—each poster, flyer, and photo is preserved and arranged with deliberation, and the whole thing is varnished over into one smooth surface, protecting the paper underneath.

The other walls have no posters but are no less interesting, the stones painted directly in bright patches of warm colors. But the paint isn't messy or peeling—it's practically applied, the right sort of masonry paint.

Raisa sees you looking at the walls and beams. "For a long time, I lived in state apartments, you know? Everyone was living in them. No paint like this allowed. Music kept secret. You would get arrested, questioned, back then."

You ask her when that was, and she gives you a sad grin full of pointed teeth. "Before the revolution. Long time ago."

She opens a dresser drawer, saying, "I just have to get ready—" but pauses. She looks back at what you're wearing: the same damp clothes you arrived in. "But you are cold!" she exclaims, as if she'd forgotten this was something humans experience.

She rummages around in a box with a random selection of clothes that look clean but like they definitely don't belong to her. "These are left behind," she says, "from parties." You think about the huge empty rooms full of dust and Casimir's thunderous looks, trying to imagine when they last threw a party in the castle.

You feel strangely at ease in Raisa's presence as she searches. There's an electricity to her, an easy chemistry that makes you feel like you could tell her anything and she'd have your back—or that, if you wanted, you could easily find a different kind of companionship.

She finds thick, stretchy leggings in about your size and a T-shirt that says *metaldeath* in unreadably jagged letters. Gesturing at the fire, she invites you to change and hang your wet outer layers on the fire screen.

"I won't look!" she says, sitting down on the bed and making a show of covering her eyes and turning away to make sure you understand.

Then, as a throwaway afterthought, she adds: "Unless you *want* me to?" Her voice is cheeky and a little rough over the words. It sounds like a genuine, impulsive proposition—though she also seems perfectly happy just to chat.

- Change clothes while she looks away and talk to her. **TURN TO PAGE 199.**
- Strip and ask her to watch. **TURN TO PAGE 204.**

MORE THAN YOU CAN CHEW

As the adrenaline of the bike ride fades, you realize the weird wine from dinner has really started to kick in. As you finally stand still for a moment and listen to someone trying to tell you the rules of the game, you realize your head is still swimming.

The rules are impossible to understand from this explanation, and the words glide smoothly off you, absolutely none of it absorbed whatsoever.

Someone hands you a ball, but your throw goes so wide it disappears into the kitchen. You find yourself giggling at the werewolf who sprints after it to get it back.

Someone on your team tells you to drink from a cup of dubious cleanliness full of a dubiouser pink liquid. You're in way too deep to refuse at this point, with a large circle of people and monsters looking at you, so you knock it back—and you keep on doing that every time someone puts a cup in your hand.

As the game goes on, you find yourself entranced by the arc of the ball through the air toward the mystifying, many-layered mountain adorned with cups. You're not sure how much time elapsed or what happened, but your team seems to lose—possibly your fault—and you're given almost a whole pint of the weird pink stuff to chug.

You're not sure what happens after that. Later, your gran sends you a photo in which you're upside down on the dance floor, attempting some kind of headstand move you've never done before in your life—a moment you have no memory of whatsoever. You think your mind being blank is probably a good thing.

TURN TO PAGE 254.

A CHANGE OF CLOTHES

You change clothes as Raisa looks away with her eyes covered. She fills the warm, quiet room with comfortable chatter as you strip out of your cold, wet outer layers to hang them by the fire. She's talking about how difficult it was to get a generator installed at the castle so her record player and tape deck would work.

"I've done it before—we used to have parties in chemical factory basement, where secret police cannot find. You use wires for big speakers, not so hard. The danger was if they catch you."

You don't interrupt as you change into the borrowed clothes, and she goes on matter-of-factly, as if this was all a normal part of life to her once. She uses "secret police" interchangeably with "Securitate," so from your grandmother's occasional mentions, you gather she's talking about the old Communist regime more than thirty years ago. All three vampires must be older than they look.

"When I was young, my parents were very scared of the secret police—suspicious of neighbors, everything. They turned people in, worried and sick about what people think of us. You can't live like that, I think."

She falls quiet, hands still over her eyes.

"You're done?" she asks, and when you say yes, she uncovers her eyes and smiles when she notices you've been listening. "Sorry," she says in a brighter voice. "Parties make me think of the old times. But it's good, you know—it's good to remember."

You're much warmer now that there's nothing wet actually against your skin and your outer layers are only slightly damp—you could easily put them back on over the top. But Raisa doesn't seem in a rush. The moment feels still and comfortable.

› Put your outer layers on and go to the party. **TURN TO PAGE 208.**

◆ If you have the marker **A CRISIS SHARED**...

Raisa gives a wave of her hand to indicate you could sit down beside her.

With this marker, you can also choose to sit down and ask Raisa more about her earlier life. **TURN TO PAGE 201.**

WEREWOLF HOUSE PARTY

The large room is crowded with a mix of ordinary people and . . . *others*. Big figures covered in fur loom above the crowd, with heads that look halfway transformed to wolves', drinking beers through straws to avoid the teeth. You see people with shimmering scales running up the sides of their faces and others that look horribly corpse-like—all just chatting and laughing like this is normal.

Over to your left, the sofas have been pushed back and a ball of colored lights plugged in to create a makeshift dance floor. A few people are dancing, and more are arguing about what music to put on. Upbeat, heavily distorted guitars blare out of the speakers.

To the right, there's a group of people who've set up a complex game that looks like beer pong. Paper cups of an unidentifiable, lurid pink alcoholic punch have been arranged on a table with stacks of empty cans and boxes in an elaborate many-layered setup, with toy cars and plastic tracks leading up and down. As you watch, one team gives a huge cheer as they land a ping-pong ball in a particularly precarious cup that's balanced on the top of a table, several shoeboxes, and a ukulele. Someone plucks the cup from its perch and chugs the contents.

In the middle of the room, a group including Raisa surrounds a table covered in empty cans, where two seated figures compete to see who can chug a beer fastest. One is a werewolf, the other a much smaller human, and as she finishes her beer and slams the empty tin back down on the table, you realize it's *your gran.*

She yells your name as she spots you across the room. "You miss your flight!" she cries over the crowd. You nod back, completely at a loss for what to say. *This* is why she couldn't drive you to the airport? She calls out again, slightly tipsy, "But you come to the party! This is good! The party is always good."

Before you can reply, the werewolf next to your gran pulls her into conversation, and you hear her explaining loudly that you're her grandchild and saying the word "*Anglia*" in such a derisive tone that you immediately know she's saying you live in England. You're not sure exactly how many beers she's had at this point, so you forgive her—but she seems to have slightly forgotten you're there.

- Go hang out with your gran. **TURN TO PAGE 210.**
- Join in with the game of beer pong. **TURN TO PAGE 205.**
- Head to the dance floor. **TURN TO PAGE 212.**

THE PARTIES UNDER THE FACTORY

Leaving your outer layers by the fire, you come and sit next to Raisa on the bed. She still looks contemplative as she looks at the wall papered with posters and record sleeves. When you ask what it was like growing up, she replies easily.

"Well, my parents wanted me to be a good, quiet girl. That was safe," she says. Still looking at the wall, she grins, but there's something hard behind it. "So of course, I wanted opposite."

You ask her about the secret parties, and she leans back to stretch out on the bed, talking animatedly and stretching her arms out above her to gesture.

"Small parties are easiest to keep secret. But still good! In the bad times, all TV had only one channel for only a few hours—electricity rations, you know. Life was hard but also boring. So we got special records, banned books, and we could share them. Factory is not close to houses, so we played music loud. There I could kiss girls as well as boys without any danger."

She lets her arms fall over her head back onto the blankets.

"For a long time we were not caught. It was a secret joy, you know, you carry it in your heart even in the factory, even on a hard day. Me and my friends, we were young, we feel invincible."

You ask whether they were caught.

"Yes," she says simply, as if it was inevitable.

She rolls her head to look at you. "Some of my friends escaped, went back to living quiet, avoid trouble. Some taken, in work camps or dead in prison. I would be, also. But August saved me."

She lapses into silence. The fire crackles. "It is a long time ago, now," Raisa says quietly.

- Put your outer layers back on and go to the party. **TURN TO PAGE 208.**
- Ask Raisa about how she met August. **TURN TO PAGE 202.**

RAISA AND THE SMUGGLER

You lie back on the bed so you're next to each other, looking up at the ceiling. After having talked honestly about your own life at dinner, Raisa now seems happy to share in turn, her words coming easily.

"My friend had a secret contact who gets music records from the West. One day she sends me to pick up the package instead, so I meet the contact: August.

"Most people did not like August. They move unnatural in the dark like a cat—yes, okay. I understand people do not like this. But the big reason is that August is not a man in the way people wanted. Even my friends thought August was dangerous—too obvious they were enemy of the state. But I liked this! August is not afraid.

"And anyway, when August eats, it is like an animal eats—to stay alive. So I like August. Dangerous but good. More good than my mother, because my mother turns in 'enemies of the state,' you know? For my mother it's a choice, to be cruel.

"After the first time, I always do pickups with August. We talk about music. After time passes, I give August blood. In exchange, they smuggle food into town. Even in food shortages, rationing, when farmers have to give crops to state, still all houses here had food—we told them it's government aid. We smuggle petrol generators for extra power to hospitals. Everyone knows there is smuggling. Nobody asks questions. We keep people safe and alive."

Raisa pushes hair out of her face with a pained expression, eyes on the ceiling. "But eventually someone informs. One of our friends turns on us. We don't know who—only one day in the factory, two friends are missing. I know what is coming. My hands shake on machines all day. When I walk home, men in uniforms follow. I broke one nose before they got me in a truck.

"They took me to a dark room and have questions, questions. They want confessions. They want many arrests. I will not give them. They know I had a friend who was pregnant and I helped get her medicine to stop it. She cannot afford a baby. But it's not allowed, you know. They want more babies, more workers.

"And the police, they know I did this, and they hate me. They beat me. They were killing me," she says, voice level but absolutely sure.

She turns her head to look at you. "But then I hear screams. And I know August has come. The door breaks, the men die, but it's late—I am already dying. So August asks if I want to live." She runs a hand over her pointed canines. "I know what it means.

"And I am so angry, and times are so bad, and I want to keep helping. So of course, I say yes." Raisa's eyes shine bright like a flash on steel. "I am never sorry for it," she says, fierce and resolute.

For a while, you lie there on the bed together. Her black hair is spread messily out behind her head as she looks up at the ceiling again. You're not sure what to say, but she seems comfortable—both nostalgic and grim, glad at having a chance to reminisce. You imagine her at a forbidden basement party, ready to enjoy herself as a form of resistance, never sure whether it'll be her last.

She turns her head toward you again and gives you a wistful smile that curves her round cheeks. "You're a good listener," she says softly. You can see a faint messy line where her long eyelashes have smudged mascara against the skin.

Then she stands up and stretches, letting the moment break.

She goes over to the fire and hands you the dry clothes with a smile. "I don't want to miss the party," she says simply. "Let's go."

You pull the clothes over the top of your borrowed ones.

TURN TO PAGE 208.

NO BEATING AROUND THE BUSH

You tell Raisa yes, you do want her to watch, and her eyes widen in gleeful surprise.

She shifts around on the bed until she's leaning back on her arms as if to get a better view. She runs her tongue unconsciously over her sharp teeth, waiting.

You pull off your wet outer layers without much ceremony, but she watches hungrily as the skin is revealed. She lets out a considering hum of pleasure, running her hand down her own chest with no sense of self-consciousness, enjoying the touch. You hang the clothes over by the fire and turn to face her with a thrill of anticipation.

She gives you a casual shrug, beckoning you over to the bed with a grin. "We should wait a *little*," she purrs at you. "Better for clothes to dry, yes?"

As you approach the bed, she pulls you down into a rough kiss with no preamble.

Her sharp canines graze over your lips, the curves of her body soft where they press against you. She kisses as if it's the simplest thing in the world—as if you want each other and that's all there is to it. She runs her hands over you in uncomplicated enjoyment at the feel of it, and you find yourself leaning into the touch and returning in kind. As your brain tries to catch up with your body, she moves against you, playful and responsive.

Raisa efficiently and thoroughly finds out exactly how you like being touched. She seems to enjoy watching as she makes you unravel completely and leaves you gasping with your mind wiped clean.

Afterward, you lie panting on the bed, still shocked from the whirlwind. Your entire body feels good. Raisa rolls upright with a grin, going to grab your clothes from beside the fire. "You see?" she says, picking them up. "And still lots of time for the party."

Body still tingling, you pull on borrowed clothes and your own mostly dry ones on top, along with gloves, an anorak, and a motorbike helmet Raisa thrusts at you.

Raisa puts on a black corset that exaggerates her soft curves, along with a fishnet top and a ragged scrap of band tee. Her hair's still half sticking up from your hands grabbing at it, and the effect is one of untamed, gorgeous disarray. She winks as she catches you watching and pulls on a biker jacket with studs all across the shoulders. "Let's go."

She leads you to a converted garage and has you sit behind her on an old-school motorbike. Wrapping your arms tight around her waist, she grinds her hips back toward you with a laugh as the engine flares into life and the outer door rolls up to reveal the howling wind outside.

TURN TO PAGE 206.

MYSTERIOUS PINK LIQUID PONG

As you head over to the table—and the various stacked boxes and plastic track adorning and extending the table—you hear two of the half werewolves having a loud disagreement. You realize they're speaking English, one with a definitely German accent, trying to find the best common language.

One particularly corpse-like guest wanders off to the kitchen, giving you a space to slip through and enter the circle.

"Think about it, bro: The storm is the best time for skinny-dipping! It's dramatic," says a particularly muscly werewolf in a circle skirt and a tank top. "The others are waiting."

"No, Mila, you'll make the teams uneven!" another says in a voice that sounds like a dog's whine.

"Just find someone else," says Mila, turning and coming face-to-face with you. "Hey! You're Raisa's friend, right? You should come and play!" she tells you, holding on to your forearms with the sincere friendliness and intensity of someone drunk and having a good night. "I have to go swim in the lake."

Her eyes widen, excited. "Or you can come swim in the lake! Bring Raisa!" She waves at a slightly confused Raisa and disappears through the kitchen and out the back door.

> Join the game of beer pong. TURN TO PAGE 209.

> Go to the lake with Raisa and the werewolves. TURN TO PAGE 213.

THE MONSTER MASH

Raisa drives *fast*. Her unnatural reflexes and familiarity with the terrain let her race through the forest, swerving around trees and hurtling through the branches as you cling on for dear life. You're heading downhill, and at one point you see the headlight illuminate only rain and air ahead as you shoot out over a precipice—Raisa whoops as you try not to faint in terror—before you land hard on the road, skidding round to a right angle and continuing on without stopping. Your teeth feel like they're rattling out of your skull, but you feel undeniably alive.

The road swerves around the edge of the mountain and downward. You skid through sheets of rain, a whirl of trees and tarmac whipping by in the circle of light in front of you. You have to periodically close your eyes to focus on holding tight to Raisa, your dinner, and your sanity.

The roller-coaster movement slows and shakes. You open your eyes again to see you're shuddering along a dirt track toward the lights of a big house surrounded by trees and fields, where you hear a bass beat thumping out from the lower floor.

Raisa, who's obviously been here before, turns into a covered barn and brings the bike to a stop. You find you're breathing hard in the helmet and pull it off to pant in the cold night air, wired and full of adrenaline.

"You're good?" Raisa says, slapping you on the back with a big grin. You manage to nod as Raisa walks back out into the wind and the dark, beckoning you behind her, barely giving you time to catch your breath. She runs the distance between the barn and the front porch, unnaturally fast as she vaults over the railing from the side and skids to a halt on the dry wooden decking in front of the main door. You follow at a more human pace up the steps as the door creaks open.

In the doorway is . . . a normal human. She's pale skinned and wearing black—a floaty dress with sleeves that drape over her hands so you can just see the tips of her fingers and their black nail polish.

"Mara!" Raisa yells excitedly, asking how she is and introducing you before you're even through the door. Mara gives you a little wave as Raisa tells you, "We can't use the castle, so Mara is hosting this year—she has a big house." It's not much of an explanation, but Mara adds nothing more, only steps back as if to let you both in.

You're walking in toward the sounds of laughter and music and taking off the anorak when you realize Raisa is still hovering outside the doorway and Mara has started to giggle.

"Oh, you're *so* funny!" Raisa says, laughing indignantly back. "Every time, it gets more funny."

“Hmm, well,” says Mara—they’re both speaking in English for your benefit, you assume—“*this* time I will invite you in. Come in, Raisa.”

Raisa practically bounces inside, and as she comes in sight of an open doorway to the left, you hear excited yells of “Raisa!” and what sounds like an actual howl. You see a very big, very hairy guy with a wolflike head pull Raisa into the room as she laughs, and you’re left slightly stunned with Mara in the corridor.

Mara smiles at you with the same dreamy and contented expression as before, completely unperturbed by the large wolf-man in her house. “Welcome!” she says, taking your wet anorak and hanging it up on a set of pegs where various jackets are scattered, both hung up and chucked over whatever objects used to be underneath before the thick layer of coats arrived. “Please, eat anything, go anywhere. My house is your house!” says Mara earnestly. She points out a charger near the coats, and you gratefully leave your phone to charge for a few minutes to let the battery get back above 10 percent.

- If you have the marker
  DEAD PHONE . . . REMOVE IT.

Mara is just pointing out the kitchen at the end of the corridor when someone emerges, calling for her. She excuses herself with an apologetic smile, leaving you alone. Music thumps loudly in the room off to the left that Raisa disappeared into—the main part of the party.

- Go into the main room to your left.
  TURN TO PAGE 200.
- Follow Mara into the kitchen.
  TURN TO PAGE 226.

TELL RAISA YOU'RE READY

Raisa seems to stir herself from her thoughts when you tell her you're ready. "Okay!" she says, turning her mind toward the party. "Okay, yes. One minute, I have an idea." She doesn't bother to warn you as she strips her top half down to her bra, puts on a fishnet top, and fishes around until she finds another T-shirt in a drawer—this one cut raggedly to make it a vest.

She pulls it on with a grin, then points meaningfully at her chest, which now has a matching *metaldeath* logo on it. "It's good, yes? Everyone knows we are friends."

She pulls on a new jacket with even more patches and rows of spiked studs along the shoulders—her formal biker jacket, maybe—and then tosses you a helmet from under her bed, though she doesn't get one for herself. "Humans heal slow, need to be careful," she says by way of explanation.

She hands you warm socks, gloves that look waterproof, and a big anorak to protect against the rain, and you put them on along with your shoes.

Raisa leads you out of her room along a dark corridor and into what you realize is a converted garage full of retro and half-taken-apart cars with styles going back about a hundred years. In the middle, a big old-school motorbike stands pride of place, finish battered here and there but gleaming and well cared for.

Raisa swings her leg over the motorbike and pats the seat behind her. She nods approvingly as you climb on and put your arms around her waist in a way that feels like a hug. "Hold on."

The engine growls as she revs, and the bright headlight flares to life—significantly better than the one on the terrible car.

Pressing a button on her keys, a slatted door rises up and out of the way ahead of you, leaving a stone archway that looks out onto the stormy night. "See?" she calls back to you over the roar of the engine and the wind outside. "Generator!"

TURN TO PAGE 206.

THE TOURNAMENT

◆ If you have the marker **FULL OF WINE . . . TURN STRAIGHT TO PAGE 198.**

◆ Otherwise . . . **KEEP READING.**

There's a cheer as you say you'll make up the team. You manage to figure out the rules, and by starting more sober than the other players, you have a distinct advantage in being able to see the ball and control your limbs.

You get a lot of encouragement and slaps on the back, and when you do land the ball in a cup, your team gives you a disproportionately massive cheer. Either they assume being a human is a bit of a general disadvantage you're overcoming or they're all just really drunk and cheerful—either way, just giving it a go seems to be getting you a lot of high fives and whooping noises, and you don't end up having to chug too much mysterious pink liquid.

Finally, with only a few cups remaining, it's your turn. Everyone hushes each other noisily in preparation for your throw. You can hear the beat of music and chatter from the other end of the room. You aim the ping-pong ball carefully.

It does not go where you were aiming: a cup balanced high on a shoe. Instead, the ball bounces off a toy car—sending it zooming around a loop—and lands neatly in a hidden cup with a crown drawn on it in permanent marker.

A massive cheer goes up as you hit the extra-special secret target. All the werewolves are losing their minds, and the game disintegrates, winners and losers forgotten, because you're being lifted up on their shoulders and they're chanting your name. Below, you spot Raisa in the cheering crowd, and she gives you a wink, delighted.

◆ Gain the marker **PARTY ANIMAL.**

As the chant dies down and you're lowered back to the floor, the crowd disperses. But from now on, you're greeted heartily by random wolfish strangers wherever you go.

› Head to the dance floor. **TURN TO PAGE 212.**

› Out on the back porch, the werewolves who were heading down to the lake seem not to have actually gone yet. To get Raisa and join them, **TURN TO PAGE 213.**

GRAN HANGOUT

While you're still wondering how you'll get through the crowd to your gran, she notices you moving forward and yells for the others to make room, and everyone immediately shifts to fulfill her request.

"You're here?" she asks genuinely, making it a question, and you explain what happened with the car and the castle.

She doesn't address the fact that her going off to a massive party left you imperiled on a dark road in the night, but her face lights up when you mention Raisa. She shouts Raisa over, who gives your gran a massive side hug around her shoulder.

"You know Raisa!" your gran says enthusiastically. "Before the revolution, I went to Raisa's parties. Me and your grandfather! The times were very bad, but the parties were good! Raisa is so good."

She leans in, slightly drunkenly. "They watch over us, you know. Some people don't like it, but they do. They protect us." That's another revelation like a slap to the face—your gran knows all *about* the vampires. She made you memorize the forbidden road because she knows *exactly* where they live. She nods to confirm when you ask. "But the forest is dangerous right now," she says darkly, and Raisa nods back, commiserating about something they've clearly discussed before.

You mentally count the years. Raisa and your gran aren't the same age—but if Raisa was young in the '70s and just stayed young, the gap might not be nearly as big as it looks.

Raisa tells you a wild story about an underground gig she and your gran went to in the city, back under the Communist regime. "But halfway, police come in—everything is shut down! Because bands were forbidden from singing in English then," she explains. Apparently, the only reason they both made it back to the bus home without getting arrested is your gran punched a policeman hard enough for them both to get free.

And Raisa has more stories—she tells you animatedly about a band your gran used to love who hid in speakers to smuggle themselves over several borders to West Germany. Your gran tells you that at one point she had a chain of contacts who got her bootleg records from the USSR, forbidden Russian music produced outside the state apparatus, illicitly cut onto X-ray prints from hospitals and passed around the scene.

Her favorite song, she tells you grinning, was about a woman in a criminal gang who gets deservedly shot. "Because she betrays friends!" your gran says, and then spits on the ground to make her point more clearly.

Someone else arrives, and your conversation moves on to more recent matters, lighter things. You're introduced to several half-transformed werewolves—not all of them speak English, but they give you big thumbs-ups when they realize you're related to your gran, whom they all seem to know. "Don't worry," your gran tells you in a stage whisper. "It's controlled, like changing only halfway. They only eat you if changed all the way," she says not entirely reassuringly, slapping you on the back.

The chat is punctuated by arguments about what music to play and various people trying to talk to your gran—old friends and monsters from all over Europe keep coming over to give her huge hugs. You eventually gather that your gran was telling the truth: This is a big deal of a party, a once-a-year reunion kind of thing. That's why she wouldn't drive you to the station.

Some of your gran's friends are younger than she is, and others are apparently long-lived creatures. You gather that most see your gran only once a year, or they usually talk to her only on the phone. You think back to her animated phone calls you assumed were with doddering old ladies in the town and were too fast for you to understand the Romanian. The old ladies from the town who are here are laughing and drinking, a few with massive tattoos and jackets covered in studs, doddering or not—you think you see one having a wrestling match with a werewolf out the window.

You give your gran a warm hug and stand up to let her talk to her friends.

◆ Gain the marker **GRAN PAL**.

"You must go, have fun! Not stay with an old lady!" she says, charitably trying to pretend that she's holding you back rather than far too popular to hang out with you. She lets out a cackle of laughter as she waves you farewell, which slightly undermines the pretense, before being subsumed into a rowdy crowd of friends and admirers.

› Join in with the game of beer pong. **TURN TO PAGE 205.**

› Head to the dance floor. **TURN TO PAGE 212.**

THE LIVING ROOM DANCE FLOOR

You move into the crowd under the swirl of colored lights. There's a real mix to the kinds of dancing—there's a slightly corpse-like woman laughing and jumping up and down with her friends in the corner, several people with closed eyes just nodding and bopping along to the beat. A werewolf finishing a very pink drink provocatively grinds up against an old man with a long beard who obviously knows how to dance only if it's headbanging. It feels like basically anything goes.

You see Mara at the edge of the dance floor, putting on a slower song on someone's phone that sounds like '80s new wave. She glides into the crowd to sway like a tree in the breeze, arms lifted high over her head and then swinging down to wave at her sides like she's casting spells—and she looks completely absorbed in the moment.

One of the people jumping in the corner is saying something that turns into a chant of "Dance-off!" and moves to the phone jacked into the speakers to put on something familiar with slickly produced vocals and a beat that thumps through your body.

The man with the beard comes over to argue, managing to cut off the beat for a moment and switch to a song with an enormous amount of dramatic electric guitar solos—before being overruled. "Air guitar *is* a type of dance-off," he's saying crossly as the beat thumps back to life. Mara looks slightly bereft, her floaty arm gestures pausing in the air as the music changes, but she looks ready to move aside and let things go in any direction. So does everyone else, to be honest—the thing that's most unpopular is the constant changes of music.

- Leave it on the hits and go for it in the dance-off. **TURN TO PAGE 221.**
- Challenge the man with the beard to an air guitar tournament. **TURN TO PAGE 219.**
- Put it back on Mara's playlist and dance with her. **TURN TO PAGE 225.**
- Lurk at the edge of the dance floor—you realize you can avoid the dancing completely by just hovering near the edge. To pass as much time as possible lurking around, sipping at drinks, and avoiding interacting with anyone, **TURN TO PAGE 228.**

THE LAKE

You bring Raisa out to the back porch, where the werewolf called Mila enthusiastically persuades her to come down to the lake. Raisa seems immediately committed, and the werewolves sitting outside whoop and get up to join you.

There's a lull in the rain, but the wind still gusts overhead, and you see the occasional crack of lightning glimmer in the sky. Ahead of you, the werewolves tear downhill across a wet meadow, and you and Raisa follow behind. Though Raisa could easily catch up, she keeps pace with you instead, laughing in the rain.

Through a clump of trees, you emerge out onto the shore of a lake. The water looks inky in the darkness, and the dark shapes of forested mountains rise up behind it, just visible in the full moon. The scene is haunting and beautiful—even with werewolves yelling and cannonballing off the end of the jetty ahead of you.

Raisa has already tugged off her combat boots, unselfconsciously stripping down to her underpants in the light rain and sloshing into the water with a yell at the cold. She gives a big shiver—though you're sure she doesn't feel the cold as much as a human would—and splashes away to float on her back, looking up at the moon.

You strip off your layers and walk ankle-deep into the freezing water. But before you can move forward to join Raisa, you notice someone else.

Just ahead of you, half-hidden behind a clump of reeds, stands an ethereal figure with delicate features, pale skin, and long, wet hair. She's wearing a long white dress, the wet fabric clinging over the curves of her hips and billowing out where it reaches the water at her knees. Her full, wet lips part as she sees you. She looks a little shy to be caught here—but then her eyes slip down over your body with a look of appreciation. She gives you a coy little smile, gesturing as if you're welcome to join her.

- Join the woman in the reeds. **TURN TO PAGE 216.**
- Tell Raisa where you're going before joining the woman. **TURN TO PAGE 214.**
- Head over to join Raisa and the werewolves. **TURN TO PAGE 215.**

WINGMAN

You call out to Raisa across the water as you gesture toward the figure. Raisa turns, frowning as she treads water, and you realize she can't see past the reeds. She swims over to the side a little before she catches sight of the ethereal woman, at which point she makes such a big expression of raising her eyebrows that you can see it clearly in the moonlight.

She looks over at you with a head tilt that says "Really?" but then gives a shrug that seems to say "Okay, sure!" along with a grin and a thumbs-up.

◆ Gain the marker **WINGMAN.**

"I'll be here!" she yells, then goes back to drifting contentedly in the water.

TURN TO PAGE 216.

SKINNY-DIPPING WITH GOTHIC DRAMA

You give the ethereal woman what you hope is a friendly wave but head off in the other direction, and when you glance back, she seems to have disappeared.

You wade into the freezing lake, moving your feet carefully over the smooth stones and slimy water weeds as you make your way up to your waist, the cold knocking some of the air out of your lungs. Something moves in the wet tendrils around your ankles, and the shock makes you fall in the rest of the way, your whole body splashing down under the water. You splutter to the surface and gasp in air.

◆ Gain the marker **LAKED.**

Raisa must have noticed the splash, because you see her gliding over with a grin, effortless in the water like a seal or a river otter.

She seems unselfconscious about her bare chest and unconcerned about being out in the dark lake ringed with pitch-black forest—brazen and brave. It makes you feel almost safe with her, and your body relaxes a little in the cold water.

Farther away, the werewolves are whooping and splashing around.

You float out to where it's just shallow enough to stand, and Raisa throws her arms out, gesturing at the mountains in the dark. "It's beautiful, huh?" She grins, eyes bright.

It is beautiful, you agree. It's beautiful and wild and dangerous—a bit like Raisa. As the wind blows through the trees, the rain patters on the surface of the lake, rough and ghostly in the moonlight. Raisa tosses the wet hair out of her face, close enough for you to reach out and touch. Her cheeks round in a smile that looks like it's inviting you closer. You feel very full of adrenaline.

› Kiss her. **TURN TO PAGE 218.**

› Go and join the werewolves together. **TURN TO PAGE 220.**

› Tell her it's fucking freezing and you want to head back. **TURN TO PAGE 224.**

THE WOMAN IN THE REEDS

You move toward the enchanting figure waiting for you.

As your feet slosh through the cold water, the tall reeds close off your view of the rest of the lake, and the sound of voices grows quieter, replaced by the whispering movement of the wind through their stems. Your eyes lock with the pale, beautiful woman standing ahead of you, and the cold barely seems to matter. It's just the two of you in your own little world, out of sight of the others.

You can hardly help your eyes moving down to drink her all in as you draw nearer.

The woman notices your look and gives a sweet, lovely smile at the attention. She reaches out a hand toward you, and you raise a hand back without thinking—but she must have gone a few steps farther in. You wade deeper into the water to meet her.

She runs a hand through her beautiful hair, and then, still smiling, she slowly slips her dress from her shoulders.

She lets it fall, baring her pale skin from the waist up, unashamed and lovely. She looks like a painting, you think dreamily, and you reach out toward her, wading deeper, closing the gap.

She pulls your outstretched hand to her, gliding it down the wet skin at her neck to cup her full chest. She lets out a soft noise of pleasure when you take her lead and continue, moving your other hand to slide down her back. Her breathing quickens, and she pulls you forward to meet her lips, opening her mouth against yours to moan against your tongue. You kiss back, mesmerized by the feel of her body under your hands. She feels cold in the water, and you move your body closer to keep her warm. She slides her hips up against you with an urgent press, kisses growing clumsy in her eager hunger.

She pulls the dress the rest of the way down, throwing it aside to let it float through the water like a ghost and sliding back onto a rock just under the surface behind her. Her lovely pale eyes beckon you onward, and you follow without thinking, deeper into the lake.

She draws you forward until you're pressed together, guiding your fingers under the water to rest where she wants them.

Hidden behind the reeds as the storm winds shake the trees far above, you slide together in the inky water, her hands hungry over your skin as she touches you and pulls you in. She says no words but makes soft animal noises of longing as you move, enraptured, pressing your face into her wet, pale flesh. Delicious friction builds, the nails of her other hand digging into you. Your body's growing numb, but you hardly feel it.

The ethereal woman's hands cup your face as you try to get your breath back. She slips off the rock and into the water, still holding your face in her hands as you're pulled forward. You're not sure what more she wants, at first—your slow mind can't quite figure it out.

She's still smiling beautifully as she drags your head down under the surface with her.

◆ If you have the marker **WINGMAN . . . TURN TO PAGE 45.**

◆ Otherwise . . . **TURN TO PAGE 44.**

MOONLIT ROMANCE

In the inky lake in the rain and the light of the moon, you step forward through the water and slide your arms over Raisa's shoulders to press your mouth against hers.

She melts into the touch and kisses back with a deep "mmm." Her arms move around your waist to pull you instinctually closer and press you to her bare chest.

You break away, breathless, but your arms stay looped around each other. Raisa's body isn't warm, exactly, but it's soft and lovely, tantalizing under the dark surface of the lake. Her dark eyelashes are stuck together as she gives you a little grin. There are wet strands of hair plastered to her forehead, and you ruffle them up, making her laugh.

Her eyes linger on yours for a moment, and it feels as if she's really looking at you for the first time. Her wet hand moves along your jaw, and she kisses you again, softer this time—almost tentative.

When her body pulls away from yours, you let out an involuntary shiver. "Oh, we need to move, to stay warm," she says with a big, exaggerated wink, but when you laugh, your body shivers again, this time from head to toe. Her mouth falls open, her lips framing an O.

"Ah! I mean it!" she cries, rubbing at your shoulders and looking around—out to the werewolves and back toward the shore.

- Go and join the werewolves together. **TURN TO PAGE 220.**
- Tell her it's freezing and you're ready to head back. **TURN TO PAGE 224.**

TRIBUTE

The man with a beard triumphantly gains control of the music with your help, and the room is filled with face-melting guitar solos. He explains his tournament idea, and a young woman with a mohawk enthusiastically organizes the crowd in several languages until the dance floor consists of an audience huddled around an arena of combat in the middle. In the center, two participants go head-to-head pretending to shred on the guitar, whirling and headbanging as the rowdy crowd eggs them on. People shriek and shout for the victor while the woman stands on a chair insisting on hands up for a vote, discusses the winner with the bearded man, then declares who survives this round to go on to the next.

You let yourself embrace the situation and be carried away by the building excitement—when you're picked as the next contestant, you throw yourself in with intense gladiatorial seriousness. You headbang like a warrior whose life hangs in the balance. Your fingers fly over the invisible fretboard. You move with the music like a very violent interpretive dancer. In the grand finale you skid spectacularly across the floor on your knees and endure the carpet burn.

Was it good? You have no idea. But your absolute dedication proves extremely popular with the crowd, and your slightly embarrassed opponent is banished to the outside of the circle, laughing. You prove victorious over and over until it's you and the man with the beard in the finals, whirling around each other in increasingly furious mimed, spectacular drama. It's not really clear who wins because by the end, everyone has joined in, jumping and yelling. You thought you noticed Raisa over the crowd at one point, grinning at your dedication.

◆ Gain the marker **MUSICAL THEATER.**

The dance floor turns into a rowdy mass of people choosing their favorite songs that everyone knows the words to, and you find yourself briefly the most popular person in the room. People clap you on the back, keen to hand you drinks and drag you into their circle to dance.

You're not sure how much time passes as the mood carries you along, triumphant, but eventually Mara returns to put on something slower and you find people have started to drift off, most still giving you high fives as they leave.

TURN TO PAGE 228.

WOLF GAMES

You swim over to the werewolves, who immediately begin a kind of splashing battle. Raisa darts around to dunk one of them with unnerving speed, and it's quickly obvious that as a normal human, you're not well matched to the game. Perhaps realizing this, one of them—Mila, you think her name was—gives you a yell of warning and ducks down underwater and under your legs so that when she stands again, you're up on her shoulders.

Another werewolf who seems to be Mila's girlfriend does the same with Raisa, and the game turns into play-wrestling on their shoulders, as if you're trying to get Raisa down into the lake—though you're sure she's humoring you and your human-level strength.

Eventually, you both tumble back into the water, laughing. Mila lifts herself back up onto the jetty with her extremely big, furry biceps and jogs back to shore—and before anyone can stop her, she grabs all the clothes she can find, including yours and Raisa's, and starts sprinting up the hill with them.

◆ Gain the marker **HONORARY WOLF.**

You and Raisa slosh out of the water as a couple of others go tearing after Mila.

Raisa hurls herself forward and seems to disappear as she moves lightning-fast to intercept. After a very brief tussle, she reappears with your clothes and most of her own, too. Something about it being completely fucking freezing and Raisa being so at ease makes the whole thing very nonerotic and also nonembarrassing. When you've pulled your wet clothes back on, she gives you a big, dramatic high five.

She grins at you fondly for a moment before you both laugh and start back up the hill, with the wild night around you ruffling the long grass in waves.

"You're fun!" Raisa says, absolutely genuine and sounding impressed. She says it like she's paying a serious compliment—and it warms you all the way back to the house.

TURN TO PAGE 222.

DANCE-OFF

Mara drifts off with the bearded man as the group of (ghoul?) friends gain control of the speakers. Bass thumps through the room, and you end up dancing in front of a man with shimmering eyeshadow in a clear circle at the center of the crowd. You are not better at dancing than he is. His hips move effortlessly in time to the beat, shifting fluidly through dance styles that leave the crowd watching in awe.

Outmatched, you bow to his superiority and just try to have fun. He laughs good-naturedly, and more people start to gather around, encouraging you—so you just throw yourself in. As the tracks change, you combine every dance move you can possibly think of: club moves with '70s disco, stuff you've seen in videos with cheesy wedding dances, salsa and bhangra, pirouettes into moonwalking into the worm.

◆ Gain the marker **MUSICAL THEATER.**

Is it a *success*? Well, you certainly draw attention. It makes people laugh and cheer you on, and the guy opposite and his friends join and dance back with you. You notice Raisa over the crowd at one point, grinning at your extremely goofy moves.

But it also has kind of a magic effect. No matter what anyone else tries, they can't be the weirdest or most embarrassing person on the dance floor: You have that covered. Shy bystanders see you looking ridiculous and that it's not a big deal, and they join in. A woman shows you how you're actually supposed to do salsa; an older American werewolf steals the spotlight demonstrating how they really danced at the disco.

People start choosing tracks that have a specific dance, then teaching anyone who doesn't know it until the dance floor synchronizes in a lively, playful mess. A guy who definitely knows ballet puts on a remix of something classical with a dance beat overlaid, and most of the room tries spinning and moving along on tippy-toes. The guy with a beard puts on a headbanger, and then the man with eyeshadow puts on old songs everyone knows and shouts the words along to. Everyone wants to welcome you into their circle to dance, and you find yourself talking and laughing with one group then another.

You're not sure how much time passes as the mood carries you along, but eventually Mara returns to put on something slower and people start to drift off, most of them waving fondly to you as they leave.

TURN TO PAGE 228.

WARM SHOWER

Back at the house, Raisa takes you upstairs and turns on a sputtering but hot shower that sprays down into an old-fashioned bathtub.

In the indoor light, you can see how much mud and grime you're covered in from the lake, and you both step in fully clothed to wash it off.

When Raisa gets out, you strip off your wet clothes and put in the plug. You let the clean bath fill up with hot water while Raisa uses a hair dryer on both your clothes on the other side of the shower curtain. You feel you've come a long way since stepping out of the terrible car, and you relish feeling clean and warm and safe again. Heat creeps into your body as the water flows over you, carrying the tension away.

After a while, the whole room has warmed up, and you hear Raisa turn off the hair dryer, patting your clothes and sounding pretty pleased with herself.

"*This* time, we keep you dry." She laughs. You see the shadow of her messy hair through the curtain as she comes to sit on the floor next to the bathtub, leaning back against it to keep you company. You turn off the shower to sit down in the hot water, basking in the steam.

She chats at you from the other side of the curtain. "So did you swim in a lake before?" she asks, and then she asks about the sea, and the nearest sea to London, and whether you like swimming. "You have a bath where you live?" she asks, and then, suddenly very serious, "Okay, big question: Do you have favorite shampoo smell?"

She listens cheerfully and giggles easily when you say anything even remotely funny. It feels domestic, comfortably intimate.

The party still seems to be going by the time you make it back downstairs, though the elaborate beer pong setup has half toppled over and people have started drifting off back home and to other parts of the house.

There's still a crowd on the makeshift dance floor, where Mara sways contentedly, looking completely lost in the moment.

Raisa moves some coats and a bottle to curl up with you on a squashy sofa to talk. You swap stories about anything—parties you've been to, food your gran makes, favorite films. The conversation moves easily by, and you find yourself absorbed in everything she says.

She tells you everything with animation—glimpses at surviving a difficult past, wild stories about vampire parties, ideas she has for modifying old cars, or inconsequential anecdotes about good dogs she's met. She tells you about some of the people at the party, with equal interest given to infamous joyriding werewolf Big Georgi and old Ana-Maria from the village who makes an incredible cheese pie. "Like nothing else, I swear. You have to try it!" she cries seriously.

Eventually, someone calls Raisa's name from the corridor. She gets up reluctantly with an apologetic smile, heading out the door with a "Back in a minute!"

But a minute passes, and then five, and she has not yet reemerged.

> Head to the dance floor. **TURN TO PAGE 212.**

> Look around for Raisa. **TURN TO PAGE 228.**

HOW DO YOU KEEP ENDING UP WET?

Raisa laughs. "Okay, okay, yes, it is very cold. You are only just getting dry earlier, as well!"

You both wade out of the water and pull on clothes that cling over your wet bodies.

Some of the werewolves have emerged, too, and one races up past you on all fours, chasing another who's stolen their clothes.

You and Raisa walk slowly back up the hill, shivering slightly in the faint rain, the night wild around you, wind ruffling the long grass in waves.

Raisa's arms are folded over her, and she looks down at her untied boots as she walks contentedly beside you. "Me and my friends, we used to come down here in the dark, after parties sometimes, to swim. It's not like this in the summer, you know—it's nice. But even in cold—it makes you feel alive, no?"

You can't help smiling back at her, teeth chattering.

"It's good! Not all of us get to feel alive!" she says, laughing, bumping against you good-naturedly as you walk up toward the house.

TURN TO PAGE 222.

NEW ROMANTIC

You encourage Mara to put her own playlist back on, and her face lights up in a genuine smile. "Please, everyone," she says in a floaty voice that somehow carries across the room, and some of the people jumping apologize when they see her face. Everyone seems to like Mara and is happy to concede to her choice of music.

Despite her outfit, her playlist turns out not to be confined exclusively to '80s goth, expanding out over the decades and including a few old songs most people know the words to and sing happily along with.

You dance opposite Mara, matching your movements to hers, and she laughs delightedly when she notices. She unselfconsciously shows you some of her dance moves, which you try to copy, letting your limbs move loosely through the air like you're underwater. You let yourself get swept up as the music flows through you, closing your eyes and moving fluidly like nobody's watching. Mara comes in closer like she's drawn toward you, dramatic and playful. It feels like you're the only two people in the room, moving in tandem harmony.

You're not sure how much time slips hypnotically by, your arms wafting around as all the tension drains out of you. People come and go on the dance floor, voices singing to choruses, the world drifting comfortably around you. When you open your eyes, you see colored lights bathing Mara's carefree expression in blues and purples.

After a while, a young woman comes up alongside and tries to join in. Mara looks so pleased and surprised that you feel a pang in your chest—how often does she get to share the music she loves? Several of the first person's friends join, and eventually the whole dance floor is people swaying and twirling. You spin Mara around slowly, and her expression is very open, breaking into a smile full of emotion as the whole room seems to move around her.

◆ Gain the marker **GOTH ADMIRER.**

Eventually, a very apologetic werewolf who looks fairly out of it approaches Mara to tell her something got broken upstairs. Mara, still perfectly calm, gives you a lovely smile as she tells you she has to go. But before she leaves, she leans in through the dark under the lilac lights and kisses you on the cheek.

TURN TO PAGE 228.

FIND ME IN THE KITCHEN AT PARTIES

In the kitchen, Mara is pouring alcohol into a big soup pot while talking in a kind and slightly spacey way to someone with icy-blue skin that you're not sure is makeup. A black dog with thick curly hair and a friendly, excited expression winds between her legs and looks up at you eagerly as you enter.

You notice Mara pouring the end of an unlabeled bottle of spirits into the punch. She then adds half a jar of brightly colored sweets and, finally, a mysterious spherical bottle full of a green liquid so bright, it looks like it might be glowing.

In the pot itself, the punch seems to be a very intense magenta somehow, fizzing slightly in a way that may be carbonation or possibly something stranger. Someone with bright golden eyes like a cat's scoops a paper cup from a stack with a strangely clawlike hand and helps themself. They sip at the drink without any injury—it must be safe and free for anyone to take.

Out the far door, you see people smoking on a back porch, talking and laughing together.

- Talk to Mara—ask how she knows Raisa. **TURN TO PAGE 229.**
- Get yourself some of the punch. **TURN TO PAGE 231.**
- Befriend the dog. **TURN TO PAGE 232.**
- Avoid speaking to anyone in the kitchen and go outside. **TURN TO PAGE 234.**

WINE-PUNCH COCKTAIL

You fill your cup with punch—it's more than you meant to put in, but it's too late now. You start drinking it, and before you know it, you've finished the cup. That was a pretty big cup, actually, and you're surprised you managed to drink it all so fast. Was it fast? How much time passed? Did someone refill it for you halfway? The room blurs around you.

The punch tasted weird but really good, actually. What does that remind you of?

The wine, you realize. The wine you drank at dinner. The huge, very big glass of strange and mysteriously strong wine you drank all of, probably only about an hour or so ago—if your understanding of the flow of time can be relied on at all anymore. You've been running on pure adrenaline since the bike ride, barely remembering the dinner at the castle.

But the wine and the wooziness are definitely hitting you again now with full force, like a punch directly to the head—which you guess is exactly what you just had. You laugh and realize you're standing on your own.

You put down the cup of punch and try not to lurch sideways. You try to turn the lurch into a casual lean on the counter, although the counter seems much more slippery and elusive than you remember countertops being.

Someone with eyes that remind you of an owl's and strangely feathery hair tries to engage you in conversation. You're so completely unable to follow that you're not even sure whether they're speaking in English or Romanian. Is the owl look a costume, or is it this person's face? Are those contacts? What do normal eyes look like? You feel like you've forgotten.

The night slips away—possibly into a blissful and immediate sleep, possibly into a long night of noisy, messy catastrophe. Either way, the time is lost to you, and you'll never know.

TURN TO PAGE 254.

OUT IN THE CORRIDOR/2 A.M.

A few hours after midnight, the party eventually quiets down in the main room.

One or two werewolves snore on the sofas beside the last dancers, who are picking slower beats they can sway or make out to. Most of the people you recognize or who speak English seem to have dispersed. Outside the window, the rain still falls, but now it's a soft patter in the dark night.

Out in the corridor, you open a few doors to look for Raisa. You find a small room where a few women are having a deep conversation in a language you don't know and another where several people seem to be sleeping in a big pile. You open one door to find four figures, including a large werewolf, passionately intertwined—in a position that looks more complex and athletically challenging than actually pleasurable—and quickly apologize before closing the door again.

As you return to the main corridor, you think you can hear talking somewhere outside and open the front door.

◆ If you have the marker **GRAN PAL... TURN TO PAGE 237.**

◆ Otherwise... **TURN TO PAGE 236.**

BLOOD DRIVE

"Oh, everyone knows Raisa!" says Mara dreamily. "Everyone in town knows about the vampires, I think. Some people are superstitious, they stay away, will not talk about it, but everyone knows. And people know Raisa best; she comes to town the most. Lots of us send them blood."

She says this like sending someone blood is an ordinary transaction or a gift basket. You get the impression that almost nothing you say could surprise or offend Mara, so you prompt her to actually explain what she means.

"Hmm," says Mara, as if figuring out how to explain it to an outsider. "Well, you must know that in the old regime, before the revolution, there was so much hunger. There were lines for bread and shortages of everything—medicine, food, fuel. And so the vampires would smuggle things in, over borders. And when Raisa joined them, it became a big project. They could move through the dark with nobody seeing them, scare and knock out guards, eat the police."

Mara stirs the punch, and you can't tell whether her expression is contemplative or absent-minded. "The vampires kept everyone fed. Most people are too young to remember now, but their parents do, and they pass it on. And so we kept them fed in return, and we still do."

Mara smiles at you vaguely, gets herself a big cup of the punch, and slips out of the kitchen and into the main party, giving you a little wave as she goes.

The noise of the music thumps through from the living room—along with a cackle of laughter that sounds strangely similar to your gran's.

› Head into the living room. **TURN TO PAGE 200.**

› Get yourself some of the punch. **TURN TO PAGE 231.**

› Befriend the dog. **TURN TO PAGE 232.**

I'LL COME TO THE PARTY, BUT YOU CAN'T MAKE ME ENJOY IT

You may have agreed to come along to this party, but nobody can make you participate. You borrow the phone charger from the corridor, bring it into a small side room, then close the door. You sit down in the chair and plug your phone in again—and realize that, now that you're down the hill, you have one bar of signal.

- To call Andrei and get away from the noise of the party: **TURN TO PAGE 233.**
- Or to stay here on your phone all night: **KEEP READING.**

You spend the night looking at videos on your small phone screen that get increasingly less funny, and you speak to absolutely nobody. When a small group of slightly spaced-out werewolves opens the door and asks if they can come and hang out, you tell them the room is full.

You get suggested a weird video by a social media algorithm desperate for your attention and fall down a rabbit hole of similar ones, finding yourself compelled to keep watching just to figure out what on earth is happening. It has millions of views. You don't have the will to click away. It doesn't matter what happens at the end. It's not worth it.

Ads play between the videos for things you don't want or need but will seep into your mind and make you feel self-conscious about parts of your appearance and behavior you hadn't thought about before. The people running the marketing companies have you where they want you: enthralled and miserable. You don't enjoy watching any of it, but it passes the time, hours ticking by toward the end of the night and the end of your life.

In the twilight before sunrise, Raisa pulls open the door. You manage to pull your attention away, face lit up in the numbing light of the phone screen glow. "Where were you?" she asks, and you don't know what to say.

You climb stiff and exhausted back onto her motorbike, and she brings you back to where the terrible car sits at the side of the road, barely giving a wave before she speeds away up toward the castle before the sun rises.

TURN TO PAGE 264.

MYSTERY PUNCH

◆ If you have the marker **FULL OF WINE . . . TURN STRAIGHT TO PAGE 227.**

◆ Otherwise . . . **CONTINUE READING.**

You take a cup of the punch, which turns out to be extremely sweet and slightly bizarre tasting, but you sip at it and half listen to the conversation around you and let the room get slightly fuzzy.

The noise of the music thumps through from the living room—along with someone swearing loudly that you definitely think sounds like your gran.

› Befriend the dog. **TURN TO PAGE 232.**

› Head into the living room. **TURN TO PAGE 200.**

› Head outside. **TURN TO PAGE 234.**

BELOVED

As you stretch your hand out toward the dog, Mara appears, slipping between a few people as she weaves around the party. She tells you the dog's name is *Clătită* and that it means "pancake." The dog is so, so excited to see you but behaves herself with an admirable restraint and does not jump up at you.

You pet the dog, who wriggles with excitement, moves around you in circles, and comes back to be pet again. You stroke her absentmindedly as Mara asks whether you drove here, seemingly completely unsurprised when you explain your car broke down and you ended up at a vampire castle. "It's good you didn't get eaten on the way," she says, seemingly quite serious, though it's hard to tell with her dreamy voice. "Caz would never, though. And August usually will not, if you're nice."

You end up sitting down on the floor as the dog nuzzles into you and curls up in your lap, extending her face along your leg to look up at you pleadingly if you withdraw your hands. You talk to several more people who come through the kitchen, who are all delighted by the dog, too, and talk to you a little. But with Clătită in your lap, there's not much pressure to reply or keep a conversation going.

You're talking to the dog in a slightly silly voice (which seems to be greatly appreciated) and rubbing her head when you realize Raisa is watching from the doorway with a massive smile on her face. She gives you a thumbs-up before ducking back into the main party.

Eventually, Clătită wanders off. But the dog, and everyone who saw you with the dog, kind of loves you now.

◆ Gain the marker **BELOVED BY ALL.**

The noise of the music thumps through from the living room—along with a voice that sounds weirdly like your gran's, yelling at someone.

Out on the back porch, a quieter group of werewolves still seems to be smoking and chatting, and it seems like you could avoid talking to people by heading that way.

› Head into the living room. **TURN TO PAGE 200.**

› Head outside. **TURN TO PAGE 234.**

TAKE ME HOME

You dial Andrei's number from the slip of paper in your pocket.

It isn't midnight yet, and he picks up after a few rings. When he answers, you feel suddenly on the spot. You try to explain that the highway was diverted and the small road through the mountains was too dangerous and then that you were taken in by vampires—and wonder whether he's going to think it's some weird joke. But instead he sounds serious when he replies, "Now where are you?"

You feel a surge of relief as his car pulls up in the rain in front of the house—an oasis of normality in an overwhelming night.

Andrei leans over to open the passenger door, and you climb in and slam it behind you. He gives you a nod but seems slightly unsure of what to say, haltingly offering you his guest room. "It is more quiet," he says, gesturing at the loud thumping bass coming from the werewolf party, and you nod in agreement.

As you drive back to the village, he sits in shy silence for a few minutes, then clears his throat gruffly to put on music. It's soft, soulful guitar that puts you at ease as you sit beside him, winding through the rain, away toward streetlights and normality.

When you ask whether he knew about the vampires, he makes a small noise of agreement, but it sounds slightly disapproving. "Everyone in town knows these creatures. In old bad times, they bring us food, if we, uh, give blood in bags from doctor. A good trade. So we do not try to hurt them, but—I think it is better to leave them alone. Not all safe. Some, dangerous.

"My sister, Mara, she is very friendly with all these creatures, but—" He shakes his head. "She is crazy, a little crazy. I do not go to her parties. I do not go along the death road. It's, um, what's the word—to tempt fate." He glances at you as he drives and gives you a small, shy smile. "I am glad you are safe."

TURN TO PAGE 235.

THE BACK PORCH

A group of werewolves sits on a slightly grimy arrangement of white plastic chairs, smoking and chatting quietly, mostly in English, and looking out into the night.

The back of the house looks out onto a field that slopes downhill into dark clumps of trees below. The rain is lighter now, scattering in the wind, and the full moon has emerged from behind the clouds.

One of the werewolves raises their hand in a small greeting as if you're welcome to join. Another is talking about how her girlfriend's obsessed with the idea of going skinny-dipping down at the lake, even though it's almost November—the others whoop in encouragement until they all seem pretty keen. "You're Raisa's friend, right?" says a werewolf in a sleeveless denim vest, turning in his chair to look at you. "You should both come to the lake! It'll be sooo crazy in the storm."

Away to your left, you see the main room through the slightly open curtains, where several groups of people are joking and laughing, and someone seems to be trying to throw a ball into a cup stacked on top of a shoe and a small guitar.

Farther along the porch to your right, you see another door leading into a small, quiet room. Inside you can see a comfy chair—and remember the charger in the corridor. You could avoid talking to people if you went through there.

- Get Raisa and join the werewolves down at the lake. **TURN TO PAGE 213.**
- Head back inside to the main room. **TURN TO PAGE 200.**
- Escape to the quiet room to avoid speaking to anyone. **TURN TO PAGE 230.**

NIGHT AT THE HUMAN FARMHOUSE

Andrei's old-fashioned farmhouse is tidy and homely. He seems slightly nervous, careful about your comfort, showing you up to a small room with a big, squashy bed and warm rugs over the wooden floor. He offers you cocoa and a tub of homemade biscuits he must have made himself—since it seems to be just him and a big, gentle herding dog living at the house. The well-behaved herding dog comes to nuzzle quietly against your legs as the storm howls outside, as if to make sure you're safe.

Andrei offers to wash and dry your clothes and hands over a fluffy towel and a big, clean T-shirt for you to sleep in. Then he frowns to himself and goes to get you loose bottoms, a sweatshirt, and extra blankets. "Do not be cold," he says, pressing them into your hands.

He seems both prepared for and very unused to guests, shy at having you close by. He carefully shows you the shower, turning pink as you lean in to see and brush against his arm. He meets your eyes, then moves away quickly as if slightly overcome. He busies himself bringing you a new spare toothbrush, pointing out shampoo. "Anything, please use," he says quietly before ducking sheepishly out of the room. Once you're changed and ready for bed, he hovers gruffly in the doorway, still slightly pink. "This one is my room," he says, gesturing at another doorway. "If there is anything you want . . ."

He flushes a little more, eyes lingering on your lips for slightly too long. "I did not mean—sorry, I will—good night." He turns to leave.

- Tell him there is something you want—invite him to bed. TURN TO PAGE 240.
- Tell him you want a kiss good night—but nothing physical. TURN TO PAGE 116.
- Let him go. Go to sleep and go back to London the next day. TURN TO PAGE 265.

AWAY FROM THE NOISE

You step out onto the porch that rings the house. You stand still for a moment, looking out at the dark road in the drizzle.

A car crowded with people drives out from the garage, blaring music. You can't make out the figures, the headlights illuminating the rain as the car turns out of the driveway, then recedes along the road into the night.

You hear Raisa's voice from the side of the house, calling your name. The noise is half lost among people laughing and talking—at a party full of people she already knows, she's still looking out for you. It fills you with warmth against the chill, and you follow around the porch to find her.

TURN TO PAGE 238.

THERE'S AN AFTER-PARTY, AND YOU'RE NOT INVITED

You step out onto the porch that rings the house. You stand still for a moment, looking out at the dark road and listening for any sounds in the drizzle—and then your gran bursts out of the door behind you with a loud "There you are!"

She slaps you on the back. "I'm too old! Too old to stay past two with this noise," she says, voice slightly hoarse from yelling over the music. "My friends, we have our own after-party," she says, pointing. Sure enough, you now see a group of laughing, shouting people climbing messily into a truck. An old woman covered in scales—who you think might have visited for tea once—is obviously the designated driver, trying to herd the rowdy group to sit properly in the seats.

Your gran turns to you. "Look, your life in England, it is depressing," she says with her usual forthrightness, grabbing on to your arm to get you to walk her toward her friends. She's giving you a pitying look. "When you say about your job, it makes me want to throw the boss from a cliff. *And I would do it,*" she says, deadly serious as she looks you hard in the eyes. "I have done things.

"What I mean," she says, voice back in the register of sweet old gran, the special voice she uses to hoodwink shopkeepers into giving her discounts, "is you can stay here any time. You can come back tomorrow with bag if you want. We sit around and do nothing. We watch movies, play cards. I make you *sarmale*. You help with house, help with garden. Now I know you can party, we party!"

Behind you, you hear Raisa's voice from the side of the house, and you realize she must have stepped out a side door. She calls your name, but it's half lost among people laughing and talking to her. But she's still looking out for you—it fills you with warmth against the chill.

Your gran gives you a big wink. "But maybe there are other people you can stay with, huh!" She gives you a wave as she hobbles off to where her friends are shouting for her in the drizzle. "If you get plane back tomorrow, you call to say you arrive safe. If you don't, you call to tell me gossip!" She cackles as a younger friend opens the door for her, and she packs into the back of the truck next to the others. She gives you a final wave out the window, and you hear the sound of electric guitars as the speakers blare to life. You watch the truck speed off in a spray of mud before going around the porch to find Raisa.

TURN TO PAGE 238.

THE END OF THE NIGHT

Raisa breaks into a huge grin as you come into view, waving you round to a door into a busy room. There's a man sat smoking in the doorway with a friend fully asleep in his lap, and behind him people sit talking and laughing as the party winds down. Five or six people sit lazily on a bed with Mara, slowly emptying a huge bowl of curly fries.

Raisa takes your hand, leading you through and down onto a squashy sofa beside her. She takes out a bottle with an inch of dark red liquid in the bottom, taking a sip, then running her tongue around her teeth in pleasure. "My friends, they donate," she says with a shrug. "Stops me getting too hungry. The others can eat animals. But they are good hunters and less hungry—they are old, you know."

She looks out at the cozy, crowded room. "Every year before, we had the party at the castle. It was all three of us, together." Her face creases in a frown. "I know the change is because of danger in the forest, I understand. But still, I'm sad the others don't even try to come here. They could turn up before sunset or find a new place for a party—they could make it work, but they are stuck in their heads."

Raisa flumps her head back against the sofa, her messy, dark hair spread around her. She turns to look at you in the low light. "They are used to always a little loneliness, to bad things. And they let it take over. It's easy to get used to misery. People can live with so much, no?"

She pauses before she continues. "I grew up in very bad times. Difficult to get food, heating, electricity. Say the wrong thing, you're in big trouble, always scared. And bad for women—inspections every month to stop abortion, *nothing* private. Misery, always." She moves closer, her voice low. "But still there are moments that . . . *break through*. The times to just play, try something new. You have to make it happen! When I had parties secret from government, it was important not just because it was good and fun. It was *hope*. Resistance.

"The world wants to grind a person down, make only a perfect worker, like a machine. A perfect worker does not dream, does not have beautiful, messy life—people in power want it simple, to cut away all things that are not necessary." Raisa looks up at you, her dark eyes bright. "But the times to play, the small things that are not necessary—that's where *life* is."

◆ If you have two or fewer markers in total . . . **TURN TO PAGE 239.**

◆ If you have three or more markers in total . . . **TURN TO PAGE 244.**

WORDS OF ADVICE

"You should remember that," she says, putting a hand on your shoulder. Her eyes stay on yours as if she might be about to say something more—but then someone calls her name, and her eyes drift away. In a party full of life and people and strange creatures, you've not quite done enough to hold Raisa's attention—not made an impression amongst the noise.

Raisa jumps up, called away by a group of friends wanting to hug her before they leave. You see the curve of her easy smile as her head turns away, and then she moves out of the room to speak to someone else, and you don't see any more of her.

Mara comes over to you, tired and smiling, and leads you up to a small spare bedroom as the music below winds down and conversations start to peter out. You find yourself exhausted once you lie down, and the next thing you know you're coming awake to light through the blinds and Mara putting down a mug of hot water with mint leaves floating in it beside you.

She disappears downstairs while you drink it and pull your clothes back on. Out the window there's a gray drizzle across a beautiful but ordinary landscape. The spell of last night seems to have broken, and the castle seems far away—almost a dream. When you move down the stairs, everyone is human again: bleary and half-dressed on sofas or sitting talking on the floor. Mara moves carefully among them, but there's nobody else you recognize. You go to sit in the hallway for a while to charge your phone some more.

◆ If you have the marker **GRAN PAL**...

There's a ringing from an old landline on the wall, and when Mara moves unhurriedly to pick up, she gestures that it's for you. Your gran sounds hungover but chipper on the other end of the line. "I just call to make sure you did not get eaten!" she says with a hoarse cackle. "And to remind you, you can come stay if you like. I am serious about this!"

With this marker, you can go back and stay with your gran. **TURN TO PAGE 247.**

◆ Otherwise...

Mara comes up to you with an old woman who doesn't speak much English, who might have been a werewolf doing a lot of arm wrestling last night. This morning she just smiles placidly, inviting you out to her old car to give you a lift. She takes you back to the terrible car, and you return to London. **TURN TO PAGE 265.**

COUNTRY HOSPITALITY

You draw Andrei over to the bed, and he follows, his hand not leaving yours as he sits down beside you. The soft mattress dips so you both slip closer together. The rough fingers encircling yours move, tentative and reverent, over your arms, coming to rest at your jaw.

You're aware of how big he is, even when sitting down. At first he's slightly awkward, cautious with his movements, as if afraid of being too rough. But when you kiss him and pull him down, he softens, shoulders falling as he sinks into your touch like a relief. His gentle hands grow firm as you deepen the kiss. His smile is still shy, but his careful movements are capable, kisses turning hot and earnest as he takes his time stripping away the layers between you.

For a moment, his dark eyes meet yours, and the raw desire there burns through your body. He presses his face into your neck as if to cover his naked want, his rough jaw and hot breath and soft sounds muffled against your skin.

Even as heat builds to a crescendo between you and his movements grow breathless and urgent, he seems to make an effort not to rush, savoring taking his time.

Afterward, he lies beside you, sweaty and spent, eyes moving appreciatively over you.

"When you came to stay next door, I wanted to talk, but"—he spreads his hands with a slightly embarrassed shrug—"I did not know how." He moves toward you slowly, as if giving you a chance to refuse, then kisses you, soft and warm. You fall into a deep, satisfied sleep.

Andrei wakes very early in the morning—in a half-sleeping haze of contentment, you watch his big form move to the door and carefully close it behind him before you doze off again.

When you wake up properly, you find him setting down a laden tray beside you. On it are a pat of butter in an old-fashioned dish, pots of honey and several homemade jams, and what looks like fresh bread, still warm. He's brought tea and coffee—he offers you both and takes the one you refuse.

In the light of day, he's quiet and slightly gruff again, not quite sure how to behave around you, but when you ask about the jams, his voice warms and grows more confident. There are some that seem to have no translation: "Rosehip and plum, but not jam. A little different," he says, describing the process of how he made it and telling you the names. "It's about, uh, how much sugar?" He points out a kind of fruit jelly, and when you ask about it, you discover there seem to be old customs around it. "Just for honored guests," he says with a quiet blush.

He offers to pick up your things from the terrible car, then take you on to the station. But as you're getting ready, you make an offhand comment about how you're not looking forward to returning to your horrible flat—it's not very appealing compared to being brought breakfast in the big, soft bed—and he pauses.

"If you must go back, I understand. But I have many rooms, always lots of work here . . ." he trails off. His dark eyes are earnest—serious and hopeful about inviting you to stay.

› Stay with Andrei. **TURN TO PAGE 242.**

› Go back to London. **TURN TO PAGE 265.**

SPRING BLOOMS

You help out at the farm over the winter, learning some of the less strenuous work to begin with. Andrei's big hands move skillfully over the machinery, firm with the tools and gentle with the lambs and the seedlings. He wakes early and reliably and leaves you breakfast on the bedside table. You sleep in the guest room, but he often ends up joining you.

As the year goes on, you watch the mountains and meadows bloom into beautiful spring. You find a simple and surprisingly satisfying spreadsheet keeping track of numbers, which Andrei hates filling in with a force. You offer to take over and help him finish half-completed forms for sustainable farming schemes, to his immense gratitude.

You slowly start learning Romanian, and you find he's still fairly quiet but extremely funny and quick-tongued in his first language.

One spring afternoon as you're walking the path along the edge of a field, you meet two women who run a neighboring farm. You realize they can't be married here, but they're definitely a couple—one knows Andrei from school, and they invite you both over. Over dinner and the same plum brandy your gran drinks, you all get on like a house on fire, and from then on they start to visit you regularly. Andrei bakes when they come over—crusty bread and savarin cake and elaborate loaves full of berries and spices.

Your friends crowd into a video call to meet Andrei, and he shows them the house, then gruffly invites them all to stay. When he goes off-screen to check on a stew, they all tell you he's out of your league and that they're looking up flights to Romania right now.

Your friends pack up your stuff from your shit flat and send it over, along with the news your landlord has lost his business and a lot of money after being taken to court for providing flats "unfit for human habitation."

When your boxes arrive, Andrei reverts back to being gruff and shy for a moment. "I want to ask you . . ." he says, but he can't seem to get out the rest of the sentence. You question him in Romanian until you figure out he wants to invite you to move your things into the master bedroom. You pull him into an embrace, then move into his room, smiling all the time as you fill the drawers with your things.

You see your gran often. When you tell her you'll be staying with Andrei, she tells you bluntly, "This is good. You had sad life in England. Depressing." Sometimes she invites you over to what sound like pretty wild parties. You and Andrei occasionally make an appearance—and you're sure you see werewolves drinking in the garden a few times—but you don't make a habit of it.

You find a home in the old wooden house full of the smell of bread, in the steady comfort of routine and the strong, gentle circle of Andrei's arms. There are always things to do, but you see them satisfyingly finished—the literal fruits of your labors sold on and shipped out, baked into pies that fill your mouth with sweetness on slow afternoons. There is time to notice the dew on spiderwebs, the frost over the earth, the clouds as they slip through the sky—and the first new leaves that emerge, hopeful, into the spring.

THE END

Want another adventure? See what else there is to do: **GO TO PAGE 266.**

LIFE OF THE PARTY

Raisa leans toward you and puts a hand on your arm. She looks impressed—almost enraptured, dark eyes wide. "I know you get it. You feel bad at home, but you come here, and you try new things! *Crazy* things. And—*playful*, you know? I like it so much." Her hand slides down to yours, and she squeezes it warmly. "When did I last meet someone like this?"

She leans back as if remembering there are other people in the low-lit room, though none seem to be paying you much attention and several seem to be falling asleep. "Come with me," she says, still holding your hand, then leads you through the people scattered talking on the floor, out past people smoking by the window and looking for their coats to go home.

She takes you up the main stairs, then up another narrower set until you're in a room built into the roof with sloping wooden ceiling beams. You both have to duck to avoid hitting your heads, but you follow her over to the mattress laid out on the floor, where she sits down and throws the thick, soft covers over your legs. The mattress is at the side of the room, beside a low window, and Raisa opens it outward to lean out, resting her head on her arms to look out over the view. Cool air flows in, and you pull the blanket up over both of you as you move alongside to join her.

The clouds have cleared a little, and there's enough moonlight to see the whole shape of the valley: the undulation of hills and dramatic rise of rocky mountains; the dense, prickly coat of forest spread over the slopes; the reflected stars glimmering on the lake far below.

Under the lip of the window, you're sheltered from the rain, but the wind tousles Raisa's hair as she looks out at the landscape, keen and awake even in the small hours. "When you see the world like this, it makes you want to go out and see it, no?" she says. You agree—though maybe not at 3 a.m. in the rain.

"No." She laughs. Her eyes are intent as they lock on yours. "Witching hour. Time for something more quiet." Her face is close—closer than an ordinary friend—but she looks at you curiously, waiting for your lead. Raisa's company feels easy and comfortable. You think she'd enjoy kissing, touching, anything you want to give—or she'd also happily welcome a more platonic intimacy: a partner in adventure.

› Kiss her and invite her to bed. TURN TO PAGE 246.

› Share the bed but platonically. TURN TO PAGE 245.

PARTNERS IN CRIME

When you don't move to kiss her, Raisa gives you a broad smile and leans her head down to rest against your shoulder instead, looking out over the landscape, perfectly content. You sit close and comfortable, talking softly and laughing, until the music below quietens, then stops, and light slowly begins to creep into the sky.

◆ Gain the marker **PARTNERS IN CRIME.**

Before the sun rises, in the pale blue of the early morning, Raisa leans far out the window and starts to talk about the things in view.

She points out a distant mountaintop in the blue mist and the last rain and tells you about the steep climb it takes to get there. She leans her head on her arms and peers down at the lake as she tells you how she used to visit as a child, when travel outside the country was restricted and they couldn't afford to go farther anyway. She moves your arm until you're pointed in the direction she means, head resting next to yours until you can see where she's looking: a road winding through the hills she tells you is perfect on a motorbike.

She tells you who lives in some of the houses on the other sides of the valley, then tells you about friends who used to live there long ago, friends who died in the revolution more than thirty years ago. Her whole world is spread out and mapped before you—and you realize she's never really been much farther than you can see now.

When the first rays of the sun appear over the horizon, Raisa reaches her hand out ahead of her for a moment, stretched out of the high window and into the drizzle. She winces as the sunlight hits her fingertips but lingers for just a moment, feeling the sun on her skin anyway.

Then she pulls her hand inside, giving you a wistful smile as she closes the window and curtains.

As you curl up together under the thick, soft covers, you find yourself bone-tired, and you fall into a contended sleep beside her.

TURN TO PAGE 248.

REBEL GIRL

You move forward to press your lips to Raisa's, and you feel her grinning through the kiss. She pulls you down to the mattress, laughing.

She kisses soft and open, but her hands move over you with an eager roughness, finding what makes you react.

You both make it only halfway out of your clothes, fumbling breathlessly as she makes soft animal noises of pleasure into your mouth. She's still wearing the studded jacket, her top underneath shoved up toward her neck to bare her full chest, where one hand plays, which you replace with your own.

She undresses you, eager and laughing, pulling off your shirt impatiently. You see her eyes on your pulse at your neck and her tongue running over her lips as she grabs tight to your hips to put you where she wants you. As you begin to move, she tips her head back in a husky shudder of relief with no self-consciousness at all. You find she gives herself without restraint—or any effort to keep herself quiet.

Once serially satisfied, she pulls you forward with her eyes wild, as if barely able to stop, and before you know what's happening, her teeth sink into your neck. The pain turns golden as the sensation building in you stretches out into a long, suspended moment, a giddy intensity that spreads through every nerve in your body.

You feel her stop sucking, but she holds her mouth there, her head nestled in the crook of your neck as the world slowly returns to normal.

You're not bleeding when Raisa pulls away. Her pupils are blown wide, and she moves slowly, almost like she's a little drunk. "Thanks," she says slightly thickly, and you don't point out that she didn't ask. She runs a hand absently over your arm, as if she's pleased you're here, and eventually you disentangle and flop down onto the bed and under the covers.

You lie close, but not touching, and you feel Raisa press a kiss onto your shoulder before you fall into a very deep and satisfied sleep.

TURN TO PAGE 248.

INSIDER

Your gran—still in last night's clothes—comes to pick you up and gives you a big hug when you get into the car. She turns up the slightly discordant folk songs on her car's old cassette player on the way home and sings along with enthusiasm and not much accuracy, laughing. "I will teach you the words," she says seriously. "It's good you learn."

Back in the house, the two of you decide to order food at 4 p.m., and you sit eating under blankets in front of the TV while she tells you every crazy story about nights out with vampires and makes some implications about a wild night with a werewolf. You ask incredulously if this was when your grandad was alive and regret it when she tells you enthusiastically yes, and how much he also enjoyed big, strong werewolves when he was younger. She cackles delightedly at your groaning reaction and insists you make her a tea.

"We cannot tell outsiders about creatures, but if you find out on your own—nothing we can do!" she says, pleased. "And now you know, my friends, they visit. And my friends, they have children, grandchildren who will like you. We will have dinners, parties."

The day after, you finally tell your boss to fuck off over the landline in your gran's hallway, and when you hang up, you find your gran cackling with glee, breaking out the plum brandy and starting to bake a cake in celebration.

◆ If you have the marker **GOTH ADMIRER** . . .

Mara finds excuses to come and visit often—bringing a new recipe for your gran or a new tea blend as a present. She visits her brother, Andrei, much more than she used to, your gran says, with a twinkle in her eye. Mara clearly wants to get to know you better, and when she finally asks you shyly over for dinner on what's clearly a date, you can choose to go. **TURN TO PAGE 249.**

◆ Otherwise . . . **TURN TO PAGE 96.**

YOU SURVIVED THE PARTY

You wake late in the morning to see Raisa with bed hair and a band tee, grinning and brandishing a piece of toast and a mug of coffee at you.

She snuggles down under the blankets alongside you as you slowly wake up, as if you always share a bed together and have known each other for years.

"So listen. I have been thinking," she says, eating a bite of the toast she brought you. "I think often about driving away, actually. I am tired of being locked away with old, sad vampires. I love them, but I want to go around new places, you know? I want to meet all the people and see life in the world. I want to hear music I haven't heard! And eat new food, even if it's not good for me to eat so much human food. I can have a little, so it's okay. I need money to go, but Caz will give me some, I am sure."

She turns to look at you, and her grin is slightly nervous. She tucks a strand of dark hair behind her ear, which does not make her hair look less messy at all.

"I can go alone, maybe, but—it's easier to go with someone with blood." She gives you a grin, but it falls into a more earnest smile. "And you know, when you are not alone, it's easier to laugh when things go bad, also. It's a crazy idea, right? But it's good, I think. Come with me, traveling. If you don't enjoy, you go home. It's no problem."

The valley outside is gray in the drizzle, lighting the edge of Raisa's tired face in cold light—but she looks so earnest, so full of energy. There's sunlight turning the edges of one of the clouds silver, and the rain glistens on the mountain roads below.

- Agree to travel with Raisa. **TURN TO PAGE 252.**
- Decline. Get a lift back to the terrible car and return to London. **TURN TO PAGE 265.**

◆ If you have the marker **GRAN PAL . . .**

Before you can reply, Mara knocks on the door, telling you your gran has called, offering to pick you up if you want to go and stay with her for longer.

With this marker, either you can tell your gran you'll be traveling with Raisa and **TURN TO PAGE 252** or you can choose to go and stay long-term with your gran instead. To live with your gran, **TURN TO PAGE 247.**

GOTH GIRLFRIEND

Mara is cooking when you arrive, wearing a long skirt and an oversized sweatshirt she pushes absentmindedly up her arms when she laughs. "Hello, hello, welcome!" she says, ushering you into the kitchen, where she happily fries potatoes and onions in paprika, adding spices haphazardly to a pot of vegetables as the dog winds around her legs. "We have a guest—do you remember?" she says seriously and dreamily to the dog.

Mara pours drinks made from the elderflower in her garden and asks you to taste-test the vegetable soup, smiling shyly as she holds the spoon carefully to your mouth. You don't need to exaggerate—they're both some of the best things you've ever tasted. Her cheeks round as she smiles and flush as you compliment her.

After dinner you sit together on a battered sofa in a low-lit room draped with wall hangings and blankets and cushions she must have embroidered herself. Her favorite music plays softly on old speakers, and she listens to you talk with her whole body turned toward you, eyes bright and ready to laugh at any joke.

She leans in and kisses you shyly at first, then when you respond, earnest and carried away. It reminds you of how she dances, losing herself in the feeling and delighting at the sensations in her body.

Your gran teases you mercilessly when you return home the next day, but from then on continually asks you how Mara is and when you'll next go to visit her.

You find that Mara loves making things. When you ask, she shows you excitedly: She's been learning to make eco-friendly soap by watching videos on her small laptop, scrawling improvements out in a big handmade journal. She asks your advice about the scents and spends a month perfecting them, making box upon box of stock that fills up one of the downstairs rooms.

She takes the soap to a market in town every Sunday, and you help her pile it into her car. She laughs as she stacks a box on your lap in the passenger seat and puts on her favorite music as you wind through the misty forest toward the town. You bring her hot tea at the freezing stall, and when you stick around to help count change and bring boxes from her car until she sells out, she kisses you impulsively and invites you back to stay at hers.

The soap sells out the next week, too, and she hand-carves stamps for the recycled paper packaging she makes herself, hanging sheets to dry on lines she strings across the living room that are very easy to walk into by mistake.

In the spring, she carefully points out the hives at the end of her brother's garden when she visits, then shows you the candles she's made from the beeswax. When you come to stay one evening, you find she's learning to knit with some friends and started making small mushrooms and toys out of felt.

She puts a handful of candles and small felt animals for sale online, where they start to do well. You help her with taking photos, holding colored card backgrounds and lights as she positions the things she's made among backdrops of old wood and flower petals, books, and teacups. She puts on music and talks to you softly as you help pack orders. She works gently, putting tasks aside when you come over tired or the sun's out, drawing you out to sit on the back porch and look over the lake with steaming mugs of tea made with mint from her garden.

She often has friends staying, all of them easygoing and happy to chip in with stamping envelopes or some big order, and she seems quietly pleased to let you stay as often as you want, too.

You split your time between Mara and your gran, who seems to approve.

Whenever you tell her you're visiting Mara, she shoos you out of the house. "Of course, go visit, get out of my way. My friends come tonight for poker and vodka anyway," she says, waving you off brusquely. "And you ask Mara for some of her cakes to bring back!" she calls as you leave.

The next Hallowe'en, Mara hosts another party—along with your new friends from town, you all spend the week helping Mara make up beds and excitedly cut out big paper decorations of bats to stick on the windows. Werewolves arrive to stay and greet you grinning with high fives, and all three vampires descend from the castle—although two seem to hide themselves away upstairs with bottles of wine and similarly ashen-toned friends. Only Raisa comes to talk enthusiastically, giving you a big wink of congratulations when she figures out how often you've been staying with Mara.

Your gran arrives like a guest of honor, scolding everyone for their biscuit recipe not being to her exact liking and for not mixing the punch strong enough. Everyone greets her fondly in return.

After midnight, you find Mara on the slowly emptying dance floor, swaying and lost in the music. You kiss her under the projected swirl of colored lights, your feet sticky on the floor and her mouth sweet from the punch. She leans into you, smiling, and the world seems to fall away. As the party fades to a murmur, you slip out the back door together to watch the sunrise with her friends—now your friends, too—as you all sit under blankets on the back step.

The pale light of the sun over the mountains lights up the mist over the lake, the whole valley spreading out below you as it comes into illuminated view. Mara's tea sends swirls of steam through the morning air, and her head is warm against your shoulder—and you realize whatever happens next, there isn't anywhere else you'd rather be than here and alive in this moment.

THE END

Want another adventure? See what else there is to do: **GO TO PAGE 266.**

THE OPEN ROAD

You and Raisa stick around to help clean up after the party while Mara hands out coffee and cooks up plates of fried potatoes for you all. After eating, you cling on the back of Raisa's motorbike and go return the terrible car to Andrei, who apologizes profusely and seems very nervous around the vampire. You retrieve your case and check in with your gran before setting up in Raisa's room at the castle.

For a couple of weeks, the two of you look over maps and chat about your plans over boxes of pastries from town. You look up travel guides on a very dated computer in the garage while Raisa noisily fixes up an old car and customizes a touring motorbike for the warmer weather, with a proper second seat and compartments for spare clothes and bottles of blood.

Once, you join the other vampires at dinner, and when Raisa starts talking about your travel plans, Casimir gives her a stern look. He seems to address you instead, perhaps hoping you'll be more receptive to his warnings. "A rogue vampire stalks the forest, too powerful for the three of us to kill. That's why the party can no longer be held at the castle and the forest is so dangerous at night.

"I feel . . . uneasy about you leaving with this creature still at large," he tells Raisa stiffly in his deep voice. "It's the two of *us* he holds a grudge against and seeks to kill"—he gestures at himself and August—"but he is violent, vindictive. He may hunt the two of you to strike a blow at us."

Thinking back to the party, you ask if the werewolves could help take the rogue vampire out on the next full moon, and Raisa nods eagerly. "Yes! You see? Like I said"—she looks over at you—"with you, we can persuade them for sure," she says enthusiastically.

Casimir scowls through dinner and leaves early, seeming to think werewolves unlikely to help anyone. But Raisa goes to talk to him regularly over the next week, and she returns to tell you confidently that she's wearing him down.

◆ If you have the marker **HONORARY WOLF** or **PARTY ANIMAL . . . TURN TO PAGE 255.**

◆ Otherwise . . . **TURN TO PAGE 253.**

GATHERING THE PACK

"You have to go talk to werewolves on your own," Raisa tells you, sprawled out on her bed. "Everyone keeps wolf forms secret. A vampire visiting is too suspicious."

So you go knocking on doors in town alone—most of the werewolves seem to remember you from the party and know your gran, and they're willing to hear you out. You explain it's to help you and Raisa and focus on how it'll keep the town safer, and in the run-up to the full moon, you end up gathering a decent-sized group willing to help.

Raisa becomes familiar: the shape of her voice when it echoes in the corridors, the things that make her laugh, the expressions she pulls when she's talking about the things she cares about. She shows you her favorite music, and you drive into town after dark to see her friends and visit your gran and try everything on the menu at a couple of the old restaurants.

"It will be no problem," Raisa says confidently as she readies herself on the night of the full moon—wearing one of her lesser biker jackets "so no bloodstains." She looks at you warmly from the doorway before she leaves her bedroom and points at the record player. "Play something loud," she says.

You spend a tense hour listening to her noisiest records, the beat thundering along with your heart as you wait, trying to ignore the howling outside the windows.

But it's not too long before Raisa returns, splattered with blood. "All good," she says. "He is dead." She doesn't give you the details—"*Messy*" is all she replies with a wince. "But not so hard, with many of us."

Outside the room you see August bringing the werewolves bandages and some kind of concoction in small bottles, which causes some excitement—it seems to be the thing that makes their transformation "controllable." The mood seems easier, like bridges in long disrepair are being rebuilt. As Raisa washes the blood off, Casimir thanks you seriously. He hands over an envelope of euros and a credit card, along with good wishes and a lot of advice for the trip. August tells you to have fun and to bring back pictures—both seem relieved to have this rogue vampire finally dealt with.

By the time you're ready to leave, all three vampires have been talking more, raising ideas of their own travel plans over dinner. Raisa seems relieved in turn. "I felt bad about leaving them here all sad," she tells you one night, flopped down on the blankets beside you in bed. She gives you an earnest grin. "But now, they will be okay, I think. Thank you."

TURN TO PAGE 258.

THE MORNING AFTER THE NIGHT BEFORE

You wake up feeling like you died several weeks ago.

Slowly, you realize you're lying on a sticky floor in a stranger's house. On the sofas nearby, a couple of people who might have been wolves yesterday are lying sprawled mostly naked, one of them with a pair of glasses drawn on their face in permanent marker. How old are these people? How old are you, and what was your name again?

Your stomach lurches as you move, and you let yourself drift back to sleep.

When you wake again, you hear engines driving away outside the window and several people clattering around in the kitchen. You wonder whether one of the engines was Raisa, racing away up the hill, or whether she left to go elsewhere in the night. You were too drunk to notice or keep track of her—and now you see no sign of the vampire and have no way to contact her again. The memory of the castle feels hard to hold in your mind, like a dream.

Looking around at the chaos and hearing some of the laughing conversations, you wonder how much you missed last night.

You manage to sit blearily up, and Mara puts a mug of hot water with mint leaves floating in it in your hands, then goes off to speak to someone. She returns with an old woman who doesn't speak much English—and whom you think might have been a werewolf doing a lot of arm wrestling last night—and the woman gives you a lift back to the terrible car in her only slightly better one.

TURN TO PAGE 265.

ONE OF THE PACK

"You have to go talk to werewolves on your own," Raisa tells you, sprawled out on her bed. "Everyone keeps wolf forms secret. A vampire visiting is too suspicious. It's why we only see wolves at parties." She rolls over to grin at you. "But they love you! It will be good."

When you go knocking on doors in town, you discover she's right: You're now kind of a legend among werewolves.

Everyone seems thrilled to see you. You get invited excitedly inside, fed tea and cake, and find yourself being questioned about who you met and told outlandish, exaggerated accounts of stuff you did at the party.

In the run-up to the full moon, you easily gather a huge team of people eager to help you, however they can, including several friends of friends who drive across borders to get there.

Raisa becomes familiar: the shape of her voice when it echoes in the corridors, the things that make her laugh, the expressions she pulls when she's talking about the things she cares about. She shows you her favorite music, and you drive into town after dark to see her friends and visit your gran and try everything on the menu at a couple of the old restaurants.

On the night itself, Casimir seems slightly bewildered at the size of the group that shows up to help, greeting you and Raisa eagerly.

"It will be no problem," Raisa says confidently as she readies herself—wearing one of her lesser biker jackets "so no bloodstains." She looks at you warmly from the doorway before she leaves her bedroom and points at the record player. "Play something loud," she says.

You spend a tense hour listening to her loudest records, the beat thundering along with your heart as you wait. You hear howling outside the windows—but it all seems to be over very fast. Raisa returns out of breath and gives you a thumbs-up, not even covered in that much blood. "All good," she says. "He is dead. Easy, with so many friends," she grins.

A formal and slightly uncomfortable Casimir invites the werewolves inside afterward. He seems unsure of what to do—surprised that it was done so easily, apparently unused to having so many people on his side.

August seems to know a few of them and brings out some kind of herbal mixture in bottles. From the excited conversation, you gather that this is the werewolf medicine that makes the transformation safer—restraining it halfway before they can turn truly bloodthirsty and uncontrolled, a more dangerous form you've managed to avoid seeing. The werewolves seem very grateful, and a couple who came here from farther away give you the credit for the connection. August opens several bottles of wine, and a few of the triumphant guests end up staying over, curled up on the floor by the fire in Raisa's room in borrowed blankets. By the time they all leave, even Casimir is speaking to them with more ease—he seems to have started rebuilding bridges that had previously long fallen into disrepair.

The following night, Casimir invites you to dinner and thanks you seriously. He hands over a thick envelope of euros and a credit card, along with good wishes and a lot of advice for your travels.

August tells you both delightedly to have fun and to bring back pictures. Both seem relieved to have this rogue vampire finally dealt with.

By the time you're ready to leave, they've been talking more, raising ideas of their own travel plans. Raisa seems relieved in turn. "I felt bad about leaving them here all sad," she tells you one night, flopped down on the blankets beside you in bed. She gives you an earnest grin. "But now, they will be okay, I think. Thank you."

Your new friends in town tell you that word is now spreading about the incident among European werewolves: vampires who dealt responsibly with their most dangerous members and were not afraid to ask for help and forge an alliance. It also makes you and Raisa even more famous among them.

Later as you travel, you find yourselves invited to parties every month at the full moon, in almost every city in Europe. Everyone's always excited to see you, whether you recognize them or not. You usually take them up on their wild suggestions for their honored guests: breaking out onto the roofs of famous landmarks, spending a night in supposedly haunted woods or abandoned buildings, or climbing a mountain to watch the sunrise.

But you also meet less loud people who insist you come to stay with them once they're back in human form. You end up spending a month sleeping on people's sofas in Berlin after a huge party there in an old warehouse. At one point you end up staying in the spare bedroom of a werewolf with a huge villa who flies you out to a music festival where you all share a VIP tent.

The werewolves fill up bottles of blood for Raisa—always while in human form, she says, as it doesn't taste the same if they've transformed—so she stays easily in control. It lets her go wherever she wants, even in a hoodie and gloves on overcast days, exploring cities without having to worry about feeding on you or whether she's brought enough with her.

And as you get to know people, you get invited more often into people's houses, to come and sleep on their floor or come to their cousin's wedding.

And Raisa loves it—you see her face light up getting to meet people's kids and dogs. She likes helping with random errands—babysitting and house painting, Christmas shopping and elaborate cooking, or helping make food for Suhoor before she goes to bed at sunrise. She likes driving out to fast-food chains at 1 a.m. to bring food back to a party, or giving people lifts to the emergency vet or to their office team's early-morning football matches before the sun comes up.

It's only a few days a month, but it feels like having a huge extended family. You feel so welcome and so full of love every time, and the two of you always drive back brimming with stories and ideas, ready to go anywhere and do anything.

TURN TO PAGE 258.

ROAD TRIP

Over the winter, you and Raisa fill the car with blankets and snacks and drinks and discs for the old CD player. You take highways to a handful of big cities nearby she's heard of but never been to, where she marvels at everything from the churches to the landscapes to ducks she sees on the river.

You meet new people in the bars and stay in the clubs until closing, taking your time to see the sights and the landscapes. You stay in grimy little motels and bed-and-breakfasts in the mountains where the hosts make everybody coffee in the mornings. You stay in noisy hostel dormitories, where you occasionally make incredible friends with the other guests and agree to travel with them for a while or give them a lift to their next stop. Other times, the other guests are a nightmare and you end up sleeping in the car or dragging your blankets out into the corridor to sleep.

You stay in people's spare rooms that they advertise online and sometimes find you're eating dinner with their families, who tell you eagerly about the country and the local foods and the best things to see in the city. Raisa carefully eats only a few mouthfuls before surreptitiously sliding the rest of the meal over to you or the dog.

In the spring, you head north and then east on her motorbike, clinging on as she races along the huge, wide roads, and get a first glimpse of the wide plains of the Steppe.

In the summer, she takes you on the Transfăgărășan, the famous road that winds up and up into the southern Carpathians, hairpinning up over bridges, past waterfalls and trails of sheep that span the rocky slopes. Raisa tells you it was built brutally by the military when she was young as she looks out over the landscape—now busy with tourists eating from food vans at the tops of peaks.

Next you follow the mountains around into Slovakia, then head toward the Alps. You both love taking the advice of fellow travelers coming from another direction or whomever you last stayed with—whatever the local owners of guesthouses and spare rooms insist are their favorite things to see.

◆ If you have the marker **PARTNERS IN CRIME . . . TURN TO PAGE 262.**

◆ Otherwise . . . **TURN TO PAGE 260.**

UNSPOKEN AND LOUDER THAN WORDS

You and Raisa don't define what's between you, but you find yourself learning the shapes of her smile and her body, the two of you drawing closer, comfortable and inexorable, without any mention of it ever passing your lips.

You ask if she wants to share a bed in a hotel to save money, and she grins back at you like she knows that's not what you're asking. "Sure!" she says cheerfully, and once the door is closed, she kisses you hard up against it and leaves you gasping. She steals kisses in crowded bars and behind motels next to crowded highways. She pulls you into the back seat of the car on dark nights in secluded places. She finds new places in which to sink her teeth and drink you in, and she drives you slowly to pleasurable desperation, playful all the while as she goes. She makes sure to catch your attention as she strips in the low light in mountain cabins, locks the doors provocatively in grimy hotel rooms and shared accommodations in a way that makes you laugh and catches the breath in your throat at the same time.

She yells "I love you!" at a gig when you boost her up to help her crowd-surf, and you're dazed for a moment, because you thought you saw something there in her eyes when she said it. And then you see her saying the same thing to a bouncer five minutes later when he gives her the same boost up over a barrier—and then she says it again later on the way home, to a big dog.

But she does learn your patterns, inside out. She learns what you like, and you realize slowly how much energy she spends trying to give it to you. She holds your hand tight in crowds and your body close against hers in the night. Once, when a man looking for tourists' money pulls a knife on you in a back alley, Raisa moves faster than you've ever seen to slam him to the ground. You make her let him go, but you're not sure what she would have done if you hadn't. Her eyes are intent afterward as she holds your face in her hands. "Nobody will touch you when I'm around," she says, serious and wild. "Nobody you don't want."

When she drinks blood from the bottles she brings or feeds on you in the night, her movements grow loose and honest, as if she's finally able to relax. She curls her body next to yours and strokes her hands idly over your skin. Sometimes she tells you she's never met anyone like you before, or she tells the story of how you met like it's a fairy tale, like it's one of the best things that could have happened to her. She doesn't need to articulate what there is between you—it's there, anyway, burning hotter than fire and speaking louder than words.

And when you travel, you watch fondly as Raisa talks to everyone and says yes to everything. She introduces you to new people she just met, and you find yourself at parties in castles and caves where she throws her arms around you to kiss you in the dark. You spend all night tucked away in cafés where musicians jam in the corner and invite you to talk afterward in whatever language you can find in common. You spend evenings in intimate underground bars with the old owners who regale you with stories until the wee hours and invite you to meet their families the next day.

And when you're exhausted, you go back to the castle and the town and your gran, to familiar faces waiting to see you and happy to hear your stories about everything you've done. A pile of your stuff accumulates in Raisa's room, and when you give up on your terrible flat and abandoned job, your friends send the rest of your stuff over.

One day, you go looking for Raisa, following the sound of her singing along to old records, and find her covered in a paint-spattered band tee in a big room next to hers. She's painting huge stripes over the stone in bright, chaotic, beautiful colors. "Ah!" she yells when you come in. "It was going to be a surprise! So . . . you have your own space, if you want, sometimes." But then she frowns up at the wall and starts laughing. "But maybe you should help choose colors?" You end up covered in paint as you kiss her.

You spend as long as you want back in the town: lazy, hot summers with Mara by the lake and surrounded by snow in the winters, when Raisa puts on records to dance to before pulling you into bed. When the other vampires are around, they're keen to suggest what city you should go to next—and now they're traveling, too, only some of their advice is a hundred years out of date. There's a home waiting for you there now, for whenever you want to come back and stay—but for now there is so much world, and you've still seen only a glimpse of it.

THE END

Want another adventure? See what else there is to do: **GO TO PAGE 266.**

PARTNERS IN THE HIDDEN WORLD

Raisa talks to everyone and says yes to everything she can. You find yourself at parties in castles and in huge ancient caves. You spend all night tucked away in little restaurants where live musicians jam in the corner and invite you to talk afterward in whatever language you can find in common. You spend evenings in intimate underground bars with the old owners who regale you with stories until the wee hours and invite you to meet their families the next day.

And when you're exhausted, you go back to the castle and the town and your gran, to familiar faces waiting to see you and happy to hear your stories about everything you've done. A pile of your stuff accumulates in Raisa's room, and when you give up on your terrible flat and abandoned job, your friends send the rest of your stuff over. Raisa starts painting a bigger room that adjoins hers in bright, chaotic, beautiful colors, ready for you to spread out.

You spend as long as you want back in the town: lazy, hot summers with Mara and her friends by the lake and surrounded by snow in the winters. When the other vampires are around, they're keen to suggest what city you should go to next—and now they're traveling, too, only some of their advice is a hundred years out of date. There's a home waiting for you there now, for whenever you want to come back and stay—but for now there is so much world, and you've still seen only a glimpse of it.

Raisa is physically affectionate and easy, slinging an arm over your shoulder or linking her elbow through yours, nudging you happily with her hips as you walk together. She learns your favorite foods and the things you do when you're tired. You know the contours of each other's conversation and jokes and voices. People assume things—mostly that you're a couple in a particular sense, but you and Raisa don't really mind.

You explain to your friends back home: The two of you are closer than with anyone else. You're best friends and partners in life (or death) with a bond that's not any lesser just because it doesn't look like the kind of romance people expect. You fall asleep next to each other, curled in strange beds and on futons or living room floors, and it feels like home because you're together.

The two of you travel through the world side by side, curious and vibrant—ready to listen and dance and try everything new that you can. Sometimes when you drive at night on roads through the country or the mountains, Raisa will pull over and sit on the hood of the car to stare out in the darkness, wind whipping through her tousled hair. When you come to sit next to her, she grins back at you, sharp and wild. Each of you burns brighter and braver with the other at your side. Out in the void of night, the lights of distant houses twinkle—the whole world is before you both, hidden and impossible to predict, just waiting to be discovered.

THE END

Want another adventure? See what else there is to do: **GO TO PAGE 266.**

GO BACK TO LONDON, THE EXACT SAME

You go back to London. Absolutely *no vampire adventures for you, thank you very much.*

The forest looks ordinary in the gray daylight, and the terrible car starts up on the third try and makes it to the station without falling apart. The airport in Bucharest reminds you of all other airports, and there's not enough legroom on the plane. You watch the clouds disappearing beneath you as your night at the castle grows more and more distant, like a fever dream or an old movie you've forgotten the name of.

Your terrible job is still waiting for you—it turns out nobody wanted to take it when they advertised. Your boss buys nicer instant coffee for the break room once as if that might solve any internal crisis you're having, and it does absolutely nothing to improve anything.

A rat dies under the floorboards in your flat, and a new leak opens up along the window—your landlord refuses to fix it for several years, until you hear one day that he's been arrested for tax fraud and you have to go and live somewhere worse and more expensive.

Sometimes at crap parties on the other side of London that took an hour and a half to get to—ones where when you arrive, everyone's too far gone to hold a conversation—you try to tell people about your night at the castle. Once, someone listens to you rapturously describe your cool gran and the beautiful mountains.

As you insist that you could have been eaten by hot vampires at any time that night, they ask you why you came back.

You don't really know what to say.

THIS IS YOUR LIFE NOW! THE END!

You've survived the vampire castle by avoiding most of it.

See what else there is to do: **GO TO PAGE 266.**

To restart from dinner, **GO TO PAGE 28.**

RETURN CHANGED

You return to London a little bolder than before.

The terrible car makes it to the station without falling apart, and in the light of day the forest looks ordinary—manageable. The airport in Bucharest reminds you of all other airports, but you wander through the shops restlessly and impulse-buy a paperback. You dislike it so much you end up talking to the person next to you on the plane about it, who turns out to have read and hated the same book. The bond of derision gives you a little glimmer of warmth toward the stranger—and the world.

Back in London, you tell a friend about the castle and realize it sounds like a fever dream, so you move on to talking about your gran instead. But next week, the friend invites you to a showing of an old cult vampire film, which she never would have before. *Why not?* you think, and you go, and you have a great time.

You go back to your job, and it's terrible. Was it always this bad? After a break, you're even more aware, more suspicious than ever that your boss paying you late all the time is not just immoral but illegal. You find a citizen's advice place to ask about it and discover you were right. With their help, you send a strongly worded letter about your employment rights and consequences if it doesn't get fixed, because surely that's better than nothing.

You're not sure if it's the letter itself that does it or if it's you talking in the break room until everyone else is aware and angry about it, but something scares your boss so much that next month, everyone gets paid on time and in full, and it goes on that way. And now everyone at work also wants to buy you a drink down the pub. You start figuring out how to do the same with your landlord, too.

Sometimes you try something you'd never have done before. Your friend invites you to a restaurant in a prison, or you try a local bar's costume party speed dating, or follow up an ad for a pole-dancing class that also offers trapeze. Because when you cast your mind back to that night at the vampire castle, you think, *well*, if you did that, of course you can do this. And the next year, you think, hey, why not visit your gran again? It was great last time. And if you end up on the forbidden road, you can see whether some of the same old faces are still around.

THE END (. . . ?)

You survived the vampire castle but didn't unlock its secrets.

See what else there is to do: **GO TO PAGE 266.**

ACHIEVEMENTS

Download a digital version to print at **hari-illustration.com/vampirecastle**.

Check off each achievement you manage to earn! Try getting three in a row on a single play, or for the badges below, play a few times to check off a whole row across both pages.

BEAUTIFUL DISASTER	Obnoxious Be killed by August	Explorer Be eaten in the crypt	Told you so Be killed by a werewolf	Party on Pass out at the party
LORE MASTER	Gran lore Learn who your gran punched and why	Was that sarcasm Ask August how to become a vampire	Seven days Climb down a well	Déjà vu Find out how August died
THRILL SEEKER	Smoothie Be fed on by a vampire	Brat Disobey Casimir	Sugar baby Go to Paris for free	Guillermo Help kill a vampire
MAIN CHARACTER	Final girl Flee the castle before sunrise and survive	Crushin' it Free the ghost (sensually or not)	Fuck it Move to the beach	Cottagecore Move to a farm

NEW GAME?

Discover more in the vampire castle:

› To restart from dinner, **TURN TO PAGE 28.**

› To restart the night *after* dinner, **TURN TO PAGE 33.**

Fairy-tale ending Die at the bottom of the lake	**Almost had it** Die at a bus stop	**Speedrun** Die before you reach the castle	**Why did you buy this book** Go home and nothing changes
Moonlight Discover August's "experiment"	**The old kingdoms** Learn where Casimir grew up	**Underground** Learn when Raisa became a vampire	**A glint of chains** Learn about the murder in the house
Public service Help kill a billionaire	**Secret main quest** Make friends with a dog	**Road trip** Travel around Europe	**Do it all** Get 5+ markers in one playthrough
Goth gf Help sell small felt animals	**Musical theater** Win(?) a dance-off	**One of the pack** Become an honorary werewolf	**Creature of the night** Become a vampire

ROW 4
COMPLETE:

SPECIAL THANKS

Huge thanks to the guest artists and to everyone who helped playtest this book: in particular to Mal, Eve, Letty, and Lin for always listening to my ideas; to Peony for London advice and Sam for car advice; and to my darling experts on the subject of hot vampires, Amanda and Alex. Nobody's opinion on these characters was more important than yours.

Thanks to supporters on Patreon for your thirsty and motivational comments, to Jasmine Walls for additional editing and feedback, and in general to Louise Lamont and my agent, Jessica Mileo, for your support and willingness to encourage the niche romance ideas I bring you—you are greatly appreciated.

GUEST ARTISTS

› **VINCENT CECIL**
(vincentisvintage.com | vincent-is-vintage.carrd.co)
Casimir "Brief Candle" and "Creature of the Night" endings

› **OTAVA HEIKKILÄ**
(otavaheikkila.net | @Claystorks)
Casimir "Blood Bank" ending

› **VAL/BISHOP WISE**
(valkwise.neocities.org | @ValKWise)
Casimir "Patron of the Arts" ending

› **ALEX ASSAN**
(alexassan.com | @AlexAssanArt)
August route: intro, "Butterfly Kiss," and hunger paths

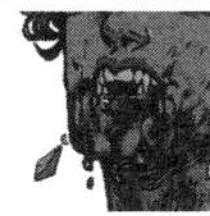

› **LIO PRESSLAND**
(kroov.club | @Kroovv)
August "Monster" and London endings

› **BAYLEIGH UNDERWOOD**
(iceghostart.com | @iceghost.bsky.social)
Raisa route: intro, moonlit romance, and "Road trip" and "Partners" endings

› **MAL MARWOOD**
(malacandrax.com | @Malacandrax)
Luka and Andrei: intros, endings, and "The Transformation"

› **ROWAN MacCOLL**
(rowanmaccoll.com | @SkulkingFoxes)
"The Woman in the Reeds," "Nothing Can Save You Now," and "What Did I Tell You?" endings

› **ASHLEY McCAMMON**
(avmccammon.com | @Draculing)
The ghost and the gardens

› **SHAZLEEN KHAN**
(shazleenkhan.com | @Shazleen.jpeg)
Mara intro and ending

› **HARRIET MOULTON**
(harrietmoulton.co.uk | @HattersArts)
The countess

› **ANINE BÖSENBERG**
(anineillustration.com | @AnineBosenberg)
Your gran's house

ABOUT THE AUTHOR

HARI CONNER is an award-winning author and illustrator, mostly of queer romance comics and illustrated books.

Hari grew up in London—if you can't tell from this book—and now lives in Scotland. They're generally rumored to be an unholy creature beyond mortal ken, or possibly a Victorian ghost who gets emotional thinking about trees.

› **DRAWINGS BY HARI**

(@haridraws)

Cover; objects, buildings, bedrooms; Casimir's main route, Raisa's "Unspoken and Louder than Words" ending, August's "A Late Foxglove" ending; achievements

NOTES PAGE

Write down any **MARKERS** here, or track your route by writing down page numbers.

NIGHT AT THE VAMPIRE CASTLE

A CHOOSE-YOUR-OWN ROMANCE

The authorised representative in the EEA is Simon and Schuster Netherlands BV, Herculesplein 96 3584 AA Utrecht, Netherlands. (info@simonandschuster.nl)

Andrews McMeel Publishing
a division of Andrews McMeel Universal
1130 Walnut Street, Kansas City, Missouri 64106

www.andrewsmcmeel.com

25 26 27 28 29 RLP 10 9 8 7 6 5 4 3 2 1

ISBN: 979-8-8816-0185-0

Library of Congress Control Number: 2024952861

Editor: Katie Gould
Art Director: Hari Conner
Designer: Diane Marsh
Production Editor: Kayla Overbey
Production Manager: Julie Skalla